AMANDA BRITTANY lives in Hertfordshire with her husband and two dogs. When she's not writing, she loves spending time with family, travelling, walking, reading and sunny days. Her debut novel *Her Last Lie* reached the Kindle top 100 in the US and Australia and was a #1 Bestseller in the UK. It has also been optioned for film. Her second psychological thriller *Tell The Truth* reached the Kindle top 100 in the US & was a #1 Bestseller in the US. All her ebook royalties for *Her Last Lie* are being donated to Cancer Research UK, in memory of her sister who lost her battle with cancer in July 2017. It has so far raised over £7,500.

Also by Amanda Brittany

Her Last Lie
Tell the Truth
Traces of Her

I Lie in Wait

AMANDA BRITTANY

ONE PLACE. MANY STORIES

HQ
An imprint of HarperCollins*Publishers* Ltd
1 London Bridge Street
London SE1 9GF

First published by HQ 2020

This edition published in Great Britain by
HQ, an imprint of HarperCollins*Publishers* Ltd 2020

A catalogue record for this book is available from the British Library.

ISBN: 9780008362881

MIX
Paper from
responsible sources
FSC www.fsc.org **FSC™ C007454**

This book is produced from independently certified FSC™ paper to ensure responsible forest management.

For more information visit: www.harpercollins.co.uk/green

Printed and bound in Great Britain by
CPI Group (UK) Ltd, Croydon CR0 4YY

For Kev, with love.

Prologue

Present Day

Me

'Maddie? Maddie, is that you?' It is. I know her voice. She's in the next room. 'Maddie! Maddie, please help me!' I tug at the chain trapping my wrist to the bedstead. It cuts into my flesh. Makes fresh wounds.

'We're heading back to Drummondale House on Friday,' she's saying. 'It's the anniversary of Lark and Jackson's disappearance.'

'Maddie, please!' I yell. Why can't she hear me?

'Robert feels there may be something we missed that night. I'm not sure what to think, but I'll keep you updated. Wish us luck!'

'You're wasting your time, Maddie,' you say. And of course, you are right.

The sound of your laptop snapping closed brings me back to reality. Maddie isn't there at all. You were listening to her vlog.

I close my eyes, fatigue washing over me, my usual thoughts carrying me to nightmares: How did I let this happen? How could I have been so stupid?

I have no idea how long I've slept, but I'm now alone, and the place is in darkness. I shuffle up the bed, ears pricked on alert for the sound of tyres rolling over the ice-packed ground. My sore, watery eyes pinned on the window, waiting for a glimpse of your car's headlights to cut across the grubby glass. But it's silent, and I wonder if you've gone back there – back to Drummondale House.

Chapter 1

Present Day

Amelia

He took her. Jackson Cromwell – my mother's lover. He took my teenage sister. He took Lark from us. I know he did. And sometimes, looking back – eyes wide open – I wonder if I should have reacted when I saw the way he looked at her, the way he flirted.

It's the anniversary of her disappearance this Friday. Twelve long months of not knowing where Lark is – whether she's alive or dead.

My ex-partner William couldn't cope with my outpourings of grief following my sister's disappearance. It couldn't have been easy for him listening to me repeat the same tragic words, desperate to explore my feelings, desperate to cope with what had happened. I went from numb to feeling too much, to numb again, all with the aid of too much wine.

In fact, I still hadn't come to terms with her loss when, seven months later, my mum died. Imagine a car wreck – well that was me in human form.

But a few weeks after her funeral, life took an upward turn. I discovered I was pregnant. For three months a tiny baby had been growing inside me and I'd been too swept away by grief overload to realise. It was a miracle, and for the first time in ages, bubbles of happiness fizzed.

'It can't be mine,' William said, when I broke the news over his favourite meal of guinea fowl and gnocchi.

'Of course it's yours,' I said, placing the little stick telling me the best news ever onto his side plate, and trying to smile despite his tactless comment.

'That's got your pee on it, Amelia,' he said, pushing it away. 'Are you positive it's mine?'

'OK, for one …' I held up my index finger '… I've only slept with you in all the time I've known you. And two …' I burst into tears.

William jumped up, grabbed a serviette – he always insisted we had them on the table, as I had, still have in fact, a habit of getting 'stuff' on my face when I eat – and thrust it into my hand.

'OK, great, I'm going to be a dad,' he said, and left the room. He'd barely touched his gnocchi. I guess the pee on the stick hadn't helped.

So this portrays William in an awful light. But, in fairness to him, he'd been through my hell with me, and was no longer 'Fun-Loving Will' the man with the amazing smile who I met on a night out with the girls three years ago. He was a faded, tired version. In fact, I couldn't recall the last time he'd smiled. He wanted out of our relationship, but, at the time, he didn't have the heart to leave a woman weighed down by a bucket-load of tragedy. And now, a baby – our baby – would trap him forever.

*

Things improved after that. We began picking up the scattered pieces of our relationship, and I tucked the loss of my mum and

4

sister into a little velvet box at the back of my mind, determined to move on with my life – our lives. It's what Mum and Lark would have wanted, I told myself. And I desperately wanted to make William happy.

But that small snatch of happiness lasted no time at all. My life, the life I thought was back on a safe, even road, plummeted into another deep dark ditch, and I wasn't sure I'd be able to climb out this time. After awful stomach cramps I prayed were IBS, I lost our baby at five months pregnant.

So, it's been a tragic year – a year of heartache and loss. I've heard people say bad things come in threes. But how does anyone stay strong when said bad things hit one after the other? One! Two! Three! Wham! Bam! Slam!

Lark vanished.

Mum died.

I lost my baby.

I'm not going to lie; I wondered what I'd done in a previous life to deserve such sorrow.

I tried so hard not to be that woman who everyone felt sorry for. 'Poor Amelia – nothing goes right for her.' 'Oh, Amelia, love, it could only happen to you.' Or worse, the woman people crossed the road to avoid, fearing her misery was catching. But it was impossible. I was that woman wallowing knee-deep in self-pity, and I hadn't got a clue where to find the strength to pick myself up; still haven't. In fact, I fully understand how some women lose their mind following a miscarriage, as I'm pretty close to losing mine right now.

With the loss of our baby, my life with William was over. He'd seen the worst of me – not a pretty sight. Couldn't take any more. Wasn't strong enough. He said, as he touched my cheek gently a week after our loss, his fingertips drying my skin, 'I can't do this anymore, Amelia.' He'd lost his baby too, he said – he was in pain too, he said – but I know he never felt the same kind of screwed-up agony I felt.

5

He stayed around for two months after that, spending a lot of time at his mum's, or crying on the shoulder of an ex-girlfriend. He never did tell me her name. Did he think I would knife her on a lonely street?

For a while it was as though my baby – the little girl I had so many plans for – was still with me. But eventually, with time, I accepted there was an empty place inside me where I once felt her flutter – a timid butterfly trying out her wings for the first time. I'd felt so sure she was happy. I'd held my belly so often, talked to her, sung to her. But we can never be sure when happiness will be snatched away from us. I know that now.

*

'Amelia, have you got the contract for Jennings and Jennings?'

I look away from the office window, and up at Malcolm. My boss is out of breath, and needs to lose a few pounds before he keels over. His tone, as always, is anxiety-tinged, his face stretched into a shiny-cheeked smile. He won't make old bones at this rate.

'You need to shave off that ridiculous moustache, Malcolm.' I've wanted to say that for years, if only to help him find his soul mate. No wonder he's single. 'You look like Hitler.'

His eyes widen, as much as they can in their puffy sockets, as he touches the hairy culprit under his nose. 'You need more time away from the office, Amelia.'

'I need forever,' I say. I haven't even turned on the computer and it's almost midday. I've spent most of this morning gazing out at the grey day. Thinking. 'Can you give me forever, Malcolm?' I ask, in a maudlin tone – that's pretty much my only tone right now.

'Take more time out if you need it. You're no use to us here.'

'Cheers for that.'

'I think you know what I'm saying, Amelia.' He strides off, in his creased shirt and too-short trousers.

I've got to go home, or hide in the loos for the rest of the day.

I fidget in my swivel chair. I won't get paid if I go home. I've had way too much time off already. The thing is, I can't afford the apartment now anyway, not since William left. I need to do something – something else, something to make life worth living again. But then how can I do that without Mum, without Lark, without William, without my precious unborn child?

I look out of the window once more. The tall buildings of London surround me, and The Gherkin feels so close. I'm tempted to open the window and lean out – try to touch it. I would fall, of course. Tumble to my death, and possibly make headlines in The Metro. But then nobody would care. Not a single soul would miss me – except perhaps my dad, and possibly my brother Thomas.

I roll my chair back over the plush carpet, put the photo of William in the bin, and my Thor figure, that Thomas bought me a few years back because I told him I love Chris Hemsworth, in my bag. I grab my jacket, rise, and head for the door, throwing one look over my shoulder at the rabbit warren of desks. Nobody looks my way. I'm right. Nobody will miss me.

Outside, I dash towards London Bridge Underground, pushing through the crowds. I won't cry, I tell myself. I'm all cried out.

*

'William, it's me. Pick up, please.' I'm pissed, sobbing into my phone, my cat curled on my knee, her purr giving me comfort. Drunk-me is far too needy, and I seem to turn to her too often lately. 'Call me, please. I need you right now.' It's the tenth time I've called and it's only seven o'clock. Ten times he's ignored me.

I throw my phone across the room. It hits a photo of us in Rhodes. It clatters on the dresser. The glass cracks. Were we even happy then? I know it was difficult when Mum got cancer, and everything that followed was impossible – William struggled with me struggling, which made me struggle even more.

I look at the empty wine bottle, before burying my head in

my hands until the tears stop. And then it hits me. I need my dad, to feel the comfort of his arms around me. But I can't take off to Berwick-upon-Tweed and leave my cat – who now looks up at me as though she knows what I'm thinking. 'But if I stay here, sweetie, I'll go crazy,' I say, tickling her soft ears.

Later, after crying on my neighbour's doorstep – a kindly twenty-something with pink hair – she gives me a much-needed hug. 'You've been through hell, Amelia,' she says. 'Of course I'll look after your cat. Take as long as you need.'

'Thanks so much,' I say, wishing I knew her name – but it's far too late to ask her what it is; we've been chatting for months.

I return to my flat and call Malcolm, realising, after apologising profusely for letting him down at such short notice, that he sounds relieved I'm taking time off.

'Great. Super,' he says. 'Brilliant!'

'I'll be taking an early train to Berwick-upon-Tweed and probably won't be back for a while. Is that OK?'

'Of course, Amelia. Please, please don't hurry back.'

I end the call, flop down on my bed, and close my eyes.

Chapter 2

Present Day

Amelia

I caught the early train from London and it's now 10 a.m. I'm relieved to be here, standing on the doorstep of the house I grew up in, waiting for Dad to answer the front door.

'Surprise!' I cry, as he opens the door. I dive in for a hug, breathing in his familiar aftershave, almost knocking him over, despite him being six foot.

'Amelia!' he says as I release him and step back, noticing he's dyed his hair black and seems to have sprouted a moustache – moustaches are clearly invading my world. I'm close to telling him it does nothing for him, and the black hair makes him look as though he's fallen headfirst into a barrel of tar, when he adds, 'What are you doing here, love?'

He seems happy to see me, but there's something else. Something I can't quite put my finger on.

'Well I'm pretty much waiting for you to invite me in.' I rub my gloved hands together as a blustery wind catches my hair and blows it across my face like flames. 'It's bloody cold out here – snowed all the way from the station.'

'Yes, sorry.' He opens the door wider.

My throat closes as I look down the narrow hallway, and memories of Lark and Mum flood in. This is the house where I spent my childhood and teens. A four-bed modern detached that looks out over a huge expanse of grass leading to the River Tweed. A once crazy, noisy, happy house, that now feels far too quiet. Only Dad and Thomas live here now, and I'm guessing my brother is in his bedroom – once the dining room where we all shared happy meals, now extended to accommodate my brother's needs.

Dad's stepped to one side. 'Come on, love, you're letting the cold in,' he says rubbing his hands together, bringing me back to the moment. I will myself to move, heave my rucksack off my back, and edge past him. He closes the door behind us.

'So what brings you all this way?' he says, following me into the kitchen. He picks up the kettle and gives it a little shake before flicking it on. 'Nothing wrong, is there?'

Yep, just about everything.

I shake my head and sit down at the round kitchen table. It still has the pretty embroidered tablecloth draped over it that I remember Mum buying over ten years ago.

'How's work?' I ask. Dad loves his job as curator at the local museum, and last time I spoke to him he was working on an exhibition about ancient crimes in the area. It fills his mind, leaving no space to dwell.

'Good,' he says. 'Keeps me busy.' I rest my case.

I ponder his earlier question, as he heads towards me with two steaming mugs of tea, places them on the table, and sits down opposite me.

So what brings you here?

He doesn't know I've lost my precious baby. I never told him when I found out I was pregnant. I don't know why – an amalgamation of reasons, probably. I suppose the news was far too good after everything that had happened. Maybe I didn't want to jinx it. Maybe I was convinced that only bad things happen to me now. Maybe I wanted to tell him face to face. Whatever the reason, he doesn't need to know now. He doesn't need my tragic news on top of all the heartache he's already been through.

'I've broken up with William,' I say, keeping my voice upbeat and even, as I fiddle with the handle of the mug.

'Oh, love.' He turns warm brown eyes on me.

I raise my hand, knowing if we go down the hugs road at this moment, I'll sob like a baby. 'But I'm fine.'

He throws me a sad smile. 'I never liked him.'

I smile. 'You never met him.'

'You deserve better.'

'Well yes, yes I do.' Another smile, though tears are close. I've almost accepted I'm better off without William, but it still hurts like crazy. I need a change of subject. 'So what the hell have you done to your hair? And what's with the moustache?'

He laughs. 'I'm playing Hercule Poirot.'

'A card game?'

'You know who Poirot is, you devil. Don't you come here teasing your poor old dad.'

I laugh. 'Sorry, I couldn't resist.' It's good to see Dad back performing with the local am-drams. 'Well I must say I'm relieved. I thought it was your new look. So a French detective, aye?' I'm teasing.

He straightens his back, and with a pretty impressive accent says, 'I'll 'ave you know Poirot is from Belgium.' He picks up his mug and takes a sip. 'So are you on holiday from work?'

'Unpaid leave.'

'And you're managing OK?'

I want to tell him I'm not managing at all. That I'm going to have to move out of London because I can't afford the rent, but instead I say, 'Fine, I've got a bit of money saved.'

11

'It will be good for you. You never gave yourself time to grieve after your mum.'

'Oh I don't know, I've done a ridiculous amount of crying.' My voice cracks.

'Oh, love.'

'Will it ever get any easier, Dad?'

He lifts his shoulders. 'They say it does, eventually.'

I blow steam from the tea and take a sip. 'I thought if I came to see you, stayed for a bit ...' I suddenly feel overwhelmed. I haven't been back here since Mum died, and there are memories of her, of my childhood, everywhere.

'The thing is ...' He glances at his case by the back door, that I hadn't noticed.

There's a beat before my thoughts become words. 'You're going away?' I rub my temples. I don't want to go home right now. I want to stay here with him. I meet his eyes, knowing he feels awful. 'Oh God, I shouldn't have turned up unannounced. I just wanted to surprise you, that's all.' It wasn't strictly true. I needed him. Desperately.

'Don't be daft. I'm thrilled to see you, love. But—'

'I should have called you first.' Despite him telling me each time we spoke on the phone that he keeps busy, that he'd even joined the local ornithologists, that he'd started acting again, I still imagined him sitting at home broken – like me. And truth is, I know he is broken. He's just better at plastering over the cracks than I am.

'You can stay here, Amelia,' he says. 'I'm only away for a week, and once I'm back, we can—'

'No. No it's fine.' I rise. Annoyed. Not with him, but with myself. Rattled that I assumed he would be here waiting for me, his life on pause.

'Sit,' he says. 'I'm not leaving for half an hour, and I'm all packed. We have lots to catch up on.'

I lower myself back down. 'So where are you off to?' I say, diverting the conversation into unknown territory.

'Well, that's the thing.' He avoids meeting my eyes as he runs a finger over his moustache. 'I'm hoping you'll understand why I didn't tell you.'

'Didn't tell me?' My body tenses.

'I'll be staying at Drummondale House.'

'What?' It came out high-pitched. 'Why?'

'Lark disappeared a year ago this week,' he says.

'Christ, Dad. Don't you think I know that?'

He covers my hand with his. 'I know you know that, love. I'm not trying to upset you.'

'But why didn't you invite me to come with you?' I'm hurt, upset. I pull my hand from under his, lean back, and cross my arms over my chest, knowing I'm being defensive. 'At least mention it?'

'Because … because I didn't think you would cope with it, Amelia. You've been so up and down over the last year. I thought it would be too much. I didn't mean to deceive you. I wanted to protect you.'

He's right. I've been so unstable. 'But I still don't get why you would go back to that place.'

His chest rises and falls as he takes a deep breath. 'Inspector Beynon may have given up hope of finding Lark, but I haven't. I need to check we didn't miss anything. Something that could lead us to her.'

'After all this time?'

He raises his eyes to the ceiling, tears glistening. 'I don't know. I can't explain it. It just feels right somehow.'

'Oh, Dad,' I say, softening. 'She's not in Scotland.' But there is no strength in my words. Despite the whole area being searched at the time, my mind still wanders back there. What if someone hid her underground, or deep in one of the many caves along the shoreline? We'd combed the area for hours, the police, dogs, and people from the local villages giving their support. But had we really covered every inch of the Drummondale House estate? I sigh deeply, reach over, and close my hand over Dad's.

Truth is, I've been through every possibility. At first I'd clung to the hope she took off. But when Mum died and Lark never appeared – never said goodbye – hope petered away, and lately I'd wondered if we'd missed something in Scotland too.

Dad grabs a clump of tissues from a box on the table and divides them between us.

'I need to do something,' he says, dashing a tissue across his eyes. 'Since your mum's been gone, all I can think is what if we missed something, so we thought we'd head up there.'

'We?'

He nods. 'Thomas and Maddie are coming for support.' He looks away, as though he doesn't want to see my reaction.

I feel my eyes widen. 'Maddie is your support?'

'Not exactly. Thomas is my support, and your brother needs her. You know that.'

My jaw clenches. 'Bloody Maddie. I curse the day she became Thomas's carer.'

He shakes his head. 'Please don't say that, love.' He places his hand over mine once more. 'You sound so bitter.'

I cover my face with my hands. 'She should never have said those things about me on her vlog, Dad.'

'I agree, it was thoughtless—'

'Thoughtless? She made me look—'

'I know, love, but she's young. She made a silly mistake, and you needed someone to vent your anger on. She's sorry, Amelia. The post has gone now. Please let it go.'

But I'm not sure I can let it go.

'I've rented two of the cottages,' he says. 'If you feel you're up to it, there's room for a small one.'

I look up and shake my head. I'm not sure I can face going back there.

'No.' He shakes his head too. 'I didn't think so. Although, it could be a chance to talk to Maddie – lay your demons to rest, as they say.'

14

'I quite like my demons full of energy, thanks very much.' It comes out snarky, and I'm not even sure of the point I'm trying to make.

He looks down for a moment, and then up and into my eyes. 'And we might find something that leads to Lark.'

I so want to embrace his hope.

I have three choices: One, go home to my empty apartment and lose myself down a bottle of wine every night, whilst making desperate calls to William. Two, spend time here alone in this house, regressing into my childhood. Or three, head to Scotland, to Drummondale House with my dad beside me.

Tears burn as I imagine one of us recalling something vital that leads to finding Lark safe and well. Is it really possible?

'OK,' I say before I can change my mind, a surge of hope rising inside me. What if the answer to my sister's disappearance really does lie up there in the Scottish Highlands? What if retracing our steps unearths a vital clue?

I drain my tea. 'But you'll need to keep me away from Maddie,' I say, thumping my mug down. 'Or I may just kill her.'

*

I watch from the front doorstep, as Dad lifts Thomas into the back seat of his Ford Freedom, and puts my brother's wheelchair into the boot. Thomas looks different to when I saw him last. His hair's longer, and it's tied back in a man-bun, and he's grown a beard too, which suits him.

'Robert, could you spare one of those bottles of water? My mouth is so dry,' Maddie calls out of the rear car window, as he loads a pack of water into the boot along with the bags and other provisions, including a litre bottle of gin, which looks tempting. The wind catches Maddie's silky black hair and whips it across her face. 'The weather's going to be a challenge,' she says, pulling the strands from her cheeks. 'Let's hope it's better in Scotland.'

'I hope so too,' Dad says with a laugh.

I notice the way Thomas still looks at Maddie. I can't work out if he's in love with her, and I worry she'll break his heart. A brief memory of her kissing his teary cheeks at Mum's funeral flutters in and then evaporates. I'm sure she only sees herself as his carer, and one day she'll meet someone and fall in love, and then what? Where does that leave my brother? My parents never planned for that.

'Are you getting in, Amelia?' Dad slams the car boot, and hands Maddie a bottle of water through the window.

Apprehension and the freezing weather nails me to the spot, and the earlier fluttering of snow is moving into blizzard territory.

'Amelia?'

'Uh-huh.' A deep sigh turns to mist in front of me, as I make my way down the path, almost slipping on an earlier settling of snow. I climb into the passenger seat. Slam the door. Say nothing.

'Grumpy!' Thomas says, with a laugh. 'I can see you're going to be fun on this trip.'

'How the bloody hell is this trip going to be fun, Thomas?' I refuse to look round, sense Maddie's eyes boring into my back.

'Oh come on, sis,' Thomas says. 'Don't be like that. We've got so much to catch up on.' My brother seems oblivious to the suffocating tension in the car, or the fact we are heading to where we last saw our sister; that Drummondale House was the last place Mum smiled.

Dad gets into the driver's seat and closes the door.

I finally snatch a glance over my shoulder, and Thomas grabs the moment to smile my way. He may be twenty-eight, but I still see my little brother sitting there, and recall how we used to run and play together. But that was long before he took off to America – long before his accident.

I return his smile, and turn watery eyes back to the front window.

'Should we be going in this?' I ask Dad as he starts the engine. 'The snow is pretty heavy.'

'It doesn't look great, does it?' Dad agrees, flicking on the wipers. He leans forward and looks up through the window towards the sky.

'Of course we should go,' Thomas says. 'It will be fine. I'm psyched up for it now.'

'I don't know, it looks a bit scary,' Maddie says.

'Well, let's give it a go, and turn back if it gets too bad,' Dad says, putting the car in gear, and pulling away.

It will take over four hours to get to Drummondale House, so I bring out my phone, shove in my ear buds, and begin trawling through YouTube videos, particularly enjoying a video of a cavalier puppy being taught to high-five and roll over. Eventually, despite not being tired, my eyes grow heavy – and sleep with its awful nightmares of a year ago beckons.

I'm going to where I last saw Lark.

A sense of foreboding rises. Why do I feel this is the biggest mistake of my life?

Chapter 3

Present Day

Amelia

The first two hours of the ride is silent, and by the time we get to the services in Perth, the snow has turned to rain now lashing across the windscreen.

Dad pulls onto the forecourt. 'Need to stretch my legs,' he says. And we take the opportunity to grab a takeaway.

Dad and I get out of the car, and race towards the McDonald's, and despite him using his coat as a makeshift umbrella for us both, rain splatters down my collar, making me shiver.

We are silent in the queue. We are silent returning with the burgers. We are silent while we eat in the car.

'Well at least the snow's cleared,' Dad says finally, finishing the last of his burger and screwing up the wrapper. 'I was beginning to worry we would end up snowed in in the Scottish Highlands.' He laughs. 'Imagine that.'

'I'd rather not,' I say, though the thought of it raining all the time we are there is almost as bad.

'Only another two and a half hours,' Dad says, wiping his hands with a serviette. 'You've got a splodge of something on your cheek, love,' he adds, and I instinctively touch my face, and get mayo over my fingers.

Back on the road, I find myself dozing once more. When I wake, the car's heater is pumping out a dry heat, and snow tumbles from a charcoal-grey sky once more, as though someone's tipped out a giant bag of cotton-wool balls.

Dad is crawling along at ten miles per hour and the wipers struggle to and fro – thump, thump, thump onto cushions of snow each side of the windscreen.

'When did it start snowing again?' I say, rubbing sleep from my eyes.

'About an hour ago,' he says. 'We're almost there.'

We make our way up a steep hill, skidding and sliding. 'I think we should have turned back, Dad,' I say. But there's a determined look on his face. He's desperate to get there.

As the wrought-iron gates that separate Drummondale House from the rest of the Scottish Highlands loom in front of us, my stomach flips. Memories of the last time we were here invade my thoughts, and a feeling of absolute dread rises inside me.

The gates stand open, and as Dad pulls through them onto the drive that leads to the ruin, I battle an urge to grab the steering wheel and turn the car around. We shouldn't have come. My heartbeat quickens, banging against my chest as I catch sight of Drummondale House, shrouded in snowflakes. A few years back I would have whipped out my phone and taken a picture. Put it on Facebook or Instagram. But I'm a different person now. Broken.

I sense Maddie moving forward in her seat, her breath hot on my neck. 'This weather is awful, Robert,' she says. 'I mean I love snow, but this is crazy.' There's tension in her voice. 'We should have turned back an hour ago.'

I turn and glare at her. 'Well, maybe you should have said something an hour ago.'

'It's too late now, Maddie, love,' Dad says, meeting her eye in the rear-view mirror.

I snap a look at Dad, my body tense. His eyes are back on the windscreen, and he's hunched forward over the steering wheel.

'I'm sure it will clear up by morning,' he says.

'Unlikely. I'm pretty sure this snow is here to stay, Robert.' There's a quiver in Maddie's voice.

'Well we can't go back now,' he says, blinking. 'It's too late. We're here now.'

We pull onto the snow-covered car park, and memories of twelve months ago skid into my head like a skier on a downward slope. I remember it all so well.

I press my forehead against the side window, eyes tipped towards the sky. It's blustery out there – the wind rattling and moaning as it wraps itself around tall trees that sway as though dodging its icy hands.

A sudden thump on the glass makes me jump. 'Fuck!' It's Ruth, the owner, far too close to the window, peering in at us, her small, grey eyes screwed up against the weather. I sink down in my seat, holding my chest, taking deep breaths to calm myself.

'I'll get the keys,' Dad says, switching off the engine. He leans over his seat, grabs his coat from between Thomas and Maddie, and opens the door, which swings outwards, almost ripping from its hinges. Snow invades the car.

Once outside, Dad struggles to put on his coat, wind whipping it into the air like a kite, as he pushes his body weight against the door to close it. Finally, he beats the wind, and manages to get his coat on, doing it up as he trudges through settled snow, Ruth by his side.

I glance back at Thomas. He's asleep, making puff puff sounds as he breathes. It breaks my heart that he messed up his young life. I can still recall how excited he was a few years back when a Hollywood director hired him to write a screenplay for a new feature – we all were. He'd flown to the US full of so much hope.

But he struggled. Mingling in circles where he didn't quite belong was too much for him. He began drinking and dabbling in drugs to cope, and instead of his life taking off, as it should have, he spiralled downhill. Lost control.

I gulp back my emotions, and turn back before Maddie can speak.

The cottages are a blur through the front windscreen, and I realise tears have filled my eyes. I cough, choking, as my larynx twists. I'd blocked this place out as best I could. Attempted to run from the memory.

'You do know I'm sorry,' Maddie says and I feel her move, and grip my seat. 'That I didn't mean—'

'I don't want to talk about it,' I cut in.

I hear her flop back in her seat. 'OK,' she says. 'Fine.'

We sit in silence for some time, before the car door opens, and Dad jumps into the front seat, feathers of snow covering his hair and coat.

'Ruth says we can pull up in front of the cottages for now.' He starts the engine and drives towards Bluebell Cottage where Mum, Jackson and Lark had stayed last time. He stops outside the front door, and glances over his shoulder. 'Right, let's get you two in the warm.'

'Thomas,' Maddie says, shaking my brother to wake him. 'We're here.'

He opens his eyes. 'Christ. Where are we – Narnia?' He pushes his nose against the window, and takes a gulp of air. 'When did we drive through a wardrobe?'

Maddie laughs.

'We have seen better days,' Thomas says, his voice suddenly low and level. He often quotes Shakespeare, since studying literature at university and getting a first-class master's degree. 'Now is the winter of our discontent.'

Chapter 4

Present Day

Ruth

'Finn!' I call, heading into the kitchen. 'We need to prepare the vegetables. I want this meal to be perfect.' I pick up a small knife that once belonged to my mother, and begin peeling potatoes. 'Finn!'

'For God's sake, Mum, give me time to get down the bloody stairs.' He appears, lifts a stripy apron from the back of the kitchen door, and slips it over his head.

I look up at him and smile. He's looking so much better than he did a year ago. He runs each morning before I get up, and every evening too. I reach up, stroke his hair – he suits it shorter – a tingle of satisfaction running through my body. He's finally got over his wife's affair. It took some doing but I've got my son back.

Finn picks up a peeler, begins stripping carrots with the speed and skill of a professional chef. I've taught him well. My daughter couldn't carry the baton, but Finn is the next best thing. 'So the guests are here?' he says.

I nod. 'They are Lark's family. They hope to remember something.'

He catches his finger on the blade, and winces. 'About the disappearance?'

'Mmm. I'm not sure what they hope to achieve.'

Finn shrugs, glances through the window. 'And the snow is getting deeper out there. They can hardly search the woods.' He crosses the kitchen and grabs a blue plaster from a medical box. 'This is going to be awkward. I mean do we mention what happened?'

'We let them take the lead.' I cut a peeled potato in half, and drop it into a saucepan of water with a splash. 'Oh, and I had a call from Rosamund Green this morning. She should be here by dinnertime with her daughter.'

'Really?' He glances towards the kitchen window once more, his eyes narrowing. Snow rests on the frame, like a picture on a Christmas card. 'Do the Taylors know she's going to be staying here too? I mean Rosamund wasn't exactly supportive when Lark went missing.'

I shrug. 'I have no idea.' I feel a smile stretch across my face. 'But I can't wait to see how it all unfolds.'

'Well I for one am dreading it.'

I curl a tendril of hair behind my ear, noticing how grey I'm getting. 'It will be fine, Finn,' I say. 'I'll make sure everything is perfect.'

Chapter 5

A Year Ago

Amelia

They tried so hard to hide their sadness the day they arrived at Drummondale House a year ago, the sun warm on their backs as they headed across the cobbled car park.

Amelia clung on to her dad's arm. To her, he'd always been strong. Her rock. The person she leaned on if her world fell apart: like the night she was dumped at the school prom by Joshua Williams, or the day she didn't get that weekend job at Blockbuster she'd set her heart on.

Once, when she was little, her dad had appeared in the kitchen wearing green corduroy trousers that were slightly baggy at the knees, and an equally green cardigan. Amelia called him The Incredible Hulk, and her mum couldn't stop laughing. She could never see what Amelia could see – called him a dusty historian. Maybe that's why she left him for Jackson.

Today there was no sign of The Incredible Hulk. Her dad was struggling like the rest of them. This was to be her mum's final holiday, and she'd gathered those she loved most in the Scottish Highlands.

As they strolled across the grass, Amelia released her dad's arm. Her insides were a knot of sadness and anxiety, her eyes ached from tears she tried to hold back. But she knew, like everyone else on this ridiculous venture, that she had to make it the best holiday ever, for her mum's sake.

'You OK?' she asked, looking up at her dad as they followed the rest of the family – six of them, and Maddie – towards Drummondale House reception.

He fiddled with the binoculars hanging around his neck – always a keen bird watcher – and shrugged, eyes shining. It was a stupid question. Of course he wasn't OK. He was losing the only woman he had ever loved to cancer, and he couldn't even comfort and care for her, because Jackson bloody Cromwell had moved in on her a year ago – taken her from him.

Still, Amelia told herself, her mum must care for her dad. She wanted him to be there. She touched his arm. 'We'll get through this,' she said. 'For Mum.'

'Well, it's a tough one, and no mistaking.' He rubbed his head with both hands, as though the action would scrub away the pain. 'And if I'm honest, I don't feel right being here. I don't belong with your mum anymore.'

'But she still loves you, in her own way.'

He shook his head.

'You were together for over thirty years, Dad. You had three children together.'

'Yes, but …' He looked towards the cloudless sky, his brown eyes watery. 'Bloody disease,' he muttered, his voice cracking. He'd aged. His dark hair speckled with grey, the creases on his forehead deepened. Amelia leaned into him. Rested her head on his shoulder. Finding out her mum had terminal cancer had taken its toll on them all.

'It's crap,' she said, looking towards Lark sitting cross-legged on the grass brushing a tear from her pale cheek. None of them were doing a good job of hiding their desperation. They needed to sort themselves out.

Lark looked so different to the last time Amelia saw her. Gone were the pale-blue dungarees, the high ponytail, her love of Justin Bieber. Today, she wore a flowing black dress, and black lace-up ankle boots. She was growing up fast, looked older than her seventeen years, her long blonde hair flowing down her back, her freckled cheeks masked by pale foundation, her lips painted red.

'She's refusing to go to university next year,' her dad said, seeming to notice where Amelia's eyes had landed.

'Lark?'

He nodded. 'She's been so moody lately. I can't get to the bottom of it.'

'Mum's dying,' Amelia whispered. 'She isn't coping.'

Lark looked up, and caught Amelia's eye across the expanse of grass. Her eyeliner had smudged beneath her eyes, and Amelia felt a pang of guilt that she rarely saw her anymore. 'I'm worried about her,' she said, turning back to her dad.

He nodded. 'Me too.'

The rest of the family reached reception, and Lark got to her feet and shuffled towards them, head down.

'We should probably go over,' Amelia said. 'Try to look happy.'

'Yes, of course – chin up and all that.'

They rose and linked arms. 'I'm so glad you're here,' Amelia whispered.

As they approached, Jackson – who was only six years older than Amelia at thirty-six – had taken charge, and was in full voice.

'It looks a bit small in there,' he said, peering through the bay window into reception, one hand over his eyes to block out the sun. 'I'll go in and get the keys, shall I?' He pushed his sandy-blond hair from his face with an exaggerated flick. 'Then we can unpack,' he went on. 'Have a rest and freshen up before dinner. How does that sound?'

'Good to see you taking charge,' Amelia said with a roll of her eyes. This man walked in on my family and changed everything. She bit down on her lip. What right did she have to say anything? Her fleeting visits to the apartment Mum shared with him in Tweedmouth, brandishing huge bunches of flowers that only went some way towards easing her guilt, were hardly the act of a supportive daughter. She'd been a coward hiding in London, hoping a miracle would happen and she would never have to face the loss of her mother.

Her mum, who was holding on to Jackson's arm, threw her a pleading look. She loved Jackson – Amelia knew that, even if she didn't understand why. Yes she was still heartbroken that she'd left her dad, but this break wasn't about Amelia. This was about her mum's happiness – a happiness that would be cut short long before it should have been.

'Sounds fine by me,' Amelia said, and a lump rose in her throat as her mum smiled and mouthed, 'Thank you.'

She let out a sigh, and looked away. How the hell was she – or any of them – going to get through the next few days?

Chapter 6

A Year Ago

Ruth

Ruth stood behind an antique reception desk, inquisitive grey eyes, like marbles, fixed on the couple entering. The woman looked familiar, though she couldn't fathom why, but then Ruth had met so many people over the years – visitors to Drummondale House.

'Good morning.' She moulded her face into a welcoming smile, without showing her teeth. She didn't like her teeth – far too small, her mother always said. 'Welcome to Drummondale House.'

'Hey there.' The man was American, and exceptionally handsome. His face lit up in a smile. 'I'm Jackson Cromwell, and this is my partner Caroline Taylor.'

Ruth's guests fascinated her. The anticipation of discovering more about their lives was her only pleasure outside of cooking. They always arrived smiling because they were on holiday, hiding their faults and flaws, their quirks, and deepest troubles. But what was beneath their façades intrigued her. It was like finding hidden treasure when it revealed itself – always a delight to see that they were never quite as happy below their holiday sheen. No happier than she was.

Ruth had been here all her life. Her mother had owned this small part of the Drummondale estate, and her father before her.

'Your great-grandfather won the land in a poker game from George Collis,' her mother told her once. And now it was hers – a sizeable piece of land right smack bang in the middle of the Drummondale House estate. Her mother had used the land as a camping retreat until her death thirty-five years ago. She'd been an untrusting woman. 'Ruth,' she would say, 'keep your eye on everyone you meet, and trust no one. Nobody's really your friend.' And Ruth followed her mother's advice always. Apart from that one summer when she was seventeen, when he said he loved her – and she'd believed him.

'It's stunning here,' Jackson continued, looking through the window, forcing Ruth from her memory. She couldn't help staring at him. There was something about him that drew her in.

'Aye, it is. A beautiful part of the country,' she said.

'He's been on TV and on the Broadway stage.' It was Caroline. 'He did really well in the US.'

'Sorry?' Ruth moved her eyes from Jackson to Caroline. The woman was much older than he was, twenty years, probably, and wearing faded blue jeans, a thick jumper, and a powder-blue scarf around her head. Ruth didn't need to be told this woman had cancer. Her cheeks were slightly bloated from steroids, and chemo had stolen her eyelashes, her eyebrows, the colour from her cheeks.

'I thought you must have recognised him. You were staring.'

'No, no, I don't think so.' Ruth felt wrong-footed – her cheeks burned.

'Don't worry,' Caroline continued with a small laugh. 'He's a bit of a head-turner. I'm used to it.'

Ruth held her smile, but desperately wanted to hide her face. She certainly couldn't recall seeing Jackson on TV, but there was no doubting he had the kind of look people noticed, the kind of eyes – green with flecks of hazel – that could ignite a fire inside you – something that hadn't happened to Ruth in a very long while.

Caroline picked up a pen. 'So where do I sign?' she said, her eyes fixed on Ruth, as though taking her in.

'If you could write your name in the register please, and the names of your party, and their relationship to you.' Ruth didn't need all that information, but it helped her get to know her guests better. She unbuttoned and rebuttoned her cardigan as she watched Caroline write, her handwriting distinctive, flamboyant swirling and curling on the page:

Caroline Taylor
Jackson Cromwell (partner)
Robert Taylor (ex-husband)
Amelia Taylor (daughter)
Lark Taylor (daughter)
Thomas Taylor (son)
Maddie Jenkins (son's carer)

Ruth couldn't help but notice what a complicated setup it was, with Caroline's ex-husband being with them, and a fizz of excitement ran through her. This could get interesting.

Caroline placed the pen on the register, and straightened her back, letting out a little gasp, as though the job had exhausted her.

'Thank you.' Ruth picked up the pen, put it in a wooden pot, and closed the register. 'You have the weather on your side. Eighteen degrees in late November is almost unheard of around these parts. We normally have snow by now.'

'Yes, it's beautiful out there,' Jackson agreed, as Ruth reached behind her and unhooked two sets of keys from a small rack. 'It's so peaceful too. I'm sure we'll have a relaxing stay.'

'I'm sure you will.' Ruth glanced at Caroline, who had moved towards the window, and now had her back to her.

'Bluebell Cottage, the largest dwelling, is next to the ruins,' Ruth continued. 'Honeysuckle Cottage is on the far side, backing onto the forest. There are some lovely walks down to the sea, with stunning views you'll love.' She placed the keys in Jackson's outstretched hand and smiled. 'But do be careful if you go into the woods after dark. It's easy to get lost and end up on the cliff edge.'

'Thanks,' Jackson said, once Ruth had told him dinner would be served in the conservatory at seven, and breakfast at eight the following morning.

'The electric gates are the only way in or out of the site. They open automatically if you want to leave, and there's a wee code on the key ring to get you back in again after dark.'

'Great. We saw a quaint little pub about ten miles down the road, didn't we, Caroline? We might head there one evening.'

'It all sounds lovely, Ruth,' Caroline said, turning from the window. 'I can't think of a better place to be.'

'Have a good day,' Jackson said, and Caroline gripped hold of his arm as they made their way through the door and out into the bright afternoon.

'Shall I get your wheelchair from the car, darling?' he asked her.

'I'll be fine,' she said, as the door closed behind them.

Through the window, Ruth watched as the family met up again. And as they chattered, she studied their faces, wondering who they all were. She suspected the tall man in his fifties was probably the ex-husband as he looked moody and out of place. The young man in the wheelchair was perhaps the son, Thomas Taylor, and the pretty woman with shiny black hair pushing him, was perhaps his carer, Maddie. She studied the pretty teenage girl dressed in black – unsmiling – her arms wrapped around herself, as though if she let go she would fall apart. She reminded Ruth of Kyla, and she wanted to take the girl in her arms and squeeze.

31

The door leading to the back of the cottage opened, and Ruth startled. She spun round. 'Finn.'

His light brown hair, parted in the middle, hung limply to his shoulders. His grey tracksuit bottoms were misshapen at the knees, and his black AC/DC sweatshirt stretched too tightly across his chest. She had to admit he'd lost his looks since he returned home. But he was better off without her. Better at home with his mother. Better away from his wicked wife. And now Ruth was dependent on his company again – she could turn to him when black moods invaded – when memories flooded in. It was good to have him home where he belonged.

She glanced back at the window. Jackson and his group were walking across the grass towards the cottages – she wished they would use the path.

'The big group has just checked in,' she told Finn. 'Three more guests are arriving tomorrow from the same party.' She placed her hands flat on the counter – hands she felt gave her age away. Despite her ritual of applying hand cream night and morning, these hands – her hands – told the world she was in her late fifties. That she'd had a difficult life. Maybe if she kept them tucked in her cardigan pockets she could pass for fifty. She took a deep breath. It didn't matter how old she was, not really. She could never get back what she'd lost. 'We'll meet them all at dinner,' she said.

Finn opened the door to the back of the house once more, and the aroma of the pork joint sizzling in the oven hit Ruth's senses. There was only one vegetarian this time, and Ruth had prepared a small broccoli and tomato quiche for her that morning. 'Talking of dinner,' she went on, following Finn through the door, 'let's peel the veg together, shall we?'

Chapter 7

A Year Ago

Amelia

'Caroline and I will grab Bluebell Cottage,' Jackson said, waving the keys above his head like a tour guide, the sun glinting on his hair, making it shine like gold. He flashed Lark a smile, and added, 'Lark, you can share with us.'

'I'd rather not,' she said. Her tone was calm and even, but there was something in the way her sister looked at him that Amelia couldn't quite put her finger on.

'Oh please stay with us, darling,' Caroline said, gripping Lark's hand. 'We can have some mother and daughter quality time.'

Jackson placed a set of keys in Amelia's hand. 'The rest of you can take Honeysuckle Cottage.'

'Yes, sir,' Amelia muttered, and as she turned to head away, first checking her mum wasn't watching, she saluted him. She knew it was childish, that she should, for her mum's sake, stop acting the fool.

As they walked away, Maddie was suddenly in step beside

Amelia. She linked her arm through her elbow. There was no doubting she was stunning, with glossy raven hair, a clear, olive complexion, and deep brown eyes. She had come over from America and was staying with family when she'd spotted the advertisement for a carer for Thomas a year ago. It was after some awkward interviews, including one with a man in his eighties with arthritis who Robert was certain needed a carer more than Thomas, and one with a woman who insisted she would have to bring her three Labradoodles with her because they couldn't possibly cross their legs for the four hours she would be away, that twenty-two-year-old Maddie Jenkins turned up, brightening the room.

Thomas liked her from the off, and although he'd never admitted to anyone the emotional pain he'd been under since his accident, closing himself off completely when he returned from the States, the family knew Maddie had pulled him back from the edge.

'Do you like him?' Maddie whispered to Amelia now, as they made their way towards Honeysuckle Cottage. It was one of two cottages that backed onto part of the forest that formed a semi-circle around a large expanse of grass.

'Who?'

'Jackson.' She kept darting him looks over her shoulder, a cigarette dangling from her free hand.

'I barely know him.' It was true. Amelia had seen him on the odd occasion she visited, and her observations were conflicted. On the one hand, he seemed fond of her mother, but he was also vain and cocksure of himself. She certainly wasn't his biggest fan. 'Anyway, it doesn't matter whether I like him or not, Maddie,' she said. 'As long as my mum's happy, I'm happy.'

'He's great-looking though, don't you think?' She almost swooned as they continued across the plush green grass.

Amelia glanced over her shoulder, watching as he headed into the cottage, his arm around her mum's shoulders, Lark a few steps behind. As though sensing her stare, he bolted her a look, and smiled. Yes, he was good-looking – too good-looking – tall, slender yet muscular. She narrowed her eyes. Didn't return his smile. What had attracted him to her mother? As lovely as her mum was, Jackson, with his charms and good looks, could have had his pick of women of his own age.

'Not my type,' Amelia said, looking forward once more. He wasn't. She preferred her men a little rough around the edges – and Jackson was a priceless jewel that positively gleamed. She shrugged, unhappy discussing his appearance – or him at all for that matter. Apart from anything else, her dad was only a few steps in front of them pushing Thomas in his wheelchair.

'So, how are things with you, Maddie?' It was an attempt to change the subject.

'Great.' Maddie released Amelia's arm, and ran towards the cottage, her floral dress flapping her calves.

Amelia followed and, once they were congregated around the red-painted door of the cottage where they would spend the next few days, she suddenly felt unnerved. The area was too quiet – just the rustle of trees swaying in a light breeze, the caw of a crow. She turned, taking in the ruins, shuddering at the sight of the crumbling walls, the broken statues. Why had her mum picked here and not Spain or Greece? But then she wasn't fit enough to travel, and Amelia quickly chastised herself for being selfish.

This was where her mum had spent wonderful holidays as a child and as a teenager. It held happy memories for her. This break was all about her mum and nothing about Amelia. Supressing a sense of foreboding, she stepped inside the cottage and closed the door.

Chapter 8

Present Day

Amelia

Dad drives with care, snow crunching under tyres as he heads towards Honeysuckle Cottage, where we'd stayed a year ago.

Together we carry in our luggage, and close the door against the weather.

Ruth has lit the wood burner and the cottage feels warm and cosy, after the freezing conditions outside. We stand for some moments in the semi-darkness, both lost in thought, and I know, like me, the memories of last year are flooding Dad's thoughts.

I feel that familiar sensation of tears rising. I would give anything to have everyone here with me, for the sun to beam down – for the sky to be clear and blue. 'What are we doing here, Dad?' I drop my rucksack to the floor with a thud, and flick on the light, hope of finding anything that could lead to Lark falling away.

'I'm already wondering that myself, love.' He runs his fingers through his damp hair. 'I suppose I thought ... well like I said before … that something might come to me. But now we're here it feels such a ridiculous idea.'

I tug off my boots and coat, and pad towards the window. It's bright out there, the snow reflecting light, and a full moon hovers above the ruin. It's beautiful – peaceful yet haunting.

After staring out for some time, I pull the curtains across the window. 'Was there something specific that drew you back here, Dad?' I turn to see him perched on the edge of the sofa, tears in his eyes.

'Only Lark,' he says, rubbing his face with his hands. And talking through his fingers, adds, 'I hoped to find Lark.'

I race to his side, drop down next to him, and wrap my arms around him. 'Oh, Dad.'

'Where is she, Amelia?' His tears turn to sobs, and I'm struggling. Yes, I've seen him cry – when Lark went missing, and after Mum's funeral, but it never gets easier seeing your father cry. 'Where's my little girl?'

'I wish I knew.' I'm crying too, fat tears streaming down my face – not only for his little girl, but for mine too. We're a mess – a tragic bloody mess.

We finally release each other, and he dries his eyes on his sleeve. 'Do you still think he took her?'

'Jackson?'

He nods. 'What did your mum really know about him? What did any of us know about him?'

It's true. Mum had known very little. He told her his parents had recently died, and it was only by accident she'd found out they'd been travellers. When he disappeared, she never spoke about him again.

I lean my head on Dad's shoulder, my eyes growing heavy, and before long the journey catches up with us both, and we drift off to sleep.

*

Someone is knocking at the door. My eyes spring open, and I glance at my watch. It's almost seven.

'Dad,' I say, pulling myself upright, and he stirs. The hammering grows louder. 'It's probably Maddie needing help getting Thomas over to the conservatory for dinner.'

I jump up and hurry to open the door. Maddie stubs out a cigarette on the porch, and dashes past me, bringing a flurry of snow and the smell of tobacco with her. She's togged up against the weather in a furry deerstalker hat and a navy ski suit that I can't believe she's had the sense to bring with her.

'Hey, Robert, are you ready to eat?' She aims her question at Dad, acts as though I'm not here. 'I think you'll need to carry Thomas. We'll never get his wheelchair through all this white stuff.'

'Yes, yes of course. I'll carry him,' Dad says, his earlier sadness masked with a smile.

'It's a good thing you're strong, Robert,' she says.

Dad rises and flexes his muscles, and she laughs. He likes her. Mum did too. 'She makes Thomas happy,' Mum would say, when I tried to suggest Maddie shouldn't vlog about us; that I didn't want a breakdown of our lives online for everyone to hear about.

'Are you ready, love?' Dad says to me.

I move across the room to the mirror above the wood burner and comb my fingers through my hair, catching a tangle and yelping. I look a right state, but I don't care.

'Yep,' I say, pulling on my padded jacket, and bending to pull on my fur-lined boots.

We trudge through the snow, and, as promised, Dad carries Thomas. Maddie walks along beside them. I dawdle behind, kicking snow like a sulky child.

Ruth is by the conservatory door, patting warmth into her arms. Her hair, pulled back in a ponytail, looks greyer than it did this time last year, though I'm sure she's wearing the same button-through knee-length dress and cardigan.

'He looks heavy,' she says, with a smile, as Dad carries Thomas through the door and lowers him down gently onto a chair. Maddie and I file in behind them.

'Cheers, Dad,' Thomas says, looking dishevelled, and I wonder if he's in any pain. He shuffles free of his jacket. 'Although for the record, next time I'll get a taxi.'

Dad laughs as he takes his jacket from him and hangs it up.

Once we're free of our coats the rest of us sit down. The smell of dinner cooking tingles my taste buds, and I realise I'm hungry. But as I sit, surrounded by empty chairs where Mum, Lark, and Jackson sat one short year ago, a painful lump rises in my throat, and I lose my appetite.

Ruth approaches with her notebook and pen. 'Can I get anyone a wee drink?' she says. 'Tap water is included; anything else is extra.'

'A large white wine, please,' I say as a sense of déjà vu settles heavily on my shoulders.

Once we've received our drinks, and Ruth has vanished to the back of the house, the silence between the four of us is awkward and painful, and I'm almost relieved when the door springs opens. Until I see who it is.

'Rosamund,' I whisper. As elegant as ever, she's wearing the same orange coat she wore a year ago, topped off with a flamboyant fur hat and gloves. I feel a pang of envy when I notice she's pregnant.

Her eyes meet with Dad's. And without speaking she takes a seat.

I look over at Dad for an explanation, but he looks as bewildered as I feel, and is blinking rapidly. My body fizzes with adrenalin. Not once did she visit Mum after Lark went missing. Not once did she call to see how Mum was. She never even came to her funeral.

I desperately want to know what she's doing here. It can't be a coincidence, surely. I open my mouth, about to fire questions at her, tell her she was nothing more than a fake friend to Mum, but Maddie beats me to it.

'Hey, Rosamund, how are you?' she says, fiddling with the stem of her wine glass.

'I should be asking you that question,' Rosamund says, her tone soft and caring. She is stroking her stomach as though gaining comfort from her unborn child. I know that feeling. 'You must have had a dreadful year,' she goes on. 'I'm so sorry I haven't been in touch.'

'It's been awful,' Maddie says. 'But we're coming to terms with it all.'

'Are we?' I bristle. Maddie is not part of our family. How could she possibly know how we feel? Whether we are coming to terms with things? Which I'm not.

'When ... when did you lose Caroline?' Rosamund's voice cracks, her watery eyes glancing at the empty chair where Mum sat a year ago.

'Five months ago,' Dad says.

'I'm so sorry, Robert.' She leans across the table, and places her gloved hand on his. He snatches his hand away as though burned, leaving hers redundant on the table.

'It's not like we didn't know,' he says.

'It doesn't make it any easier.' She withdraws her hand too, and removes her gloves, tucking them into her coat pocket, and sits down.

The door from the kitchen opens. It's Finn. He looks different – slimmer, healthier, his hair short. 'Can I get you a drink, Rosamund?' he says, and then smiles at each of us in turn. It's good to see him.

'Please,' she says, removing her coat and hanging it up. 'An orange juice will go down a treat.'

'How were the roads?' Finn asks, as he pours juice into a crystal-glass tumbler.

'Horrendous. I skidded twice. Elise got quite panicked and feels a bit sick from the journey. But we got here in one piece, that's the main thing.' She glances at the window. 'I can't believe the

40

rate it was falling earlier. Thank goodness it's stopped for now.' She smiles. 'Elise wants to build a snowman in the morning. I'm sure there is still a small girl in there somewhere, even though she's taller than me now.' She's babbling. Perhaps it's us being here. Maybe we make her feel awkward – nervous. Well, she can't feel any more uncomfortable than I do.

*

'I'm going to head back to my cottage,' Dad says as he finishes his last mouthful, and puts down his cutlery. Throughout the meal, the tension was tangible, and I realise now I've drunk too much wine.

'I won't be long,' I say, picking up on a slight slur in my voice. 'I'll be up at the crack of dawn, I expect, so will need a few hours' beauty sleep.' Truth is though: I barely sleep at all anymore.

'You're an early riser too, are you?' Finn says, smiling my way from where he's propped against the bar, long legs splayed out in front of him. 'I get up for a run around six – maybe you could join me.'

'Not if you paid me a million pounds,' I say with a laugh, and he laughs too.

Dad gets up, and puts on his coat.

'Well it looks as though that's my lift,' Thomas says, smiling. And once Maddie has wrestled into her ski suit, and Thomas has put on his fur-collared jacket, Dad heaves him up, and carries him through the door, Maddie following behind.

I don't move. Truth is, I'm not ready to leave quite yet. I hope to get more out of Rosamund before the evening is over. Ask her why she never contacted Mum before she died. Why she didn't come to her funeral. Why she is here now.

'I normally close the dining room by nine,' Ruth says coming through the door from the back of the house, her tone spiky. She's been popping back and forth clearing the table for the last ten minutes, huffing – making it clear we've outstayed our welcome. 'Can't you take your chatter to one of your cottages?'

'Or,' I say, 'you and Finn could join us.' I beckon them, take a gulp of my fourth glass of wine, knowing I shouldn't drink any more.

Finn looks at his mum as though for approval.

'For Christ's sake, Finn, you must be in your thirties. Surely you don't have to ask your mum for permission.'

Ruth narrows her grey eyes.

'I'm so sorry, we're holding you up,' Rosamund says, smiling at Ruth, and goes to rise. I need to strike now. I lean across the table with a jolt, grab the sleeve of her jumper, and stare into her eyes. 'Why exactly are you here?'

'Sorry?'

'Here at Drummondale House on the anniversary of Lark's disappearance? It's no coincidence. It can't be.'

She lowers her head. 'No, you're right, Amelia.'

The door that leads to the back of the house slams shut, and I look up to see Finn and Ruth have left.

'Well?' I say, eyes back on Rosamund.

'If you let go of my jumper, I'll tell you.'

I realise my knuckles have turned white, and unclench my fingers.

'I heard on Maddie's vlog that you were all coming here. I wanted to see you. Put things right.'

'But you never once contacted my mum after Lark vanished. She needed a friend, and you weren't there for her.'

'No, and I'm sorry. The truth is I couldn't cope with watching her die.' Her eyes fill with tears. 'I know I was selfish then, and I'm selfish now, but … well … I need closure. Her loss haunts me.' She dashes a tear from the corner of her eye with her finger. 'I thought if I was to see you all, ask you to forgive me, it would help. I wasn't there for her, and I can't forgive myself.' She looks at her watch. 'Oh God, I should get back to Elise,' she says, grabbing her coat, and putting it on. She fumbles in her pocket and brings out her gloves. She's about to put them on when I pick up on the low ring of her phone. She pulls it from her pocket, and presses the screen.

'Hello, darling,' she says, pinning the phone to her ear. 'Calm down, sweetheart, talk slowly, the line's dreadful.' Another pause, longer this time. 'Oh, Elise, please, not this again, you know what your father said. You have to stop—'

'What is it? What's wrong?' I say.

Rosamund raises her eyes as though in desperation. 'OK. Keep the door locked,' she continues into the phone. 'I'm on my way.' She ends the call, and I stare, my curiosity piqued, waiting for her to explain. 'It's Elise,' she says. 'I need to go.'

'Is she OK?' I ask, rising. 'Is Neil with her?'

'No, he's not with us. He's working in Wales.' She races towards the door, her coat flapping open. Stops. Glances back. 'Elise said she saw someone looking in the window.' She takes a breath. 'Someone wearing a mask.'

'Oh God,' I say, my heartbeat picking up speed.

'I'm sure it's nothing; you know what she can be like.'

I nod, recalling Elise – the way she told stories.

But then I'd seen the masks last time we were here – we all had.

'She hasn't said anything like this in a long time,' Rosamund adds. And with that, she flutters her fingers, and heads out into the snowy night.

Chapter 9

Present Day

Ruth

I rarely show my annoyance. Normally I keep it bottled up, out of reach, not for human consumption. In fact, the last time I got angry was when Finn's wife came looking for him. That woman soon scurried away with her tail between her legs. But all evening Amelia's been pushing my buttons; talking loud, inhibitions lowered by alcohol. She should take note of her brother Thomas. He remained sober – a decent man.

I remember watching my husband drink too much each night – drowning his sadness, he said. I never needed alcohol to drown mine. The thing is, people spiral out of control when they drink too much. There are no exceptions.

And now, as I enter the conservatory once more, expecting everyone to have gone back to their cottages, Amelia is still here, alone, rocking her chair backwards and forwards, sipping yet more wine as she twiddles her red hair round her fingers.

'You should leave now,' I say, folding my arms. 'The dining room closes at nine, and it's almost ten-thirty.'

Amelia looks up at me. Shows no sign of moving.

'Finn!' I call out, and he appears through the door behind me looking flushed. He's probably been out for a brisk walk; he often goes out in the evening as part of his fitness regime.

Amelia turns and smiles at him. 'Finn,' she says, swinging her arm in the air in an exaggerated wave. 'How lovely to see you again.'

'Hey, shall I get you back to your cottage?' he says, walking towards her and, taking hold of her arms, he pulls her to her feet.

'I'm sure the lass can find her own way,' I say. 'Just point her towards the door, son.'

Amelia threads an arm through Finn's and leans against him. 'You smell nice,' she says.

I grind my teeth, turn, and head back into the main house, slamming the door behind me, disgusted by the young woman's behaviour.

Chapter 10

Present Day

Amelia

Snow swirls and twirls from the night sky, and I stick out my tongue. Try to catch flakes.

'Are you a bit of a mummy's boy, Finn?' I'm clinging to his arm as he guides me through the snow, brandishing a torch to light our way. I'm regretting the amount of wine I've drunk, as I'm at that stage where crap falls from my mouth. I shouldn't use alcohol to drown out real life, but sometimes it's just too easy. 'She's ever so, ever so, much possessive of you.'

'You think?' He sounds amused by me.

'Mmm.' I screw up my nose, and stare up at him. 'It's kind of obvious.'

'I guess she's relied on me over the years. She means well.' He shrugs and avoids my gaze. 'Just cares a bit too much, I guess. She's had a hard time of it over the years. What with …'

'With?'

'Oh nothing,' he says, and despite my intoxicated state, something tells me not to pry.

'Should we check Elise is OK, do you think?' I say, as we pass Primrose Cottage where Rosamund and Elise are staying.

He shakes his head. 'It's in darkness. They're probably asleep by now.'

'But Elise saw a masked face peering in her window, Finn. That's what she told Rosamund. And remember last time?'

'It's unlikely anyone peered in at her, Amelia. We're miles from anywhere, and the weather is awful. Elise probably imagined it.'

'She's pretty imaginative,' I agree, recalling her from the last time I was here.

'And it's quite creepy around here; can play tricks with your mind.'

I stop and look about me, my eyes falling on a set of footprints heading from Primrose Cottage towards the forest. 'Oh God, who made those?' I clench tighter onto Finn's arm, my heartbeat picking up speed. 'Someone else is here, Finn. Oh God, Elise was right.' I sound a bit manic.

Finn is silent for a while, his eyes on the footprints. It appears that whoever made them walked to Primrose Cottage, and returned the way they came.

'Do you think Rosamund has seen the footprints? Should we tell her?' I say.

'Tomorrow. Whoever it was has gone now.'

I shudder, unsure whether it's from fear or the freezing conditions. 'But—'

'Amelia!' It's Dad, hurrying through the snow towards us in his long winter coat, his arms folded around his body.

'You can head back now,' I say to Finn, releasing him. 'My dad will walk me the rest of the way.'

'Oh. Right. OK.'

'Thanks for bringing me this far – you're very kind.' I rise onto my toes, and kiss his cold cheek.

'No problem.' He raises his gloved hand in a wave, before turning and trudging back, his head down.

Dad and I carry on towards our cottage.

'I was getting worried about you,' he says. 'Though I shouldn't have been. Finn seems a nice guy.'

'Get that look off your face, Dad. He's not my type.' It's a lie. I like him. But a relationship, or even a brief fling, is the furthest thing from my thoughts right now, especially when a possessive mother looms large. I open my mouth to tell him about the footprints, but he speaks first.

'Odd that Rosamund is here, don't you think?'

I nod. 'She says she needs closure, Dad. Wants us all to forgive her for not being there for Mum.'

'Oh, I see. Well she won't be getting any forgiveness from me, that's for sure.'

I glance over my shoulder at the footprints, and back at Dad. He looks brighter than he did earlier. Any mention of anything odd will bring him tumbling down, and his thoughts will be back with Lark. I need to give him at least the rest of the evening off. I'll tell him in the morning.

*

I rise at six, and pad towards the bedroom window. My head thuds, my mouth is dry, and regrets fill my head at the things I said to Finn last night.

I pull back the curtains. It's still dark outside, but the lights on Rosamund's porch are on, haloing Elise crouched with her back to me in front of a rather splendid-looking snowman. She's clearly still a fan of pink; the hat she's wearing is the same one she wore on the beach a year ago, but the pink jacket is paler – more grown-up – and her fair hair is longer, several inches peeking out of the bottom of her woolly hat. As she rises and pushes a carrot into the snowman's head, I see she's taller, no longer a child but a young woman.

Unbidden memories flood my head of playing in the snow with Mum and Dad when I was a child, and my throat closes round them. I turn from the window, and shiver. It's not cold in the cottage. The central heating is on and, if anything, it's too warm. It's the simple thought of being here again – where Lark disappeared – where we were all last together.

I close the curtains again. I need water – lots of water – and head downstairs, where I gulp back a tumbler full, and flick on the kettle. I hear Dad's footfalls on the stairs, and make him some coffee, and myself some tea, and leave the kitchen.

He's sitting on the sofa, and I place the steaming mug on the table in front of him. 'Thanks, love,' he says, as I kiss his head.

I perch on the edge of the armchair, cradling my mug of tea. 'Rosamund and Elise have built a great snowman,' I say, before taking a sip.

He smiles. 'You used to love the snow,' he says. 'Lark not so much. She used to cry if her hands got too cold.' I hear a crack in his voice. 'And Thomas used to throw snowballs at me when I came home from work.'

I laugh. 'I remember,' I say, recalling the small boy who would run like the wind when Dad chased him.

'Do you think we should head for home today?' I say, blowing the steam from my drink.

'I've been wondering that myself.' He picks up his coffee.

'There's nothing here, Dad. We're chasing shadows.'

He nods. 'But I'm not sure how the roads will be this morning. It's been snowing through the night.' He picks up the remote control and flicks on the TV. 'Let's see what's happening in this area, shall we?'

We wait a while for the local weather forecast, before a chirpy young woman tells us the local roads are blocked until they can get a snowplough out. We're stuck here, and my heart sinks.

'Maybe it's fate.' Dad flicks off the TV, and puts the remotes on the table. 'Maybe we are meant to be here. Maybe the fact we can't leave means we will discover something.'

I can't find the words I want to say, without extinguishing his hopes further, so I stay silent, biting the inside of my mouth and tasting blood. A crushing foreboding settles on my shoulders.

What if it was a stranger who took Lark?

What if it wasn't Jackson, after all?

What if whoever took Lark is back, or never left?

What if they made the footprints in the snow last night? Looked in the window at Elise, while wearing a mask?

Dad picks up his Kindle, and I rise, slip on my padded jacket, bobble hat and boots, and take my tea onto the snowy porch at the front of the cottage.

A milky sun is rising, casting a bright light over a shimmering sheet of untouched snow. The footprints we saw on our way home last night have gone – due to last night's snowfall – though it's not falling now.

I'm lost in thought, my nose and fingertips tingling as I sip my tea, when I hear someone call my name.

It's Finn, wearing winter running gear and a beanie hat and scarf. He isn't exactly running, more stomping through the snow. 'Morning,' I call back, raising my hand, hoping he won't hate me for the way I behaved the night before. 'Not the best conditions for a run.'

He laughs. 'You're right about that, but if I don't stick to my routine, I'll give up.' He glances over his shoulder at the snowman near Rosamund's cottage. 'They've done a great job, haven't they?' He sounds a little out of breath.

I smile. 'They really have. Oh to be young.'

'Hey, we're still young.' He laughs and picks up speed. 'See you at breakfast?'

'Yes, we'll be over soon.'

'Great!' He heads away with another wave, and I take a deep breath and go back inside.

'Are you ready to eat, Dad?'

'Sure,' he says, rising and climbing the stairs. 'I'll have a quick shower first, then we can head over.'

*

We pass the snowman on our way to the conservatory, and I notice Rosamund standing in the window in her dressing gown, holding a mug. She lifts her hand in a wave, and I return the gesture. Within seconds she's gone from the window, and appears at the front door.

'Morning,' she calls. 'Can you tell Ruth we won't want breakfast this morning. Elise has gone back to bed – she was up at the crack of dawn building our new snowman friend here.' She smiles. 'And I'm feeling a bit groggy after the stressful journey here.'

'OK, we'll perhaps see you later,' I call back as we continue to trudge through the snow, trying so hard to forgive her.

Dad makes a grumbling sound. 'I don't know why you give her the time of day, Amelia. That woman—'

'I'm not keen on her myself,' I cut in. 'But she is sorry – wants our forgiveness.'

'Yes, well, she won't get mine.'

'I know. You said.' I'm frustrated by his lack of understanding. 'I just feel you should give her a chance, that's all.'

'Pot. Kettle,' he says.

'Sorry?'

'Well, you've never given Maddie a chance. Never tried to forgive her.'

'That's different,' I say, though I'm not sure it is.

I glance back over my shoulder as Rosamund calls after us, 'Second thoughts, a cooked breakfast does sound rather tempting. I'll be right over.' She steps back inside her cottage and closes the door behind her.

'Robert!' It's Maddie, waving from her cottage doorway, dressed

51

in her ski suit. 'Can we borrow your muscles again, please? Thomas is starving.'

*

'Did you hear about the footprints?' Ruth says, topping up Dad's tea.

'Footprints?' everyone says but me.

'Bit odd really,' she goes on, her hand on the side of the teapot as though her skin is made of copper. 'Finn said they seemed to come from the woods and then go back again.'

'That's weird,' Dad says.

'Aye, it is strange,' Ruth agrees, eyes searching the ceiling. 'I can't think who it could have been. The roads are blocked for miles.'

'But what if someone's been here all along?' Maddie says, her voice cracking under her words. 'Arrived before us. What if they came before the snow?'

'What size prints were they?' Thomas dips a piece of toast into his egg, and as the yellow trickles down the shell, he shoves the toast into his mouth.

'Finn said they were made by large feet.' Ruth turns to me. 'What do you think, Amelia? You saw them, didn't you?'

All eyes are on me, and Dad's forehead furrows. 'You saw them, Amelia? You never said.'

'I didn't want to worry you.' It sounds pathetic now I think about it. 'I was going to mention it this morning. I think we should tell Rosamund.'

'Tell Rosamund what?' She's standing in the doorway, looking stunning in her orange coat, her wavy blonde hair spilling from her fur hat.

'We were talking about the footprints,' Ruth says. 'Tea, coffee?'

'Tea please, I've gone off coffee since I fell pregnant.' She sits down next to Dad, and he shuffles his chair away. 'What footprints?' she asks.

'There were footprints in the snow last night,' Ruth says. 'Whoever made them walked from the woods to your cottage.'

'Oh God,' Rosamund says, peeling off her gloves. 'Maybe Elise did see someone hanging about.'

'Elise saw someone?' Dad says. 'Nobody tells me anything.'

Rosamund shudders and nods. 'Well she said she did. Said he was wearing a mask, and was looking in at her through the window of our cottage. But she makes things up. Always has done.'

'It seems odd though, don't you think?' I say. 'Especially after last time.'

'I'll talk to her again about it when she wakes up. Anyway, I didn't notice any footprints this morning.' She raises a perfect eyebrow.

'Well we saw them last night, Rosamund.' I bite into a croissant and chew. Crumbs fall onto the table. 'It's snowed since then. Covered them over.'

She shudders again. 'Don't, please, you're giving me the creeps.'

Ruth hands her a mug of tea. 'Get that down you, lass. It'll make you feel better.'

After taking several sips, Rosamund puts the mug on the table. 'Anyway, we're going to head for home today,' she says. 'I shouldn't have come. I'm not sure what I was thinking.' She's talking too fast, and her hands are trembling. 'The weather's getting worse, more snow expected later with winds of up to seventy miles per hour.'

'I think you may be out of luck, Rosamund,' Dad says, as though he's getting pleasure from his words. 'All the roads are blocked around here.'

'But we desperately need to get back to the comfort of our own home.'

Ruth rests her hand on Rosamund's shoulder. 'Don't you worry. I'm cooking a nice beef Wellington later.'

Finn appears from the back of the house. 'What you lads and lassies need is a bit of fun,' he says. 'There's a hill on the other side of the ruin—'

Ruth spins round to look at him, her eyes wide. 'Vine Hill?'

'And I've got a couple of sledges,' Finn goes on as though his mother hasn't spoken. 'Does anyone fancy a bit of tobogganing?'

Ruth storms from the room, and within seconds Dad's on his feet.

'Not for me,' he says. 'I'm not here to have fun.' He heads out of the conservatory without a word, but I can't bring myself to call him back.

I think how odd his words sounded. From the moment Mum became ill, having fun or enjoying ourselves felt wrong somehow – that if I should laugh or feel happy, then I was being disloyal to her, to Lark, then to my lost baby. Yet at this moment, a part of me wants to whizz down a snowy slope on a sledge and yell and squeal and laugh at the top of my voice.

'I'm up for it,' Thomas says. His spinal injury affects his motor skills in his legs, though his sensory functions have always been OK. But I'm still concerned.

'Do you think you should, Thomas? Dad won't be happy.'

He glares my way. 'Life is pretty crap right now, Amelia. I'm going down that slope whether you and Dad like it or not.' He narrows his eyes. 'Who's going to ride with me?'

'Me!' says Maddie, and I control an urge to thump her. 'Let's do it!'

'Great!' Finn says, his cheeks glowing.

Rosamund takes another sip of her drink, and shakes her head. 'I'm not quite sure how you can all get so excited, after just saying we may have a prowler about, and we're stranded in this awful place. No offence meant, Finn.'

My mind swirls with all the bad things that have happened, and it's as though I'm punching them to the back of my mind. 'Count me in,' I say, desperately needing to feel the freezing wind on my face – in my hair.

*

It's snowing again, and the wind is getting up, whipping the snow off the ground so it whirls and twirls in the air, stinging my cheeks.

Finn is ahead of us on his quad bike, Thomas on the back of it, clinging to him. Maddie is pulling one sledge and I'm pulling the other. They're old, handmade out of wood, sturdy.

'Almost there,' calls Finn, over his shoulder, as we make our way past the ruins, his words muffled by the wind.

Drummondale House looks like a scene from a Dickens novel, snow lying inches thick on every crumbling window-ledge, every decaying doorway – and my stomach knots, and grief floods my veins. What am I thinking being out here, about to sled down a hill in abandonment?

It's getting difficult to walk, my boots sinking deeper and deeper with every step I make. I can barely see in front of me for the falling snow. I glance back, but the view is no clearer. I'm glad we're with Finn – he knows this place so well.

'We're here,' he calls, cutting the power on his bike, and climbing off. He lifts Thomas off, and lowers him onto the snow.

'Cool,' Thomas says, flopping backwards, making the wings of a snow-angel with his arms. And for the first time in a long time, I urge his legs to work. I stare at him for a moment, and it's as he pulls himself to a sitting position I think I see his foot move. I look straight at his face, but his eyes are on Maddie who is jumping up and down as though trying to warm her feet, her scarf blowing in the wind.

'Thomas,' I say, and he turns to look at me with enquiring eyes.

'What's up, sis?'

'Oh, nothing,' I go on; deciding the movement must have been my imagination – wishful thinking.

Vine Hill is steep. I work out it heads in the opposite direction to the sea, and the foot of the slope is in walking distance of the estate owner Michael Collis's farmhouse.

Finn stomps his feet. 'So, who wants to go first? Amelia?'

'No, let Thomas and Maddie go down first,' I say. Then it

occurs to me. 'Wait though, how the hell is Thomas going to get back up?'

'I'll take the bike the long way, and meet you at the bottom,' Finn obliges. 'No worries.'

'I'm still not sure you should go down, Thomas,' I say.

'Hey, stop that,' Thomas says, his cheeks glowing. 'I'm going down. I'm all psyched up.'

'Fine,' I say. 'On your head be it.'

'You get on the sled first, Maddie,' Finn says.

She looks into his eyes and grimaces, and he puts his arm around her shoulder. 'You can trust me, Maddie,' he says. 'I know what I'm doing.'

She smiles up at him – is that adoration on her face? – and lowers herself onto the sledge.

'Right!' Finn continues, lifting Thomas onto the sledge in front of Maddie, and she grabs him round the waist, rests her face against his back.

Within seconds, Finn pushes the sledge and it hurtles down the hill, and Thomas and Maddie squeal with excitement as they zigzag through the snow, until I can't see them anymore.

'Your turn,' Finn says, smiling my way.

'Oh, I don't know anymore. Maybe I'll stay right here.'

'You need a bit of fun in your life, Amelia,' he says. 'You've been through hell. Get on the sledge.'

'Fine,' I say, sitting down and grabbing the rough rope with my gloved hands. Suddenly I'm whizzing down the slope, snow bombarding my face. Halfway down, tears spill from my eyes, but they are not happy tears, they are desperate tears, and I wonder, as the sled hits the bottom and I fall out into deep snow, whether I'll ever be truly happy again.

Chapter 11

A Year Ago

Ruth

Ruth liked this bit. The bit when her guests gathered for the first time in her conservatory to eat her delicious home-cooked meals. It was now she found out more about them – their history, their likes and dislikes, what made them tick.

She peered through the thick net curtain at her bedroom window to see the party of three – Jackson dressed in narrow black trousers and a white shirt, Caroline holding on to his arm, and the girl in black – leave Bluebell Cottage. They made their way through the darkness, Jackson brandishing a torch, leading the way like he was the Pied Piper of Hamelin. They would soon sit around Ruth's rustic pine table. She would play Mum.

The aroma of roast pork cooking floated up the stairs from the kitchen. She sniffed, satisfied. Her guests loved her cooking – her creamy mash, her buttered carrots, her tender green beans. She was old-fashioned in some ways, she supposed. Women didn't always cook from scratch anymore, but Ruth's mother had taught her from an early age, and she loved being in the kitchen – it helped give her life meaning.

She dashed down the stairs, kicked off her fur-rimmed slippers, and pushed her feet into flat black shoes, before entering the conservatory, where she moulded her face into her usual welcoming smile ready for her first arrivals.

The side door opened, and Ruth tucked a straying tendril of hair, which had escaped from her ponytail, behind her ear.

Jackson entered first, followed by Caroline.

'It's still quite warm out there,' Caroline said to Ruth. 'Can't believe it's November.'

Ruth was sick of talking about the weather, but knew it went with the territory. 'Yes, so strange for the time of year.'

'I blame global warming,' Jackson said, as Ruth gestured to the table laid out for her seven visitors. Finn had put out two jugs of water, the blue-and-white-checked napkins, and a beautiful vase of fresh flowers in the centre.

'Please take a seat, anywhere you like.'

'Where's Lark?' Caroline said, her forehead furrowing as she looked back towards the door. 'I thought she was right behind us.'

'She'll be along in a minute, darling.' Jackson took hold of her hand and led her to the table. 'Try not to stress.'

'Is she OK, do you think?' Caroline said, sitting down. 'I hope this isn't too much for her. She's barely spoken since we arrived. And those tablets she's on aren't helping. She seems zoned out most of the time.'

'She's fine, Caroline. Try not to worry. This holiday is all about you, and she needs to know that. Let her get on with it.'

Ruth's eyes drifted towards the open door. She stepped towards it, about to shut out the evening, when she spotted the girl in black – Lark – outside with the tall man in his fifties.

'But I'm not hungry, Dad,' she was saying, shoulders hunched, hands in the pockets of a knee-length black coat. Her anger was tangible. 'I don't even want to be here. It's stupid. Mum's dying, and we need to stop pretending we're a happy family, because we're not; we haven't been for ages, and we never will be again. It's pathetic.'

He placed his arm around her shoulders, pulled her close, and her eyes filled with tears. 'We're making new memories, sweetheart,' he whispered. 'I promise you'll be glad we did. This is where your mum wants to be – here with us all. Please give her that.' Despite the strength in his words, there was something in his tone that told Ruth he was struggling too. That he was finding this as difficult as his daughter.

'Fine!' Lark pushed away from him, and barged through the conservatory door. She whisked past Ruth, and thumped down in one of the dining chairs some distance from her mum and Jackson, and pulled out her phone.

The older man followed her in, threw Ruth a half-hearted smile, and closed the door behind him.

'And the bloody signal is erratic as hell,' Lark said, banging her phone down on the table, and glaring up at the ceiling.

Ruth looked away pretending she hadn't heard. What did the girl expect? They were miles from anywhere. The signal was always unreliable. She looked at her watch, still three more guests to arrive before she could serve dinner.

Once the man was seated, she padded towards the table, and pulled a notepad from her cardigan pocket. But before she could speak, the conservatory door opened once more, and the woman in her early twenties with silky black hair, and smooth olive skin, pushed in the young man in a wheelchair. She sped across the parquet flooring, making a noise like a car engine, and leaving a trail of floral perfume in her wake. 'We're here,' she said with a giggle. 'Let the fun begin.' She was American. Vivacious. Beautiful.

'Good evening,' Ruth said over her shoulder, her smile frozen. 'I'm Ruth … the owner.'

'Hey, I'm Maddie, and this is Thomas.'

Ah, the carer and the son.

Maddie moved a chair from the table, scraping the legs across the floor, and pushed the wheelchair into the space. Thomas looked up at Maddie, adoration in his brown eyes. 'Cheers,' he said.

'You are most welcome, kind sir,' Maddie said in a fake cockney accent, curtsying, before sitting down in the seat next to him.

Before Ruth could open her mouth, a woman of around thirty with red wavy hair to her shoulders, and a padded grass-green jacket, and jeans, opened the door and stepped in.

'Amelia,' Caroline said, fluttering her fingers. She patted the chair next to her. 'Come and sit down, darling.'

'You look nice, Mum,' Amelia said heading towards Caroline. She kissed her mother's cheek, and sat down beside her, unzipping her jacket, her eyes darting around the conservatory.

Caroline did look better than she had earlier, Ruth thought, with more colour in her cheeks, and a bobbed chestnut-brown wig that suited her.

'Can I get anyone a wee drink?' Ruth said. 'Tap water is included; anything else is extra.'

'A large white wine,' Amelia said without looking at the menu.

'A small glass for me, please,' Maddie said.

'Orange juice,' Thomas said, and Ruth found her mind wandering. Had he been in a wheelchair since birth? She would need to find that out.

She moved her eyes to Jackson. 'Lager,' he said, smiling at her. He was far too handsome – it shouldn't be allowed. 'And a mineral water for Caroline,' he added, as Caroline opened her mouth to speak and closed it again.

'Nothing for me,' Lark said, throwing down the menu. The lass couldn't have been more than seventeen. All that black eyeliner and bright red lipstick was far too brazen, but there was no escaping her beauty – so like Kyla.

'I'll have a lager too, please, love,' the older man said.

Ruth disappeared to the small bar area, and as she poured drinks, she picked up on the awkwardness behind her – the silences. This family were deeply troubled. This could get interesting.

Everyone but Lark began talking, and Ruth handed round the drinks, before making her way to the kitchen, returning five minutes later with Finn to hand out a silver platter of roast pork, and a tray of roast potatoes.

'I'm veggie,' Lark said brusquely.

'I know, love, don't worry.' Ruth blew her damp fringe from her forehead, as she put down the serving dishes. 'I've made you a quiche, love.'

'Christ sake, I hate bloody quiche.'

'Mum's doing her best,' Finn said, glaring at the girl.

Ruth touched his arm. 'It's fine, Finn.' And making eye contact with Lark she said, with a smile, 'You will enjoy my quiche, I promise.'

Once her guests were tucking in, and the room was awash with clanking cutlery and low chatter, Ruth looked at her son, who was leaning against the counter, staring at his phone. She hoped he wasn't messaging that wife of his. She wasn't good for him. But then she wouldn't be back. Ruth had sent her away when she came looking for him a few weeks back. She'd had an affair – cheated on her son. She no longer deserved him.

'By the way, everyone,' she said to her guests, who all looked up. 'This is my son, Finn.'

He looked up from his phone. 'Hi,' he said. 'Great to meet you all.'

The lass with the red hair – Amelia – caught his eye, and they exchanged a coy smile.

I'm afraid he's not available, dear girl. So don't go getting any ideas.

Chapter 12

A Year Ago

Amelia

Amelia glanced again at Finn who threw her another smile – a nice smile. Despite taking no pride in his appearance, there was something she found cute about him, in a dishevelled kind of way.

'Finn!' Ruth was staring at Amelia, something dark in her expression as she turned to her son. 'The dishwasher needs filling.'

'Fine.' He shoved his phone in his pocket. 'I'll maybe see you guys at the ghost tour later,' he said, leaving the dining room.

*

It was almost 9 p.m. and Amelia sat alone on the crumbling wall surrounding the Drummondale House ruins, almost swallowed by darkness. It was cooler than earlier, and she was huddled into her duffel coat, her phone torch barely lighting the area.

62

She shuddered as the moon peeped out from behind a cloud, picking out the jagged shapes of decaying walls and broken statues. The thought of exploring the woods searching for phantoms wasn't her idea of fun. She was sceptical, and not at all interested in anything supernatural, but also acknowledged the whole subject gave her the heebie-jeebies.

Her mum had been a member of the Berwick-upon-Tweed Paranormal Society before she'd moved to Tweedmouth to live with Jackson. She had always been a fan of TV shows that saw celebrities creeping round allegedly haunted locations in the dark, jumping at noises and shadows. Once, some years ago, her mum came to London to visit Amelia, and they'd taken a ghost tour around Hampton Court after dark. It had frightened Amelia, and she vowed she would never do anything like it again. Yet here she was, doing it for her mum. But then she had to really. Thomas couldn't – Finn had told him his wheelchair wouldn't be suitable for the route, and Maddie had insisted she should stay with him, and was now probably curled by the fire, updating her video log.

Maddie started her vlog on YouTube with her older sister – a TV presenter, and wannabe actress at the time. It was long before Maddie began caring for Thomas. In the early posts the sisters talked about the grief of losing their mother. Later, Maddie put on a few posts explaining that her sister was suffering with depression, so she was manning the vlog for now. Now the vlog was mainly about Thomas's day-to-day life. Amelia hated Maddie sharing her brother's life online, and stopped watching when Maddie added her mum's fight with cancer to her daily spiel. But while her mum and brother didn't seem to mind, even said it might help others in similar situations, Amelia mostly kept her opinions to herself.

A chilly breeze, as if from nowhere, made her shiver once more. She pulled up the hood of her coat, and hunched over her phone, and while she had a full signal, fired off a message to William:

Hey, You! I've arrived safely. I'm not going to lie,
it's not easy here, but I've got to get over myself and
do it for Mum. Don't forget to feed my fluffy ball of
love. Hope work is OK. Love you. A X

She pressed Send.

Watched her phone, willing William to reply.

'Amelia?'

She startled, jolted her head upwards, and grabbed her chest. 'Christ!'

'Sorry.' It was Finn coming through the darkness with his torch on full beam, wearing a top hat and black cloak. 'I was going to ask if you're ready to be spooked, but I'm guessing you already are.' He lowered the beam. 'You scare easily.' His Scottish accent was smooth, and held a hint of humour.

With her hand glued to her chest, her heart thrumming under her fingers, she continued to look up at him. 'I challenge anyone not to jump when a man looking like the ghost of Jack the Ripper creeps up on them.'

'Fair enough.'

'I'm a total sceptic, by the way,' she said. 'Don't expect to convince me.'

'I wouldn't dream of it.' He removed the hat, and laid it on the wall.

'Basically, I'm only here because my mum made me come.' She smiled. 'OK, I realise that makes me sound as though I'm about eight.'

He laughed, and sat down beside her, far enough away not to invade her space, for which she was grateful.

A silence fell between them, and she spent the quiet moments staring at her phone, willing William to return her message. Wishing he was there supporting her.

She'd arrived far too early for the ghost tour, wanting to get out of the cottage – tired of Thomas and Maddie messing about, of

Maddie's shrill laughter. The young fun-loving American couldn't help being silly and yet oddly responsible – Amelia understood that – and it was good to see Thomas happy, but if she'd stayed in the cottage any longer she would have said something she regretted, or possibly throttled Maddie.

'So do you live in Scotland?' Finn asked, as he flicked his torch on and off.

She shook her head. 'I grew up in Berwick-upon-Tweed.'

'And now?'

'Sorry?'

'Do you still live—'

'Oh, no.' She shook her head, and curled a wave of her hair around her finger. 'I live in London with my cat.' She had no idea what stopped her mentioning William. She loved him, didn't she? They'd even talked about having a baby one day. Though she'd done most of the talking.

'I've never been to London, would you believe?' Finn said with a sigh. He looked about him, and as though caught on an invisible line, his eyes met hers. 'Spent my life here with Mum mostly.'

'Mostly?'

'A brief marriage that didn't work out.'

'Sorry.'

He shrugged. 'It wasn't to be. My mum never liked her – didn't trust her, said she was the type to cheat, and then she went and proved Mum right. Anyway, my mother needs me here.' A beat. 'Christ, 'ark at me sharing my life story.'

'It's fine. I don't mind.'

He smiled. 'So you're here because of your mum? She's ill?'

Amelia turned from his gaze, keeping her eyes forward. She didn't want to talk about it – it made it too real – but still words formed in her head. A painful group of words that made her eyes sting with tears. 'We've been told she's only got six months.'

'I'm so sorry to hear that.'

'Yeah. Thanks.'

65

She was relieved when the door of Bluebell Cottage opened, and her mum, Jackson and Lark appeared. Within moments, her dad came through the darkness too from the other direction.

'Welcome,' Finn said, rising to greet everyone, and putting his top hat back on.

Amelia stared at her mum who was laughing and clapping, smiling up at Jackson, so excited. She was no longer wearing the wig she'd worn at dinner – it made her head itch, that's what she'd told Amelia – and she'd pulled on a beanie hat, a khaki-coloured parka, and a navy scarf was wrapped around her neck and covered most of her face.

Amelia straightened her shoulders and smiled. 'OK. Let's do this thing!' she said, surprising herself.

'Right, ghost hunters, follow me.' Finn strode off into the darkness, his torch lighting the ruins. And, as they set out following him, yet another shiver ran down Amelia's back. This place was creepy, and Finn hadn't even started to tell stories of ghosts and ghouls.

He led the way round to the front of Drummondale House, where it had been restored. New windows had been put in, and the façade had been repointed. It looked every bit as it would have in the eighteenth century.

'This was all in ruins when I was here last,' Caroline said.

Finn nodded. 'Michael Collis had it renovated. He occasionally rents the front section out for wedding and parties.' Finn shone his torch towards the windows. 'But not today,' he continued, moving the beam across the building, rays of light bouncing off the glass. 'Some say they have seen a face at one of the windows, when nobody is in there,' Finn continued, his accent giving his storytelling an eerie feel. He brought the torch down and rested it under his chin, and Amelia jumped and clasped her hand to her mouth to prevent an escaping laugh.

'Over one hundred years ago, a young boy was locked in his bedroom by his mother. His mother fell down the stairs and broke her neck, leaving the boy alone. By the time they were both found, the boy had starved to death.'

'Oh God, that's awful,' Amelia said, her laugh evaporating.

'The mother has been seen roaming the grounds, looking for her son.'

'Christ, this is way too freaky,' Lark said. 'Mum, can I go back now? I'm never going to sleep tonight.' It was an odd thing for her to say. Nothing normally scared Lark.

'Chicken!' Jackson said. He grabbed Lark from behind and began tickling her waist.

'Stop,' she cried, a painful laugh escaping. 'Stop, Jackson, please.'

Amelia stared as Lark fell to the ground, and he toppled down on top of her. Her mum rarely got angry, but now her eyes narrowed and her fists were clenched. There was an awkward tension as Jackson clambered to his feet. 'Stop teasing Lark,' her mum whispered close to his ear. 'Please.'

Amelia offered her hand to help Lark up, but she didn't take it, her face flushed as she jumped to her feet and straightened her clothes. The moment was odd and uncomfortable – something wasn't right.

Lark hurried towards Finn, who had moved away, her dad beside him, asking in a loud voice about the bird life in the area as though nothing had happened. Amelia looked over at her mum once more, wanting to take her in her arms and squeeze, but she didn't – too afraid of making too much of the last few minutes. This was meant to be so perfect, but was far from it. What the hell did her mum see in Jackson?

They all followed Finn, and as they rounded the other side of the building, the ruins came back in view.

'Who lives down there?' Amelia said, pointing down a steep slope at a large farmhouse some distance away. A porch light was on, but otherwise the place was in darkness.

'Michael Collis, the estate's owner,' Finn said. 'But I'm pretty sure he's away right now. He turned towards the woods. 'Right, let's go,' he said, his torch beam picking out the twisting trees with branches like witches' fingers. The heavy moon hung low in the sky, and the wind whistled through the forest. Amelia shuddered. This really wasn't her idea of fun.

It was as they all set off in front of her, disappearing into the wood, that Amelia looked down the hill one last time. Her heart jumped into her throat. Someone was sitting on a bench at the foot of the hill, the moon picking out her fair hair. Was it a young woman? A child? It was impossible to tell. But whoever was down there, she was now staring up at Amelia.

Amelia raced to catch up with everyone else. She wanted to return to her cottage, but over her shoulder the thick darkness was eerie, like swirling black smoke, and trees sighed and swayed in the wind. There was no turning back alone.

Shadows ignited by the beam from Finn's torch gave the illusion of movement of something in the trees. It was as if ghosts were watching them, conjured by their human presence – angry their peace was being disturbed.

Finn continued down a well-used path, pushing through brambles, everyone keeping up – except Lark.

Amelia hung back for a moment, waiting for her, wanting to attempt to bond with her estranged sister. Why had they drifted so far apart? They had been close when they were younger, the gap of thirteen years never a problem. Amelia had adored her little sister when she was a child. Been like a second mum.

'So what have you been watching lately?' Amelia began, feeling her cheeks flush as she realised how far removed she was from the teenage scene. At thirty, words she'd used in her teens, clothes she'd worn, even some of the music she'd listened to, were obsolete now.

'Watching?'

Amelia could barely see her sister in the darkness, struggled to work out her expression. Was it amusement? Apathy? Anger?

'On TV? Netflix? At the cinema?'

'Anything by Stephen King.'

'You're braver than I am. The trailer for It Chapter Two freaked me out.' Amelia wasn't a lover of clowns – or masks – or anything creepy come to that. 'There's no way I could watch the film.'

'You've always been a baby,' Lark said, her voice dull, as though bored of their conversation.

'You're not wrong there.' On cue a small animal darted across their path – and Amelia leapt inches from the ground, and grabbed her chest. 'What the hell was that?'

Lark laughed. 'A cat, I think. Or maybe a fox.'

Well at least she'd made her sister laugh; even if it was at her own expense.

They continued through the darkness.

'I'm guessing you know already, I'm not going to university next year,' Lark said.

'Yeah, Dad told me. Will it be a gap year? Do you hope to go one day?'

'Maybe.' She shrugged. 'Truth is, I'm feeling pretty naff right now.'

Amelia touched her arm. 'We'll get through this, Lark.'

'Yeah,' she said. 'I guess so. Anyway, I'm doing some café work for now. I just feel in limbo somehow. I know it sounds awful, but I feel as if I want Mum to die so I can get the whole grieving thing over with and get on with my life.'

Amelia's eyes widened, shocked at her sister's harsh words.

Lark came to a stop, looking ahead. 'Don't get me wrong, Amelia, I don't want Mum to die. I'd give anything to reverse the bloody cancer, for them to find a miracle cure. But it isn't going to happen, is it? And waiting around to lose her is fucking killing me. God I sound crazy, wrong, weird ... sorry.'

'I understand.' Amelia sort of did. They were in a bubble, limbo, knowing the worst was going to happen, knowing they couldn't stop it. 'But it will be far worse when she's gone, Lark. We need to make the most of the time we have left.'

'Are you two coming?' Finn called to Amelia and Lark, shining his torch towards them standing in the middle of the path. 'You need to keep up. It's easy to get lost around here.'

Amelia grabbed Lark's hand and they hurried towards him.

'There was an abbey on this land long before Drummondale House was built,' Finn said as they reached the group. 'A grey lady roams the wood, and some have seen the apparition of a monk.'

'This is so boring,' Lark whispered from behind her hand. 'I sometimes feel I don't know Mum at all.'

'It's not my thing either, really.' Amelia felt a brief connection with her sister. Though she wasn't bored, more apprehensive and on full alert.

They walked in a huddle, before reaching the far end of the wood where they gathered on the cliff edge. The moon gave the sea that stretched out in front of them a metallic, mesmerising glow. Amelia leaned forward, and glanced down at the rough waves crashing against jagged rocks below.

'Careful!' Finn cried, lunging forward to grab her hand as she took another step into a mist rising from the sea. Her foot slipped on the loose stones, and there was a collective gasp.

'You were nearly history,' Finn said, pulling her to safety.

'Are you OK, love?' her dad said, stepping forward, and putting a comforting arm around her shoulders, and she nodded.

'Tomorrow, if it's a clear day,' Finn carried on, as though she hadn't almost plummeted to her death, 'keep a lookout for bottlenose dolphins in the Moray Firth. They're a magical sight as they play together in the ocean.' He shone the torch out to sea. 'There are limestone caves below us. And there's a great project along the coast at Covesea where they're examining the archaeology of this area.'

Amelia smiled. There was a lot more to Finn than she'd first realised.

Chapter 13

A Year Ago

Ruth

Ruth pushed her trolley full of towels down the winding path towards Bluebell Cottage, the shriek of its squeaky wheels echoing in the darkness. She'd seen her guests head off on the ghost walk. They wouldn't be back for a while.

This cottage was the biggest dwelling on the estate, and Ruth always thought the prettiest, charming in a chocolate-box kind of way. Flowers always bloomed so much better near the ruins.

She opened the door with one of her keys. She liked that she had so many jangling on her belt; it made her feel important. She picked up four of the fluffy white towels she'd so lovingly washed earlier.

As she entered the cottage, adrenalin fizzed through her veins. It was naughty. She should have put the towels in the cottages prior to everyone's arrival. But then if she had, she wouldn't have a reason to enter now, would she? She wouldn't be able to get to know her visitors. And she must get to know them.

The front door led straight into the square lounge, and Ruth reached for the light switch with her free hand, flicked the switch, and illuminated the room. She wasn't interested in downstairs. Her guests rarely left any part of their personalities in the lower rooms.

Upstairs, she padded into the double bedroom, put on the light, and placed two towels neatly at the foot of the floral duvet. The smell of Jackson's expensive aftershave made her feel a little giddy. He was quite the catch – Caroline was a lucky woman.

She stepped towards the wardrobe. His jeans hung on the door, and she slowly moved her hand over the fabric, before turning to observe the room.

The couple's cases were open on the floor, Caroline's clothes folded neatly inside one; Jackson's spilling from the other onto the carpet. She knelt down. Caroline's peacock-blue cashmere jumper felt soft under her fingertips; her headscarf smelt freshly washed.

Headscarf in her hand, she stood up, noticing Caroline's chestnut-brown wig on the dresser, lying there like roadkill. She dropped the scarf back into the case and headed over.

Sitting in front of the mirror she observed her reflection. Her face wasn't particularly lined. It was more her jowls that gave her age away – much like her hands. She picked up the wig and pulled it on, tucking her greying ponytail up inside.

'What do you think you're doing, Ruth?' she asked her reflection, hearing her mother's voice in hers. 'You look ridiculous.'

She snatched off the wig, her own hair falling free. 'Stupid girl,' she muttered, looking away from the mirror, and rising.

As she was about to leave the bedroom she spotted a thick pale-blue journal on the bedside table. She padded over and read on the cover the words: Caroline's Journey.

She picked it up, lowered herself onto the bed, and opened it. Caroline's writing swirled and curled on the pages. Notes about visits to hospital with Jackson by her side, how awful she'd felt after chemotherapy, how worried she was about Lark, how she missed Amelia so far away in London. There was no doubting from her words how much she loved Jackson, but Ruth could feel in the words Caroline's sadness that Robert was no longer in her life. There were lots of mentions too of her best friend Rosamund – a dream come true that she's back in my life.

The final entry in the book was labelled 'My Last Holiday' but there were no words there – not yet. Ruth closed the book, rose, and left the room.

She made her way into Lark's bedroom, where she placed two towels at the foot of the girl's bed, and ran her hand gently over the cotton fabric of the pyjamas folded neatly on the pillow.

'Sleep well, my dear girl. Don't let the bed bugs bite.'

Three Stephen King novels were stacked on the bedside cabinet next to a half-empty can of cola.

A make-up bag on the dressing table caught her eye. She padded across the room, glancing at the door every few seconds, before unzipping it. Inside she found eyeliner, a tube of pale foundation, red lipstick.

She picked up the lipstick and smeared it over her thin lips. 'Tart,' she said, and dashed it away with a tissue.

Lacy underwear spilled out of an open drawer. Ruth went to slam it shut, but noticed a small cardboard box. She pulled it out. 'Diazepam?' she whispered reading the label. 'Why the need for antidepressants, dear girl?'

*

Back outside in the cool evening air, the door locked behind her, Ruth noticed lights on inside Honeysuckle Cottage. Finn clearly hadn't tempted everyone on his ghost walk.

She walked over, towels in her arms, and knocked on the door. Within seconds it flew open. It was the American woman.

'Hey, Ruth.'

'Maddie,' Ruth said. 'I've brought you some towels.' She

liked to remember her guests' names. Tried to memorise them. Connecting their names with something memorable. Maddie – Mad – Crazy American woman. Jackson – Jack the Lad. Lark – a beautiful bird trapped in a cage, desperate to be free …

'Thanks so much,' Maddie said, taking the towels from her, and burying her face in them. 'They smell amazing. You're so kind.' With that she closed the door.

'You don't know me,' Ruth muttered into the quiet night, as she turned back to her trolley. 'How do you know I'm kind? You don't know me at all.'

She tucked a tendril of flyaway hair behind her ear, and headed back to her cottage, the squeak of the wheels grating on her nerves. Finn would need to oil them. Thank goodness she had Finn.

Chapter 14

A Year Ago

Amelia

They made their way back through the forest. 'So this is where our final ghost roams,' Finn began. 'She—'

'So, have you seen any of these ghosts?' Lark cut in from a few steps behind. 'I mean what are you basing all this crap on?'

He looked over his shoulder, slowing his pace. 'If I'm honest, I've never seen a ghost,' he said. 'But many people have.'

'Who exactly?'

'Visitors mainly, and my mum reckons she's seen a spirit.'

'Gin or vodka?' She laughs.

'Mum doesn't drink, Lark.' His tone was harsh. He took a deep breath. 'You really are a piece of work, aren't you?'

She shrugged. 'I aim to please.'

'My mother's seen the ghost, I was about to tell you about before you rudely interrupted.' He glared back at Lark, and she shrugged again, kicked the dusty mud beneath her feet as she walked.

'A teenage girl who lost her life on Vine Hill is said to wander here.'

'That's awful, so tragic,' Amelia said. 'Do you know who she was?'

'My sister.' His tone was even, his eyes looking ahead. 'Ever since I was small, my mum's said she sees her.'

'Oh God, I'm so sorry.'

'Don't be. I barely remember her. I was only three when she died.' He turned to look at Amelia, his eyes wide. 'It happened a very long time ago, and if I'm honest I don't like the thought of her roaming here, never have.'

He looked about him, as though searching for her, before picking up speed, and Amelia dropped behind with her mum, Lark and Jackson some steps behind them.

'Did you enjoy the walk, Mum?' Amelia said, noticing how weak her mum looked.

'Yes, although I'm a bit tired now.' She sounded breathless. 'I'll sleep well tonight, I expect.'

An owl hooted in the distance, and Amelia grabbed her chest. 'I'm not sure I will,' she said with a laugh.

'I thought we might have a picnic tomorrow, if the weather holds. Ruth will prepare one for us. We can head for the nearest beach with Rosamund and her family – they'll be arriving first thing.'

'Really? You never said.'

'I wasn't sure if she would come, so didn't want to mention it before I was sure. But I had a text from her earlier. They'll be here in the morning.' She paused. 'I hope that's OK.'

'Of course it is, if that's what you want.'

'It is, yes. I can't wait to see her.'

As they pushed through some brambles, Amelia caught her hand on a thorn and winced. Her mum grabbed a clean tissue from her pocket, took hold of Amelia's hand, and pressed the tissue gently against the small tear in her daughter's skin. 'There you go,' she said with a smile, and for a moment Amelia was transported back to her childhood.

'Almost there,' Finn called from up ahead, where he was walking with Robert.

Amelia glanced back over her shoulder. Lark had fallen behind, and Jackson was running towards her. He stopped when he reached her, and took hold of her hand as though trying to speed her up. She snatched it away. What is it with those two?

'You'll like Rosamund,' her mum said. 'I used to work with her a long time ago.'

'Yes, I remember.'

'Just round the next bend,' Finn called. He was a fair way ahead of them now.

Five minutes later they finally reached the ruin.

'And that's a wrap, folks,' Finn said, flashing the torch towards Amelia and her mum emerging from the forest. 'Where's Jackson and Lark?'

They waited and waited, Amelia's eyes flicking over the wooded area.

'Oh for goodness' sake,' her mum said. 'I'll call Jackson.' She rummaged in her pocket for her phone, and looked at the screen. 'I haven't got a signal,' she said. 'Oh God, where can they be?'

'They can't be far,' Amelia said, as her dad hurried over.

'You look tired, Caroline,' he said.

Amelia nodded. 'Let me walk you back to your cottage, Mum. Then the rest of us can look for them. They've probably taken a wrong turn or something, that's all. I'm sure they're fine.'

They walked towards Bluebell Cottage, and as her mum opened the door, Amelia said, 'We'll find them; try not worry.'

'Of course we will.' Her mum touched her cheek gently. 'I'm overtired, that's all.'

But as Amelia hurried back to where her dad and Finn were waiting, she felt sure it was more than that. She'd seen the looks her mum gave Jackson, the way her hands curled into fists earlier.

'To be honest,' Finn said, as Amelia approached, 'we've only covered a small part of the forest tonight. If they've taken a wrong turn, they could be anywhere. We should probably call the local countryside ranger.'

'That's a bit of an overreaction, Finn,' Amelia said, heading off towards the wood. 'They couldn't have gone far, surely,' she called over her shoulder.

'Lark!' she cried, as they followed her. But it was so quiet – too quiet.

*

'Lark! Jackson!' Amelia yelled. They'd been searching for ten minutes now, making their way deeper into the forest. And she was about to suggest Finn could be right about the ranger, when she heard the low rumble of agitated voices in the distance. 'Lark?'

'It must be them,' Finn said, as they all picked up speed, and headed towards the voices. 'Jackson?'

The talking stopped, and everything was quiet for a moment, before the sound of someone running – twigs breaking, getting closer – reached Amelia's ears.

'Lark!' she cried, as her sister appeared through the bushes, her cheeks blotchy, her eyes red. 'Thank God.'

'Amelia,' Lark said falling into her arms.

'What's happened? Is Jackson with you?'

'Yes!' he cried, appearing through the bushes. 'I'm here. We got a bit lost, is all.'

Lark glared at him, and Amelia could feel the tension in her sister's body. 'Are you OK?' she asked, as Lark stepped away from her.

'Yes,' she said. 'It's like Jackson said, we got a bit lost, is all.'

*

'Are you OK, Dad?' Amelia said, looping her arm through his elbow, once Jackson and Lark were back in their cottage and Finn was making his way to his.

'Jackson's a dick.' He blinked repeatedly. 'I'd do anything to get that excuse for a man out of our lives. He's a bloody idiot!' He took a breath, and looked down at Amelia. 'Sorry, love. Excuse my awful language. But what was he playing at, leading Lark off course like that? I don't trust him. Never have done.'

'I don't know.' She was still at a loss to how her mum could have chosen to live with Jackson instead of her dad. Her mum had had low times through the years, but Amelia never saw the cracks in her parents' relationship – never once saw them argue.

She touched her dad's arm. 'It'll soon be over,' she said, and realising immediately her words weren't the best she could have chosen, added, 'The holiday, I mean.'

'I know what you mean, love.' He smiled, and reached into his pocket for the key to the cottage.

As he pushed open the door, she heard the TV blaring out.

'I'm heading straight to bed,' she said, walking through the lounge and taking the stairs two at a time, unable to face Thomas and Maddie snuggled on the sofa together.

'Night, Amelia,' her dad called up the stairs after her.

Upstairs, she flopped on her bed, and closed her eyes. A trip to the beach tomorrow would be emotional – childhood memories were sure to flood into her mum's head – and into hers.

She closed her eyes, and tears seeped through her lashes and rolled down her cheeks, dampening the pillow. It was almost an hour before she drifted into a fitful sleep.

Chapter 15

Present Day

Amelia

I glance up the hill I've just tobogganed down, and at Maddie standing beside me. She takes hold of my arm, and yanks me up. And as I scramble to my feet, I move away from her, making a show of dusting snow from my jeans.

'Thanks,' I say through a tense smile, dashing tears away with my scarf. 'That was so cool,' I add, deciding to fake brightness. I don't want her to know how desperate I am. I don't want her sympathy, or worse her mentioning me on her vlog.

'That was so much fun.' She looks far too happy, her cheeks glowing.

'Well, I'm freezing down here.' It's Thomas, sitting in the snow, laughing as he rolls a snowball in his gloved hands. Several pre-made snowballs are lined up next to him, and I instantly know what he's planning – still a kid at heart. Within seconds one hits me in the head, and ice-cold snow slips down my collar and down my back. I shudder. I'm not in the mood, and my

80

stomach tenses. I envy but struggle to understand his ability to be so playful.

'You can't retaliate, sis.' He picks up another. 'I'm disabled. It would be cruel.' Another hits me in the shoulder.

'Cut it out,' I say, and turn to look once more up Vine Hill. The snow has eased off, and I can just make out the shape of Finn at the top, staring down at us. He turns and walks away, and a few minutes later I hear the faraway rumble of his quad bike engine.

'It's going to take a while for Finn to ride down.' I'm concerned for Thomas sitting waist-deep in the snow. We really hadn't thought this through. I look about me, try to think what to do, and notice a bench near the trees. I remember the bench from when I was here last.

I dash over, and brush away the snow from the wood. 'Let's get you onto this bench, Thomas,' I say, noticing there's an inscription on the back. I rub the snow from it.

Kyla. Forever loved.

Footprints lead to and from the farmhouse, and I wonder if Michael Collis is there.

Maddie and I carefully lift Thomas onto the seat.

'I'm a pain in the arse,' he says, as we lower him down, both of us breathing heavily. He shakes his head in despair, hates relying on anyone – still clings to his independence as much as he can.

'You're not a pain,' Maddie says. 'In fact, you're amazing. My favourite man in the world.' She kisses his cheek.

We sit down either side of him. The sun reflecting off the sheer expanse of white hurts my eyes. Eventually, Maddie gets up and heads for the sledges.

'Do you miss, Mum, Thomas?' I say, while I've got his attention. He was never an open boy, not one to rake over his life or show his true feelings, often brushing them away with humour, or quotes from Shakespeare. When he returned from America following his accident, he folded into himself. But once Maddie arrived he began making joke after joke about his situation. Even now, none of us know how he really felt – still feels – about cutting his life in the US short. How he really feels about losing the ability to walk. 'And Lark, do you miss her?' I go on. 'Do you wonder where she is?'

'Of course I miss Mum and Lark,' he says. 'But life goes on, doesn't it? It has to.'

'Bit harsh,' I say, clapping my hands together to free the clumps of snow from my woollen gloves, as Maddie approaches, dragging the sledges behind her.

'I have to be,' he continues. 'If I wasn't, I would never get up in the morning.' His nose and cheeks are pink on his pallid face, and the furry lapels of his hat hang down over his ears. His brown eyes are bloodshot. 'That doesn't mean I wouldn't give anything to see them again. But I know it's never going to happen. Mum's dead, Amelia. And however much Dad thinks coming here will trigger something that will lead to us finding Lark – and despite supporting him in every way I possibly can – I don't believe we'll ever find her. We have to get on with our lives, sis, or we might as well be dead too.'

'Wow!' I say, now picking snow from my gloves. 'You've really thought this through.'

Finn approaches, roaring across the snow towards us on his quad bike.

'Here comes our hero,' Maddie says with a giggle.

'Gosh, that was quick,' I say, getting to my feet, as Finn cuts the engine.

'Yeah, this old thing can go pretty fast downhill,' he says, turning to Thomas. 'Let's get you on the back, mate, before you freeze to death.' He lifts my brother from the bench, and onto the bike. 'You guys need to follow the track back towards the ruin. But be careful as you go; keep on the pathway. The drop is lethal.' He climbs on the bike, and Thomas grips his waist.

'Before you go,' I say, 'do you know who Kyla is?' I point at the inscription on the bench.

Finn looks at me for some moments, before simply saying, 'That ol' bench has been there for years.' He revs the engine. 'See you at the top,' he says, and roars away.

I lead the way up the windy path, dragging one of the sledges, Maddie close behind pulling the other. Keeping to the track, we eventually reach the top of the path, where Finn and Thomas are waiting for us.

I look down the hill, and can just make out the footprints stretching across the untrodden snow from the farmhouse to the bench. 'Is Michael on the estate at the moment?' I ask Finn.

'Why?'

'No reason – just wondered.' I give an odd laugh that doesn't sound like me.

'I think he's away. You know he's rarely there,' he says, and pauses for a moment, studying my face. 'He had nothing to do with your sister's disappearance, Amelia, if that's what you're thinking. He wasn't even in the country, remember?'

'Yes, I know,' I say, feeling chastised.

'We all know Jackson took her,' he adds, sounding so certain. As certain as I'd been when I first arrived. But doubts are creeping in. What if it hadn't been Jackson?

'Hey, I'm still here.' It's Thomas, peering around Finn. 'And freezing doesn't begin to cover it.'

'Let's get you back then,' Finn said with a laugh, and he takes off across the snow. My brother flutters his fingers at me and Maddie, and winks, despite his obvious discomfort.

'Finn's great, isn't he?' Maddie says, as though she would trust him with her life. 'I like him a lot.'

I don't reply – simply turn and head towards my cottage, the snow crunching under my boots. Michael Collis was abroad when my sister disappeared, and had nothing to do with it – I know that deep down. But still my curiosity is piqued. I want to meet him. Find out more about him. Discover who Kyla is.

Chapter 16

Present Day

Me

Misty nudges my face with his nose, and the rumble of his continuous purr is comforting. He has no concept of what I'm going through. He comes and goes as he pleases through the cat flap, unlike me. There's no escape for me.

I'm on the bed where I spend almost all of my time. Waiting. There's no structure to my days. And I've given up thinking anyone's looking for me. Nobody will find me here.

I look through the window, as I tickle Misty's soft ear. Clouds move fast across the dusty-grey sky as though escaping. It hasn't snowed in a while.

I rest my face against Misty's coat, breathing him in. He smells of winter – but he isn't cold. Neither am I. The heater is on.

There is a small TV here in this tiny room. I can get a few channels, and watch endless repeats of Friends. It no longer makes me laugh.

I've given up shouting and screaming. Only you hear me. Only you answer my calls.

I lift my heavy head, thump it against the wall, and smooth my hand over Misty's silky, grey fur hoping he'll stay for a while.

Chapter 17

Present Day

Amelia

Exhausted, and freezing to the tips of my fingers and toes, I shuffle out of my damp coat, tug off my snow-caked boots, and attempt to rub life back into my feet. Dad looks up from his Kindle, his face set in a frown.

'What's up?' But I know exactly what's irking him. He didn't want me to go sledging. He thinks it's too frivolous when we are meant to be here looking for clues that could lead us to Lark.

'Come by the fire, Amelia. You're freezing.' His tone is blunt, sad. He looks back at his novel.

I rub my hands together and approach the wood burner. And once I've warmed up to the point where I can feel my extremities again, I turn my back on the fire, and stare steadily at my dad on the sofa. He looks like a once-plump teddy bear that's had the stuffing knocked out of him. 'You're annoyed with me, aren't you?' I say. Even at my age I hate it when he's upset with me.

'No.' His eyes stay fixed on his Kindle.

'You're pissed off because I went sledging, when I should have been searching for … for a pipe dream.'

'A little, maybe.' He looks up and meets my eye. 'But I know there's nowhere to look. Especially now we're buried under a mountain of snow. Coming here was a mistake. I know that now.' He puts down his Kindle, leaving it on, the large text of his sci-fi thriller glowing.

'Let's go home,' I say, twiddling my damp hair around my finger. I can think of nothing I want more. 'We could try the roads. Surely if we go slowly, we …' I stop. He's shaking his head, his forehead furrowed, as it used to when I was in my teens trying to convince him to order a takeaway, or to let me stay out after midnight.

'I want to go home too, Amelia,' he says. 'But I called the local police when you were sledging, to ask how the roads are. They said we're stuck here for now at least. Snowploughs haven't got this far yet, and with more snow expected, even the emergency services are struggling.' He lowers his head. Sounds defeated.

I sit down on the rug on the wooden floor, and cradle my knees; the warmth from the fire has thawed me out. 'Shall I put the TV on? Look at the long-range forecast?'

'No power.'

'Really?' Just when I thought things couldn't get any worse.

'It went down over an hour ago. I'm sure it will be back on again soon.'

I bury my face in my knees, my mind drifting; wondering if what I'm feeling is depression, grief, or are they the same thing? The tragedy is that I thought being with Dad was exactly what I needed to lift me, but being with him, here of all places, is making me feel worse than ever.

'So, did Thomas have a go on a sledge?' Dad says, after a while.

'What do you think?' I look up to see him raise a smile. We both know Thomas. He tries anything. It's the way he has always been. Why he is in a wheelchair.

We are silent again. Struggling to communicate. It isn't like us. We've always got on great.

'Do you remember the owner of the estate?' I ask him, eventually.

'Michael Collis?'

'Yes.'

'Yes. Well, no, obviously I don't remember him as such as he was abroad.

'Why?' His eyes sparkle as though he hopes I'm about to reveal something important.

'No reason, really,' I say with a shrug. And it is nothing. Michael Collis was definitely away that day, a year ago. And the police searched his property. I get to my feet. 'I saw his farmhouse, that's all. It brought back memories.'

His sparkle fades. 'Well, the police ruled him out of any connection to Lark's disappearance.'

'Yes, I know.' I drift towards the window and look out, thinking of the beautiful late sunshine we had this time last year. Recalling the day we all spent on the beach with Mum, the ghost walk. 'I think I'll head out again. I feel a bit claustrophobic stuck inside.' I pad across the room, and grab my coat from the hook. 'Want to come for a walk, Dad?'

He shakes his head, and picks up his Kindle once more, and I wonder why he doesn't seize the opportunity to explore. But the truth is he's already defeated, and I know how he feels. Finding Lark here is as unlikely as the chance the snow will thaw before tomorrow.

*

'Heading out?' It's Rosamund, fluttering her gloved hand. She's stomping towards her cottage in a sunshine-yellow anorak. Her grey fur hat elegantly perched on her head. Her baby bump is clearly visible through her coat, and another pang of envy shoots through me. She must have been to Ruth's cottage, as she's carrying a French stick and a carton of milk. The cottages all have small kitchens: microwaves, dishwashers, even washing machines, but Ruth sells filled rolls, bread and milk, and various other things, from midday until three o'clock daily. I realise I'm hungry – all that sledging – but it's just gone three so I've missed my opportunity. 'We're about to have a bite to eat,' Rosamund goes on, and I can't make up my mind if it's an invitation to join her and Elise, but it's the last thing I want to do.

'I thought I'd take a walk,' I call, quickening my step, which isn't easy in the deep snow, and I trip, almost falling over.

'Good idea, I might do the same later if Elise fancies it. I think I'll go stir-crazy stuck inside. You can only play so many board games, can't you?' She smiles, throws me another flutter of her fingers, and, passing the snowman that still stands proudly, goes into her cottage, calling her stepdaughter's name.

The snow is soft and crunches like meringue each time I lower my boot, which amuses me far more than it should. There's no strength to the sun, which peeks out from behind soft, smoky-grey clouds, and the wind, after settling down earlier, has got up again.

I make my way over to Vine Hill and stand at the top, scanning the area. The snowy view – which I didn't fully appreciate before, far too busy debating whether to slide down or not – is beautiful. The Scottish Highlands are stunning at any time of year, but the unblemished snow stretching for miles over fields, hills and mountains, is breath-taking. My eyes sting from the cold as they travel across the splendour, landing on Michael Collis's house. It's large – too big for just him – but being a farmhouse it suits its surroundings. A lonely place to live, I imagine. But then if he travels abroad a lot, perhaps he's glad of the tranquillity when he returns home. I wonder for a moment whether the disappearance of Jackson and Lark affected him at the time. Whether he was concerned when he returned from his travels to find two people had vanished while staying on the estate.

I set out towards the farmhouse. Trying to recall the route we'd travelled earlier, but in reverse, stepping gingerly, unsure where the path ends and the edge, which falls away to a sheer drop, begins. Eventually I reach the bottom.

After brushing away the snow from the wooden slats, I sit down for a few moments on Kyla's bench, shivering. It's isolated here – unnaturally quiet. Not a single bird singing. No animals rustling in the woods behind me. I look at the set of footprints stretching towards the farmhouse. Whoever made them possibly sat here, before walking back. Was it Michael Collis? Was Finn wrong, and he wasn't abroad? Had he left the footprints leading to Rosamund and Elise's cottage too? Had he put on a mask and looked in at Elise?

My curiosity about the man deepens. It's about a five-minute walk to his house, but my toes and fingers are numb, and the clouds are darkening. I sit for a few more minutes, debating if I can manage the walk, when snow starts to fall. I need to get back.

I rise and look up at the sky, letting the flakes land on my face, icy cold, before turning to look up Vine Hill. I squint, trying to make out who is at the top looking down at me. I see a flash of a pink jacket. 'Elise?' But she moves away before I can raise my hand in a wave.

It's almost four o'clock. I'll come back tomorrow. I have to. Something draws me to the farmhouse – to Michael Collis.

Chapter 18

A Year Ago

Amelia

Rosamund, in her early forties, muscularly slim, her wavy blonde hair shining in the sunlight, climbed from the driver's seat of a white Mercedes, looking stunning in an orange coat with large lapels.

A teenage girl climbed from the back seat, and a man in his mid-thirties in a red waistcoat and black jacket, got out of the passenger seat and stretched his arms above his head, yawning.

'Caroline, darling, how are you?' Rosamund called, waving at Amelia and her mum heading towards her.

Amelia stared at the elegant woman approaching. She'd never met her, but remembered from when she was a teenager how happy her mum had been working in Rosamund's flower shop, near the River Tweed. Having done a flower arranging evening course at the local college, and finding she had a natural talent, her mum had been thrilled when she got the job. Amelia had loved how happy her mum had been while she worked there, bringing flowers home each day, always smiling. The house always smelt beautiful, looked bright.

But then Rosamund sold the shop – never said where she was going. It had broken the bond between them. Her mum had cried that day, saying she hadn't only lost a job – she'd lost her best friend too.

'Your mum has told me so much about you, Amelia,' Rosamund said, blue eyes shining, after the two older women had embraced. She really was a mesmerising woman. 'We should play a game of tennis together.'

Amelia raised her eyebrows. She had never been good at tennis. Never been sporty.

'Ah, no, you're thinking of Lark,' her mum chipped in. 'Lark is my sporty one. Well she was, until recently.' She looked at Amelia. 'Rosamund used to be the Northern Indoor Champion.'

'Well, I wouldn't want to play you then.' Amelia knew she sounded stiff and awkward, and a strange little grunt – meant to be a laugh – was expelled from her mouth.

'Rosamund's an amazing swimmer too, aren't you, Rosamund?'

'Enough, Caroline,' Rosamund said. 'You're making me sound like a superhero.'

'Well, in some ways you are.'

Please stop, Mum! You sound far too needy. It was like she was trying to impress the most popular girl at school.

The man and teenage girl approached carrying holdalls, both smiling.

'Ah, this is my husband – Neil,' Rosamund said. 'And my daughter – Elise.'

'Stepdaughter,' Elise snapped.

Neil put his arm around Rosamund's waist. She stood taller than him, and although his stance gave off a confident, self-assured vibe, there was something jittery about him under the surface. He pushed back his neat brown hair with his fingers. 'It's good to put a face to the courageous woman Rosamund talks so much about.'

Amelia sucked in a sigh, and turned to the teenage girl with her nose in a phone with a glittery pink "E" on the case. 'The signal's bad up here,' the girl said, shoving it in her pocket.

'It's erratic,' Amelia agreed. And while she had her attention added, 'I've got a sister about your age. She's here, so maybe you two could team up. Have some fun. At least you won't be bored.'

'Does she like Monopoly?'

'Maybe. Well, she used to.'

Elise shrugged. 'No big deal if she doesn't. I rarely get bored anyway.' Her fringe was pinned back from her forehead with clips, revealing a rash of tiny freckles across her otherwise pale face and turned-up nose. She tucked her fair, collar-length hair behind her ears. 'I like to read,' she said. She was well spoken, but sharp. 'I've brought some books to study.' She looked up at her father, with her bright blue eyes, and smiled. 'I hate taking time out of school, but as long as I make use of my time here wisely, it should be OK.'

'Elise is a good girl,' Neil said, ruffling her hair, and she giggled, looking up at him once more.

The girl was different to Lark, younger by a year or so – sixteen probably – and clearly a lover of pink, if her padded jacket was anything to go by. Amelia wasn't sure they would get on anyway; Elise was still a child, Lark a young woman.

'You can pick up your keys from reception, Rosamund,' Amelia said. Turning, she pointed to Primrose Cottage at the far end of the site, and backing onto the forest. 'And that's where you'll be staying.'

'Beautiful,' Rosamund said. 'I can't wait to spend time with you all. Is Jackson here?' She glanced about her.

'Taking a shower,' Caroline said. 'We're all going down to the beach later for a picnic. I know it's November, but the sun's out. I thought it might be nice.'

'Sounds perfect.' Rosamund looked at Neil and Elise. 'Right, let's get our keys, shall we?'

Chapter 19

A Year Ago

Amelia

'Finally,' Amelia whispered, her eyes scanning William's brief message that had just appeared on her phone screen.

All good here! Cat fine! See you when you get back!

'You OK, love?' her dad said, as she shoved her phone into her pocket.

'Fine,' she said, but felt far from it.

She was snuggled into her thick Aran sweater and jeans. Despite the sun beaming down from a pastel-blue sky onto the golden sand, it was nowhere near warm enough to be sitting on a deserted stretch of beach in the Scottish Highlands.

Rosamund had opened the hamper Ruth had made, and laid out a homemade quiche, bread rolls filled with ham and cheese, and two flasks of tea, onto a tartan blanket, but so far nobody had eaten anything. It all felt too forced.

Amelia had dropped down onto the sand a few feet away from everyone else ten minutes ago, and was now attempting to build a castle with a tablespoon. Her mum seemed happy, despite the chill in the air, sitting in her deckchair facing the sea, a blanket covering her knees. She was flanked by Jackson and Rosamund, and Amelia tried hard to give the impression she didn't mind them hogging her mum, but the truth was she did, and it was clear Lark was bothered too. In fact, she'd drifted away from the gathering and was now down by the shoreline, her back to them as she kicked sand, seeming deep in thought.

Everyone but Thomas and Maddie were there. Thomas had cried off, saying he had a headache, and Amelia wondered if he was finding all of this harder than he was letting on.

'I'm sure I just saw a bottlenose dolphin,' her dad said suddenly excited, binoculars pinned to his eyes. Neil, who sat beside him reading from his phone, glanced up, squinted towards the sea, and then looked back at his screen.

Elise was leaning against the rocks a short distance away from the group, reading from her Kindle. She was wearing a pink pom-pom hat pulled low, with her pink padded jacket, jeans, and spotted wellingtons.

Lark turned towards them and raised her hand. 'I'm going for a walk, Mum,' she called. She seemed to be struggling more than ever since Rosamund and her family arrived.

Amelia watched her sister meander along the beach, tall and willowy in her flowing black dress, and jacket, the breeze catching her blonde hair. She wanted to go after her, tell her everything would be OK. But it was hard to leave, and in truth she wasn't sure everything would be OK, and eventually Lark was out of sight.

'That's pretty good.' It was Elise, by Amelia's side, admiring her attempts at building a sandcastle.

'I thought I might add a moat,' Amelia said, drawing a circle around her castle with her gloved finger. 'But I need water, and I didn't bring a bucket.'

Elise laughed, and rummaged in her rucksack. 'Here,' she said, brandishing a large empty water bottle.

'Right, let's get some water then.' Amelia rose, brushed sand from her jeans, and followed Elise towards the sea.

Once at the water's edge, Elise bent and scooped water into the bottle. 'This could take a while,' she said, as a frothy wave covered her wellington boots. 'So, what do you think of Drummondale House?' She rose with the full bottle, and, staring at it, gave it a shake.

'It's OK, why?'

'I think it's a bit eerie with those ruins and creepy statues. My wicked stepmother thought it was charming, until I told her about the masked figure, and now she's officially freaked.' She giggled.

Amelia's eyes widened. 'What do you mean, masked figure?'

'Oh, don't worry. I made it up to give her the creeps.'

'You don't like her?' She glanced up the beach at Rosamund.

'Can't stand her.' Elise screwed up her face. 'She flirts with other men, and Daddy just can't see it. Daddy says I've got to learn to get along with her, but I never will. I hate her.'

'Hate is a strong word.'

'But she stole my dad from me.' She glared up the beach. 'Christ she's coming. I bet she thinks I'm talking about her.'

'Elise!' Rosamund called as she hurried down the sand. 'Everything OK?'

'I was just telling Amelia about the masked figure, is all.' She threw Amelia a conspiring look.

'Darling, Daddy wants you,' Rosamund said, seeming to ignore the comment about the masked figure.

'Fine.' Elise handed Amelia the bottle, water splashing from it, and hurried away, skipping up the beach towards her father, the pom-pom on her hat bouncing.

*

'She can be difficult,' Rosamund said, as they ambled back up the beach. 'She's played some awful tricks on me over the past two years. But I've got used to it. Her father's away a lot, and she'd been without a mother figure for so long. Neil relied on nannies who never lasted. She put a frog in the last one's bag the day she left.'

'Maybe she needs to see a psychologist.'

'Maybe. I thought, at first, she just needed plenty of love and attention. It was a tragedy that she lost her mother so young, but I've tried so hard to give her that ...' Her voice cracked.

Amelia touched her arm. 'It can't be easy taking on someone else's child – especially a teen.'

'It's not. But, as I say, I'm trying my best.'

They reached the others, and Rosamund sat back down, and Amelia dropped onto the sand once more. She didn't attempt to make the moat around her sandcastle. Instead she rolled up her scarf, laid it on the beach, flopped her head down onto it, and closed her eyes.

The low chatter around her was oddly soothing.

'I used to come here a lot with my parents,' her mum was saying. 'I loved it. In fact, I remember Ruth from when we came camping here in the Seventies, would you believe? I'm not sure she remembers me though.'

Amelia opened her eyes, and pulled herself to a sitting position. Her mum hadn't mentioned knowing Ruth.

'Hers was quite a sad story really,' her mum continued. 'Ruth was in love with Michael Collis back then, and he loved her too. But their parents disapproved – a real Romeo and Juliet situation. Michael's father was angry that Ruth's mother owned some of the estate's land. His grandfather had lost it in a poker game, or something like that.'

'Who are Ruth and Michael Collis?' Rosamund asked.

'Michael owns the estate now, and Ruth you met on reception.'

'Ah, the strange woman.'

'A little eccentric perhaps.'

Amelia shuffled onto her elbows. The sea was calm, the sun flashing on the blue making her squint. Waves ruffled pebbles as they travelled up the beach. She turned to look at her mum – who was smiling and still talking, seeming content – and felt some of that contentment absorb into her. But beautiful moments in life are fragile. This moment wouldn't last. She knew that. How could it? She couldn't stop time. She couldn't stop her mother from dying.

'I'm going for a paddle,' Rosamund said, rising and breaking the spell. 'Anyone else?'

Amelia jumped to her feet, suppressing tears. 'I'll come.'

Jackson rose too, and she wanted to sit back down again, but knew it would hurt her mum if she did, so, when nobody else got up, the three strolled down the beach towards the sea.

Amelia veered away from them as soon as they reached the shoreline, and started looking for shells and pebbles, picking one up that shone all shades of green.

When she turned to show Jackson and Rosamund, they'd taken off their shoes and socks and were paddling, laughing as they kicked water at each other, her blonde hair swishing in the sun's rays. And although Amelia felt sure it was harmless, she was irritated by their frivolity, and couldn't help recalling what Elise had said about Rosamund being a flirt.

That's when she thought she saw it – a look between them – something almost tangible, as Rosamund pushed him over and he fell with a splash, soaking his jeans.

Amelia batted away her distrust when she glanced up at her mum who was laughing too as she watched on. I must have been mistaken, she told herself.

Chapter 20

A Year Ago

Ruth

It was gone 3 p.m. and most of her guests were still at the beach, and although she'd seen Maddie having a cigarette on the porch outside her cottage earlier, she and Thomas were now tucked inside.

Ruth grabbed a handful of clean towels and headed towards Rosamund's cottage, and let herself in. She wanted to know more about her new visitors. The woman, Rosamund, she wasn't that keen on – got tickets on herself that one – far too full of her own importance with her designer clothes, and swirling, curling hair. She was heavily made-up too, thick foundation like clay. And there was something else she'd observed when they'd collected their keys: Ruth really didn't buy the woman's fondness for her stepdaughter.

Now, the man – Neil – he seemed nice enough, in a dull, work-absorbed kind of way. He seemed to adore Rosamund, though Ruth suspected he adored the child more.

Once inside their cottage, Ruth climbed the stairs. From there she entered Elise's room.

A white nightshirt with a dog on the front was folded neatly on the girl's pillow, and a book lay open on the bedside cabinet next to a notepad and pen. Ruth picked up the pad, and perched on the edge of the bed, her hand absentmindedly stroking a fluffy toy dog. The pages in Elise's book were full of neatly written maths equations, followed by several pages of writing in French. Elise was clearly studious.

Ruth rose and placed two towels at the foot of the teenager's bed. There's nothing much to see here.

She made her way into Rosamund and Neil's room, which smelt of aftershave, and hairspray. Ruth put two towels on the end of the bed, and looked at her watch. She shouldn't hang about; they would be back soon.

She hurried downstairs once more, noticing a game of Monopoly set out on the coffee table. Silver counters: the dog and the top hat, piles of toy money laid out around the edges.

Ruth padded towards the door, and ran her hand over Rosamund's orange coat hanging on the rack. Before she could stop herself, she'd lifted it down, and slipped it on. It was far too long for her, almost touching the floor, but she didn't care. She rolled her chin over the soft collar. It smelt of expensive perfume.

Within moments she was strutting up and down the lounge, as though on a catwalk, spinning around several times. Oh, to be as beautiful as Rosamund – oh to have had the life I should have had.

The door swung open. 'What the hell do you think you're doing?' It was Rosamund. Her arms folded across her yellow anorak, her face red with rage.

'Nothing,' Ruth said, almost toppling as she took off the coat.

'How is putting on my coat nothing?' Rosamund snapped.

'Sorry. It's just so beautiful. Sorry.'

Neil and Elise appeared behind Rosamund.

'I just brought fresh towels,' Ruth babbled, shoving the coat into Rosamund's arms. 'I've put them on the beds.' And without another word, she pushed past the congregated family, and headed back to her cottage.

Chapter 21

A Year Ago

Amelia

The sun was going down, now a shimmering spread of deep orange on the horizon, reflecting on the sea.

There was no sign of Lark.

Rosamund and Neil had taken the others back to Drummondale House some time ago, and Amelia and her dad now made their way down the beach in the direction Lark had gone several hours before.

'She's lost track of time, that's all,' Amelia said, trying to keep up with her dad's long strides. But she couldn't help thinking Lark was being inconsiderate, taking off – worrying everyone – again. 'Are you OK, Dad?' she added, when he didn't reply.

'Do I look OK?' He blinked furiously. 'Sorry. Sorry, I didn't mean to snap at you, love. It's just hard enough, all this.'

'A total nightmare.'

'And now Lark has taken off, and Rosamund Green and her add-ons have turned up.' He dragged fingers through his hair.

'Why the hell your mum got back in touch with that woman is a mystery.' He kicked a large pebble. 'She hurt her, Amelia.'

'That was a long time ago, Dad. People change.'

'Do they? Do they really? In my experience people rarely change – just the masks they wear.'

'Well Mum seems happy she's here. Surely that's the most important thing right now.'

He said no more, and they continued on in silence, not seeing a soul for almost half a mile. And as the darkness thickened, Amelia's anger that her sister had taken off turned to worry.

'Where the hell is she?' she said, her feet heavy in the sand. 'Why would she take off like this?'

'She's not herself.'

She swallowed. 'None of us are, Dad.'

'No. But she's just a kid, Amelia.' His voice cracked with emotion. 'A teenager.'

It was as they rounded a bend, and the view of jagged rocks against sand and sea swooped in front of them for miles, Amelia spotted the silhouette of a young woman perched on a rock, looking out to sea, hair blowing in the breeze. She looked like a mermaid.

'Lark!' she called, as they ran towards her. 'Thank God.'

Lark looked down at them as they reached the foot of the rock, the moonlight catching her wet cheeks telling them she'd been crying.

'What's wrong?' Amelia called up to her, as her dad grabbed Lark's hand, and helped her climb down.

She shrugged. 'Mum's dying, is all. Do I need another reason to feel like crap?'

Amelia opened her arms instinctively as Lark stepped onto the sand, and as her sister fell into them, any residual anger dissipated. Lark was only seventeen, after all.

Chapter 22

Present Day

Ruth

It's almost dark, and snow tumbles from heavy clouds. I can't push my trolley along the path in this weather, so distribute the towels a few at a time to my guests.

Maddie took hers from me at the door, with a polite thank you a few moments ago.

So did Robert.

Now, I'm on my way to Primrose Cottage, soft white towels pressed against my chest as I attempt to shield them from the falling snow. My steps are quick and short along the slippery path. The heavy torch Finn bought a few months back unbalancing me slightly. I preferred the small one I used for years, but he insisted it wasn't bright enough. My foot skids across the icy pavement, and I grab the ornamental fence surrounding the cottage veranda, eyes falling on the snowman. As my eyes focus on its face, I let out a yelp.

'Jesus!' A creepy mask of a young boy's smiling face has been put on the snowman. My stomach knots. I've seen masks like this before – the face too pink, too bright; the smile too wide – and yet eyes so lifeless, dead. After a beat, I take a breath; consoling myself that Elise must have put it there.

I tap on the door, and peer through the glass. The power is still out and no candles flicker inside. I knock again. Rosamund mentioned earlier, when she bought some bread, that she was going to go for a walk, saying she hoped to take some photos of the ruins in the snow by moonlight to put on her Instagram. That's where she must be. Elise must be with her.

Deciding nobody is home, I push my key in the lock, turn it, and shove the door open a few inches.

'Rosamund,' I call into the cottage, just to be sure. 'Elise? I've brought clean towels.' I push the door open further and step inside. 'Rosamund?'

I shine the torch around. Caress the room with its beam. Despite a game of Monopoly set out on the coffee table, ready to play, and two unlit candles standing either side of the board, there doesn't seem to be anybody in.

I make my way up the stairs towards the dappled greyness of the landing and pass the open door to the shower room. It's a stunning room – the best on the site, with its double sink and ivory tiles. Finn revamped it back in the spring. He did a wonderful job.

I continue along the landing, and try the handle of Elise's room, but it's locked. 'Elise, are you in there?'

'Yep!' comes the reply.

'It's only me, lass. Ruth. I've brought towels.'

'OK.'

I step into Rosamund's room, and shine the torch towards the bed, catching sight of a scan of Rosamund's baby propped against the lamp on the bedside unit. On the bottom of the bed is an orange hooded fur bed jacket. After laying the torch down, I pick it up. Within moments I've put the jacket on and zipped it up. It's freakishly soft, and my body tingles as I run my hands over, it and pull up the hood.

I pick up the torch once more, and dip the beam towards the floor, spotting Rosamund's case. I reach behind me and with the quietest of clicks close the door. I crouch down and open the case. The clothes inside are expensive; silk blouses and cashmere are packed neatly. If things had turned out differently with Michael, these are the kind of things I would have worn.

Suddenly the room fills with light. The power has returned. I dart a panicked look about me, feeling as though I've been caught out, and bolt to my feet. The shower starts up with a shudder through the pipes, and the sound of water cascading reaches my ears. I freeze for a moment, before willing myself to move.

It's OK. I've done nothing wrong.

I place two towels on Rosamund's bed, open the door and dash from the room, and onto the landing.

Elise's door stands open. The shower-room door closed. I lean my head against the wood, listen to the flowing water.

'I'm off now, love,' I call, but there's no reply.

There's a noise downstairs. Rosamund's back?

It's OK. I've done nothing wrong.

Someone is coming up the stairs – slow and steady.

'It's only me, Rosamund,' I call out, knowing I shouldn't really be here, recalling how angry she'd been when she found me trying on her coat last time she was here. 'I'm dropping off a couple of towels, that's all.'

It's OK. I've done nothing wrong.

I quickly tap on the shower-room door, and open it. I cover my eyes as I step inside, and place two towels on the rack. 'Clean towels for you, Elise,' I say.

I turn to leave, my body tensing as panic surges through me. Before me is a figure in black. I barely have time to register they're wearing the creepy mask. Barely have a moment for the scream inside my chest to reach my throat.

The pain in my head sends me reeling.

Everything goes black as I hit the floor with a thud.

Chapter 23

Present Day

Me

You've left the bedroom door open, and I can see it hanging on the kitchen curtain rail. I don't know why it haunts me. It's only a piece of plastic, after all. But it does.

It's been there since the day you brought me here. Do you leave it there to torment me? Or have you simply forgotten it's there?

I close my eyes, my mind sifting through the same old questions, and I wonder how many times I will ask myself them.

Why hasn't anyone found me?

Will I ever be free?

Will I live to see tomorrow?

I listen for your return. I want to ask you again why you are holding me here. Hope that I will find a part of you that isn't consumed by evil. But outside there's an unbearable silence.

I sit on the edge of the bed, and pour a glass of water from the jug, lift it with weak arms to my dry lips, and swallow.

I turn as Misty clatters in through the cat flap. He's free, and yet he chooses to return each day. I wonder if he knows how much he's helping me through this. Thank God I've got Misty.

Chapter 24

Present Day

Amelia

It was dark as I clambered, breathless, to the top of Vine Hill, doubling over with exhaustion. I kept going off course, and the route was hazardous. It's taken me over an hour to get back. I was stupid, shouldn't have gone out alone in these freezing conditions.

My bladder aches from needing the loo, and every part of my body hurts, as though icy fingers touch my bones, freezing soft tissue. My ears burn, and even the inside of my nose is crystallised.

I'm relieved to see the cottages have power once more, each window alight with an orange glow.

I'm about to step onwards, desperate to warm myself by the wood burner, and maybe sneak a hug from Dad if he's in a better mood, when I hear a scream. My mind shoots back to a year ago. I stop calf-deep in snow, filled with dread.

The scream came from Primrose Cottage, and Rosamund flings open her front door and almost falls through it, gripping the doorframe and bending over as though trying to catch her breath. 'Elise!' she cries. 'Elise!'

As if a fire alarm has gone off, Dad appears through the darkness, hurrying towards Rosamund, and Finn races from the other direction.

I make my way towards Rosamund, and startle at the sight of the snowman Elise and Rosamund had so lovingly built that morning destroyed – broken, scattered. By the time I reach the cottage, Finn has taken Rosamund in his arms, and she's sobbing into his chest, and he's asking her what's wrong.

'What is it?' yells Dad, reaching them. 'What's happened?'

Rosamund lifts her head, her face streaming with tears. 'She's gone!' She pauses briefly. 'Like last time. Like Lark. Elise has disappeared. And there's so much blood.' She gasps, as though her words have punctured her heart, before turning and racing back into the cottage.

We follow, and my eyes scan the room, falling on a Monopoly board, before moving on to Rosamund's red, tearful face.

She takes a deep breath. 'I left Elise reading in her room. I wanted to photograph the ruins. I asked her to come, but she wouldn't. Oh God, why didn't she come with me?' She swallows, wipes tears from her cheeks. 'I shouldn't have left her on her own. Not after the message.'

'Message?'

She pulls her phone from her pocket, fumbles shaking fingers across the screen. 'Here,' she says, passing it to me. I read the words:

Why bring your stepdaughter to Drummondale House? You know what happened to Lark.

'Oh my God. Do you know who sent it?' I say, passing her phone back to her, and she takes it with shaking hands.

'I've no idea. It's from an unknown sender.'

'You mentioned blood?' Finn says.

'Yes. Upstairs in the shower room.'

He turns and bolts up the stairs two at a time. I follow, to see him crouched in front of a pool of congealing blood on the shower-room floor. He looks up at me. 'Christ. What the hell's happened here?'

I turn to see Rosamund and Dad behind me. 'Call the police,' I say, my voice quivering. 'And an ambulance – Elise must be hurt somewhere.' But I'm doubtful she's even alive. Anyone losing this amount of blood …

Dad takes out his phone, and looks at the screen. 'No signal … I'll try outside.' He descends the stairs, as though he's glad to escape. Within moments the front door slams, and he's gone.

Elise's bedroom door stands open. It's in darkness, but the landing light allows me to pick out the double bed, the ruffled quilt, and a book open like a butterfly on her bedside unit. Floor-length curtains are pulled closed across the window. Her pink holdall is propped against the wall.

I turn to see Rosamund behind me – so close. Shaking. Unable to keep her limbs still. She brushes her cheeks with her anorak sleeve, and I notice most of her make-up has been washed away by tears. She looks vulnerable – not something I thought I would ever see. 'I need Neil,' she says trancelike, her body trembling. 'I need Neil.'

Finn is silent, his head flopped back against the wall, a torch in his hand. 'My mum was here,' he says. 'This is hers.'

Two white towels on the floor are soaked in blood. He takes a deep breath. 'She was running late, not back from her towel deliveries, and I was getting worried. It's not like her. She's always punctual.'

There are more red smears on the wall tiles, and on the landing carpet too, as though something – or someone – has been dragged across the floor. My stomach flips as I see the streaks of blood continue across the carpet and into Elise's room.

I move gingerly into her room, and flick on the light. Finn and Rosamund are right behind me. A shudder runs through the length of my body, as we take in the streaks of blood that lead to the far wall.

Is there a body behind the bed? I want to know, but cannot move for fear.

Finn takes a gulp of air, walks across the room, and heads past the bed. He glances down at the floor, his mind clearly working the same as mine.

'What is it?' Rosamund shrieks.

'Finn?' I say through my fingers.

He looks up, white with anguish, and shakes his head. 'There's nothing here.'

Rosamund and I grab our chests in tandem, and my heart thumps under my fingers. 'Let's get some tea,' I say, turning to leave the room. It's what they always say on TV, when everything goes tragically wrong. 'We can wait downstairs for Dad, and hopefully the police will get to us soon.'

Rosamund nods. 'This is what happened a year ago, isn't it?' she says. 'What if it's the same person? What if they've returned?'

'It's different,' I say, leading the way downstairs.

'How is it different, Amelia?' Rosamund says. 'The disappearance of a teenage girl, the blood.' She buries her head in her hands.

I wander into the kitchen, fill the kettle, and flick it on.

It's as it reaches boiling point the power goes off once more, and the cottage plunges into darkness.

Chapter 25

Present Day

Amelia

My eyes, now adjusted to the sudden loss of light, are drawn to the window. The blind is up, and the full moon filters through snow-heavy trees that bend and sway in the wind. A chill runs down my spine. I'm petrified.

I turn, and make my way towards the lounge, gripping the worktops as I go. The dying embers in the wood burner cast a dim glow over the lounge. Rosamund is kneeling next to the coffee table, lighting candles with a shaking hand. And as the wicks flicker and burn I watch Finn switching his mother's torch on and off.

Suddenly he jumps to his feet, agitated. 'We need to look for them. Now.'

'Finn's right,' Rosamund says, rising too. 'Surely they can't be far. Especially if one of them is injured.' The words catch in her throat.

'But it doesn't make sense. If they left through the front door, there would be a trail of blood, wouldn't there?' My words make me shudder. There's no blood down here or on the stairs. 'We should check upstairs again before you go outside. It's freezing out there, Rosamund. Think of your baby.'

Finn opens the front door, and within seconds they are both out in the cold night, where the wind is whipping up snow into mini blizzards. Finn pushes the door closed behind them without another word.

For God's sake! They're not thinking straight. We need to check the house thoroughly first. Look for clues as to what's gone on here.

I stand, a strange sense of not being alone wrapping round my body. Is someone still in the house? I pick up one of the candles, my heartbeat quickening. I have to go back upstairs. What if one of them is hurt? Unconscious? Bleeding to death? My mind ticks over, trying to remember the first-aid course I did at work three months ago – how to do CPR. And now 'Staying Alive' plays in my head over and over, as I creep up the open-tread staircase, fearing someone will jump out when I reach the top, or step out of the shadows and attack me. The candle isn't helping, casting dancing shapes around me. There's no doubt my body is on high alert. Pulses, I didn't even know I had, warn me of danger. Telling me to go back downstairs. To wait for Dad.

I'm halfway up when the wood under my feet creaks. I hear a cry, and within nanoseconds realise it came from me. I'm scaring myself half to death. I need to get a grip.

I grasp the banister, trying to stop myself shaking, the flame zigzagging across the landing ahead of me, picking out the blood we saw earlier.

I take a deep breath and head into the main bedroom, noticing a case on the floor. I guess this is Rosamund's room, from the aroma of her perfume, and the sleeve of a silk blouse spilling from the case. The wardrobe stands open and empty. She hasn't unpacked. The curtains are pulled across the window. The bed is made.

I crouch down, and with the help of the candle, peer under the bed. Nothing. I was wrong. There's nobody here.

Then I spot it – the scan of Rosamund's baby – and my mind takes a jump to the past, and suddenly my emotions take control, and a surge of tears fills my eyes.

A sudden noise: tap, tap, tap.

I freeze, trying to work out where it's coming from, dashing the tears away with my sleeve.

I rise, heart thudding, a whir of anxiety in my ears.

Tap, tap, tap.

As my mind adjusts, I realise someone is tapping on the front door. Dad?

I hurry down the stairs, and race across the lounge. 'Dad?' I call through the door.

'Yes, let me in, Amelia, it's bloody freezing out here.'

I put down the candle, and fling open the door.

'Jesus,' he says pushing past me, bringing a gust of wind and snow with him. There isn't a part of him that isn't white. 'The signal is terrible. It must be this awful weather. I finally got a connection up near the gate, and my phone packed up before I could call the cops. Pretty sure the cold has sucked the life out of it.'

I pull my phone from my pocket. There's no signal, and only forty per cent left on the battery.

Dad crouches down in front of the wood burner, picks up a couple of logs and places them on the glowing embers, before rubbing his hands together in front of it. He looks up at me. 'No power again, I see,' he says. There's a tremble in his voice, as though the cold and fear are strangling his vocal cords. 'Where are Rosamund and Finn?'

'Out searching for Elise; Ruth is missing too. Where could they be, Dad? And all the blood … it's so scary.' I sound almost childlike, as though I expect him to have the answers like he did when I was young. 'This is freaking me out,' I go on. 'Two people

115

go missing on the anniversary of Lark and Jackson's disappearance, from the same place. Another blonde, teenage girl vanishes.'

He pulls off his woollen hat and runs his fingers through his hair. 'We have to find them, but it's so cold out there. None of us should be roaming around in these conditions, particularly Rosamund.'

I look up towards the landing. 'I was upstairs when you came to the door. It's awful up there.'

He buries his head in his hands, as though in denial.

'We need to know what went on up here, Dad,' I say, turning on my phone torch and heading up the stairs, leaving him crouched by the fire. This time I reach the top within moments, the thought of Dad in the cottage too calming some of my jangled nerves.

I glance into the shower room, my eyes falling on the pool of blood once more, before I carry on into Elise's room. I crouch down bringing the torch to floor level – looking at the bloodstains on the carpet. I rise, spotting a rom-com paperback and Elise's phone on the dresser, before heading towards the wardrobe, and yanking the doors open. A couple of pink jumpers, her pink padded jacket, a black jacket that looks more like something Lark would wear, and a pair of jeans hang inside. But there's no sign of Elise.

I move towards the window where the curtains are pulled across, and take a deep breath before dragging them open, steeling myself, ready to jump back if a body should fall.

There's nobody behind them – dead or alive.

But what I do see sends my head reeling. I fall backwards, dropping onto the bed. 'Dad!' I yell. 'Dad, come here. Now! Please! Oh God, you need to see this.'

Chapter 26

Present Day

Me

Sometimes you come to me. Want sex. Other times, like now, you don't look in on me at all.

Sometimes I think of ways I might kill you. But there's nothing here that could do the job. You don't even give me a knife to cut the food. You're far too clever for that.

When I've finished eating chicken nuggets, and an apple – I quite like apples – I feel the familiar blurring of my mind. You've been drugging my food lately. I've no doubt of that. Are you going to kill me? Is that your intention?

But I must eat. Starving to death is a painful way to die.

I lie back on the pillow, my mind swimming. There's no way out of this, I know that now.

My eyelids fall heavy over my eyes, and Misty curls beside me, warm and comforting.

Another day in hell is over.

Chapter 27

Present Day

Amelia

I flash my phone torch towards the macabre sight – smears of blood on floral wallpaper below the window, smudges of red on the painted frame, bloody fingerprints on glass.

'Someone got out this way,' I say, as Dad reaches my side. I fling open the window and a gust of snow swoops into the room. 'Someone covered in blood,' I go on, as the wind grabs the frame from my hand, and it slams against the side of the cottage, cracking the glass. I bring my torch closer to the open window. It's a sharp drop down to snow-covered bushes. There's something down there.

'We need to look outside.' I turn from the window.

'Do you really want to go out there tonight, love?' There's doubt in his voice. Is he afraid? Or maybe he's having flashbacks to a year ago, as I am. But for me those memories only make me more determined to find Ruth and Elise.

'We have to, Dad. The snow will cover every trace of what

happened by morning. There could be footprints – drops of blood leading into the wood like breadcrumbs.'

We head out of the room and onto the landing. The wood burner is ablaze now, its glow lighting the open tread of the staircase as we hurry down. I'm on a mission, and I dive across the room and throw open the front door. 'Damn,' I whisper. The wind is deadly, the snowfall heavy, and my face stings within seconds of stepping outside. I pull my scarf high around my face. Although the sky is charcoal black, the moon is bright, reflecting off the snow. I look towards the ruins, and then scan the area. There's no sign of anyone.

I turn to see Dad pulling on his gloves. He shrugs as though reluctant, but steps out behind me anyway. The door clicks closed behind him.

'We should go around the back,' I say, the wind whistling human-like as we make our way down the side of the house, towards the forest.

It's darker behind the cottage, and as we push through the twisted hedgerow we can barely see in front of us, despite my phone torch. The wind is less fierce here, where tall trees shelter us, but the open window still bangs rhythmically against the cottage wall sending a chill down my spine. I wave my torch in the general area below the window. There's something on the ground.

'Oh God … no … that's not … it can't be,' I cry.

Dad pushes past me. 'Jesus.'

I take in the body lying face down in the snow, my heart thudding. I can't move from the spot, and my teeth start to chatter. Dad crouches down, and my whole body shakes, as I hover the torch over the darkness, picking out the crumpled heap, flashes of an orange fur jacket soaked in blood. He turns the body over, and slaps both hands over his mouth. 'It's Ruth,' he whispers through his fingers.

My knees buckle, and I grab a tree to stop myself falling. 'Is she dead?' My voice is shaky, bile rising into my throat.

'Someone's hit her. Hit her hard. There's so much blood.'

'Dad?'

He fumbles with her wrist.

'Can you feel a pulse?'

After a beat he shakes his head, says, 'She's dead, Amelia.' He turns away from her body, closes his eyes. 'Who the hell would do this?'

I want to spin round. Run. But take a deep breath and flash the torch around me. There are no footprints. No trail of breadcrumbs. Nobody has escaped this scene. I look up at the window still banging against the wall. 'Somebody threw her out, didn't they?' My words are calm, on a monotone, and I know I'm in shock.

Dad looks up to where my torch is shining. There's blood on the outside of the frame. 'Or maybe she fell,' he says. 'Trying to get away from someone.'

'Who would do this?' I look about me once more. 'And where's Elise? Did she witness this? Was she taken? Did she ...?' I'm about to suggest Elise could have done this, but I stop and shake my head. Why would anyone have it in for Ruth? But then I've never understood evil. It's something that has kept me awake at night since Lark and Jackson went missing. The fear that there are wicked people out there. That someone deranged could have taken my sister. Could still have her. And now Ruth's dead, Elise is missing, and we're trapped here at Drummondale House with a killer. And the biggest question of all is how would we know if we'd met a psychopath.

I turn, eager to get away from the gory sight, and begin pushing through the hedgerow once more. 'We need to warn Thomas and Maddie that there could be a killer on the estate,' I say, the words sounding alien on my tongue. Dad is right behind me, so close I can hear his rapid breaths. 'Remember the strange footprints leading to Elise's window? And she saw someone with a mask on looking in at her.' I'm talking too fast, my breathing rapid as well, the air turning misty around my mouth as the words fall out. 'Oh God, do you think—?'

'I don't know, love. But we should probably stick together. Maybe we should all stay in Bluebell Cottage as it's bigger than the others, at least until Finn and Rosamund get back.'

'Safety in numbers,' I say.

'Safety in numbers,' he echoes.

Chapter 28

A Year Ago

Amelia

It was gone seven. The dining room buzzed with chatter, everyone relieved that Amelia and Robert had found Lark safe and well on the beach. But Amelia felt displaced somehow. If it wasn't for the hunger pangs – she'd built up an appetite walking the stretch of sand with her dad searching for her sister, and had barely touched the picnic earlier – she would have gone straight to her cottage to get her thoughts in order.

Once they were all seated, Ruth brought out trays of vegetables, roast and mashed potatoes, and a plate each with a hunk of steak and kidney pie on, and a vegetable pie for Lark. It looked and smelt good, and Amelia couldn't wait to tuck in.

Once they had eaten, and Ruth had served drinks, she and Finn disappeared into the main house.

Amelia looked around the table. Her mum and Jackson were chatting with Rosamund and Neil, and a separate conversation was taking place between Robert, Thomas and Maddie. Lark looked pale and tired as she fiddled with her phone. It was as though she didn't belong – an outcast, an outcast who chose to be that way.

Truth was, Amelia had no enthusiasm or inclination to infiltrate either conversation, and was just about to announce she was leaving when there was a tap on her shoulder.

'Are you married?' It was Elise, her tone serious. Amelia turned to see the girl's bright blue eyes fixed on her. She had an angelic face; her cheeks pinker that evening, her lips curved upwards, even when she wasn't smiling.

'No, but I have a partner. We live in London.'

'What's his name?'

'William.'

'Do you love him?' Her eyes narrowed.

'Yes, I think so.' Amelia checked herself. 'Yes, I do.'

'But he's not here with you?' She tilted her head on one side, trapping Amelia with her stare – a stare that made her feel uncomfortable. It was as though she could see right into her head.

'He had to work.' The words caught in her throat as she spoke. William should be supporting me. My mum's dying. He should be here.

Elise moved in closer. 'Do you have children?'

'No. But I would like a baby one day.'

'Rosamund wants a baby,' she whispered, from behind her hand. 'I hope she can't have one. I don't like babies much – especially hers.'

Amelia felt her eyes widen, unsure what to say. 'I have a cat.' It came out squeaky. 'Do you like cats?'

She shook her head, no. 'I like dogs more.' She moved in even closer, so their heads touched. 'I want one. But Rosamund is allergic, so I don't think we'll get one anytime soon. She's ruined everything.'

Amelia glanced at Rosamund, who seemed oblivious to their conversation, then back to Elise who slumped back in her chair.

'I looked up Drummondale House on the Internet before we came,' she said. 'A young boy died here a hundred years ago.'

'Yes, I heard,' Amelia said, recalling the ghost walk from the night before.

'It's a pretty depressing place isn't it?' Elise screwed up her nose, and looked about her. 'The atmosphere is heavy. Like it's cursed or something.'

'Elise.' It was Neil, who was sitting the other side of Amelia, and leaning forward staring at his daughter. 'Enough!'

'Flip sake, Dad,' she said, shrinking further down in her seat. 'I'm only talking.'

'I'm sorry about that, Amelia,' he said. He had a kindly face, his full cheeks reddened by the warmth of the room, and possibly the two glasses of red he'd drunk. 'Take no notice of her. It's an amazing place. We're glad to be here sharing this special time with your mum.'

Elise's face morphed from sweet to sulky as he turned back to his conversation.

'One day you'll be sorry,' she muttered under her breath, giving Rosamund a sideways look.

A few moments later Elise had pulled herself back up in her seat, and was tapping on Maddie's arm. 'Are you American?'

Maddie turned from Thomas and Dad. 'Yes, I grew up in Portland, Oregon.'

'I want to go to America one day. Daddy and I were planning to go, just the two of us, before Rosamund came along.' She looped her hair behind her ears.

'Well, it's a great place if you get to go. You'll absolutely love it.'

'Do you like playing games?'

Maddie nodded, and smiled. 'I do, yes.'

'What's your favourite game?'

'My, I don't know. Maybe Clue, which is fun. How about you?'

'I like Monopoly. I like it when I get all the hotels and money, and everyone else goes bankrupt.' She paused before adding, 'Is there an American version?'

'Aha, yes, there's even a New York edition, with Tiffany's and Trump Towers for sale.'

'Really? That's so cool. Do they have a dog token?'

'Sorry?'

'On the US boards, do they have a silver dog counter?'

'Ah, I see. Yes, sometimes. It depends which version. There are so many these days. I saw a Pokémon version once.'

Elise leaned to one side, and looked past Maddie at Finn, who had just returned to the conservatory, and was standing silently at the counter.

'I'm guessing you like dogs, then,' Maddie went on, seeming to enjoy their conversation. She took a gulp of her wine. 'I like Golden Labradors – what about you?'

'I want a rescue dog. One that's grateful I saved it and never lets me down.' She moved her eyes back to Maddie. 'So shall we play Monopoly?'

'It's a bit late,' Maddie said, looking at her watch. 'Maybe another time.' She glanced at Thomas, who grinned.

'When we do, I want to be the dog.'

'And I'll be the top hat,' she said. 'It's a deal.'

'Hey,' Elise said her eyes bright, as she glanced round the table. 'Let's play Truth or Lie.'

'OK. But only if it's a quick game,' Maddie said. 'You'll have to explain the rules.'

'It's easy. We all take it in turns to say something about ourselves, or something that happened to us, and everyone else has to guess if it's true or a lie.' She clapped her hands, and everyone stopped talking and looked her way. 'We're going to play Truth or Lie,' she said.

'I'm not sure that's a good idea,' Rosamund said.

'Well that's typical.' Elise rolled her eyes. 'You spoil everything.'

'Oh come on, Rosamund, it could be fun,' Jackson said. 'Are you up for it, Caroline?'

'I don't mind.' She sounded tired, as though she would much prefer to return to her cottage.

'Thomas?' Maddie said.

'Yep, why not?'

'Count me in too,' said Neil, rubbing his hands together.

'Yay, thanks, Dad,' Elise said. 'Love you.'

'Love you too, sweetheart.'

'More than anything?'

'More than anything.'

'Will you play, Robert?' Elise asked.

Amelia glanced at her dad. His eyes were closed, clearly desperate to shut out the evening. 'Not me,' he said. 'I'll be heading back soon.'

'Nor me,' Rosamund said. 'I hate this kind of game. Far too intrusive.'

Elise rolled her eyes. 'Amelia, will you play?' she asked. 'Lark, what about you?'

Lark didn't look up from her phone. 'Not even if my life depended on it,' she said.

'I'll watch,' Amelia said, and her dad smiled, as though acknowledging their similarities.

'OK. You start, Caroline,' Elise said.

'OK then.' She smiled, but her eyes were dull. 'When I was young I had a beautiful collie dog and we named her Lassie after the films.'

Lie. You would have told me, Mum, Amelia thought.

'What films?' asked Elise.

'They were about a beautiful dog who was a hero.' She was wearing the wig she had on earlier, and kept fiddling with it, scratching her forehead. She seemed self-conscious, and Amelia wanted to tell her she looked beautiful with or without the wig.

'The films were long before your time, Elise,' Neil said. 'And mine too, come to that.'

'Lie,' Elise said bluntly.

'Aren't you going to ask my mum some more questions first?' Thomas said.

'No, I can tell she's lying. I have a gift. I always know when Rosamund is lying.' She glared at her stepmother. 'Don't I, Rosamund?'

'Lie,' said Thomas, ignoring Elise's dig at Rosamund. 'I'm sure you would have told us about it, Mum.'

'Unfair advantage,' Jackson said with a laugh. 'I'll say lie too.' His eyes were on Lark again. Amelia had seen it before. The way he looked at her. Couldn't Mum see it?

'Lie,' Neil and Maddie said together.

'Yes, it's a lie; you caught me out.'

'Dad, it's your go.' Elise was in full control of the game, and loving every moment. She was a spoilt girl – a little irritating.

Neil tapped his lip with his forefinger. 'OK. When I was at school, a bunch of boys locked me in the caretaker's cupboard over the weekend. I had to use a bucket for the loo.'

'That's so gross,' Lark muttered, turning up her nose, eyes still glued to her phone.

'Oh, Dad, that's awful,' Elise cried. She jumped up and came up behind his chair. Wrapped her arms around his neck.

'You don't even know if it's true yet,' Lark said, finally looking up.

'True,' Jackson said. 'I bet you were a bit of a dork at school, so it kind of has a ring of truth about it.'

'How did it happen, Neil?' Maddie asked, her voice soft and caring.

He widened his eyes, and glanced over his shoulder at Elise. 'Am I supposed to say?'

'Yes, people can ask questions, Dad.'

'Well, the boys grabbed me and shoved me in there for being a swot, which, to be fair, I was.' He gave an awkward laugh.

'Well I'm hoping it's a lie,' Elise said, 'but if it's true, I'll track them down and kill them. Sometimes revenge is the only way.'

'Lie,' Maddie said.

'No, definitely true,' Jackson said.

'It is true,' Neil said.

'I guess boys will be boys.' Jackson took a gulp of his drink. 'And look at you now – doing better than they are, is my guess.'

'Oh yes.' Neil nodded. 'One of them is in prison, I believe.' He laughed. 'Though to be fair we were just kids. I forgive them.'

'You're far too kind, Daddy,' Elise said, her eyes on Rosamund. 'Too forgiving.'

'Not always, sweetheart, not always.'

The atmosphere was suddenly heavy. 'Jackson, it must be your go,' Maddie said, as though trying to extinguish the rising tension.

Jackson grinned, and there was a beat before he said, 'My parents died of carbon-monoxide poisoning in the caravan I grew up in.'

'Seriously?' Lark's eyes moved from her phone to his face. 'You're going with that?'

'I didn't know that.' Caroline's eyes widened. 'It's got to be a lie.'

Rosamund stared Jackson's way, her eyes boring into him, a puzzled look on her face. 'True,' she said.

'You're not even playing, Rosamund.' Elise screwed up her face, and, clenching her fists, turned to Jackson. 'Was it like being on holiday, all the time?'

'No,' Jackson said, leaning back in his chair. 'It was a living hell.'

'You really don't look the type to have grown up in a caravan, Jackson.' Neil narrowed his eyes. 'Convince me.'

'Well, my parents were travellers. I grew up moving from place to place, finally heading for the US on my own when I was eighteen.' He laughed, shrugged. 'It's no big deal.'

'It is if it's true.' Caroline's voice was tense.

Amelia looked over at her dad. Was he smiling? Was he happy to see a crack forming?

'I think it's true,' Elise said. 'Come on put us out of our misery, Jackson.'

'It's true,' he said.

Amelia saw the shock in her mum's eyes, her cheeks flushing.

'Did you know?' Amelia whispered, seeing the shock in her mum's eyes.

Her mum shook her head, as Jackson placed his hand over hers. 'I honestly didn't think it was important enough to tell you, Caroline,' he said. 'It wasn't exactly the best time in my life.'

'Are you OK, Mum?' Amelia asked.

'She's fine,' Jackson said, his eyes boring into the side of her mother's head. 'Aren't you, darling?'

'Of course, yes. It's no big deal. No big deal at all.'

'My go,' Elise said.

'Maybe we should call it a night,' Jackson said. 'What do you think, Caroline?'

'Yes, I'm tired. I thought maybe we could all go for a walk in the forest in the morning; it's meant to be sunny.' She went to rise.

'No!' Elise yelled. 'It's my go, and I'm having it whether you like it or not.'

Jackson glared at Neil, as though asking him to chastise his child, but Neil said nothing.

'I saw a masked figure wandering around Drummondale House last night.' Elise grinned, staring at Rosamund. 'Truth or lie?'

'Liar,' Rosamund snapped, as everyone else remained silent.

Elise glared at Rosamund. 'One day you'll be so sorry you came into our lives,' she yelled, and ran from the conservatory. Within moments, Neil and a flushed-cheeked Rosamund were on their feet too, and dashing out after her.

Thomas, who'd been watching everything unfold, sighed. 'How sharper than a serpent's tooth it is to have a thankless child.'

'The Bard,' Jackson said.

'Indeed.'

'The girl is a walking time bomb, quite frankly.' Jackson dragged his fingers through his hair. 'They really need to get her some kind of help.'

'She seems quite sweet sometimes,' Maddie said, looking puzzled by the child's behaviour.

'Well, she's definitely got it in for Rosamund,' Amelia said, rubbing her eyes, and rising to her feet. 'Actually, I think I'll head back too.' She fumbled her arms into her jacket, desperate to get away. She leaned in and kissed her mum's cheek. 'Night, all,' she said, turning and heading for the door.

'Night,' Finn said, smiling at her as she left. 'Don't let the bed bugs bite.'

Chapter 29

Present Day

Amelia

'We can't leave Ruth outside.' Thomas's brown eyes widen, as he drums his fingers on his knees. He's in shock. We all are.

'I'll boil some water on the stove, make some strong tea,' Maddie says, disappearing to the kitchen carrying a flickering candle.

'Well, there's no way I'm carrying a dead body inside,' I say, my voice shaky. I lower myself down onto the sofa, attempting to recall the one session of mindfulness I attended just after I lost my baby. But trying to focus on it isn't working; I'm a complete wreck. 'You should have seen her, Thomas. It was awful.' I cry.

Thomas moves his wheelchair closer to me, and puts on the brake. 'We need to call the police,' he says.

'Can you get a signal?' I say, tears burning my eyes. I'd tried as we walked back from finding Ruth. 'Because I bloody well can't, and neither can Dad.'

Thomas pulls his phone from his pocket, and shakes his head.

'And there's more,' I say. 'Elise has disappeared. She was in her room when Rosamund went out earlier, and now she's gone.'

Thomas runs his hand over his beard. 'Jeez. Is anyone else getting a sense of déjà vu here?' There's a twang of flippancy in his voice, but fear shows on his face. People handle shock differently, I tell myself.

Maddie walks from the kitchen with a tray of mugs. 'Here you go,' she says, passing them round. I admit I'm glad of the cuppa, the warmth of the mug in my hands. In fact, Maddie and Thomas's lounge feels oddly cosy – the wood burner chugging out a healthy heat, a row of candles ablaze on the shelf above the fireplace, such a contrast to the bleak outside. But my body is tense. Ruth has been murdered.

Dad appears through the front door. 'I've put a note on Rosamund's door,' he says, taking off his coat and hanging it up. 'Said for her and Finn to make their way here when they get back. And I've picked up our phone chargers from our cottage too,' he says to me, putting them down on the table. 'We'll charge our phones once the power's back on.'

'So where exactly are Finn and Rosamund?' Maddie asks, settling herself in the armchair, as though about to watch her favourite TV drama.

'Searching for Elise,' I say. 'And Ruth too, but obviously …'

'I think we should stay together from now on,' Dad says, putting his mug down. 'Well, for tonight at least. We should all stay here. It's for the best.'

'Really?' Thomas looks about him. 'We're all going to kip in here?'

'It's the biggest cottage, Thomas,' I say. 'If we stick together, we should be fine.' I sound melodramatic, but in the circumstances I offer no excuse.

We lapse into silence as we drink our tea, before I finally put my empty mug on the table. 'I could do with something stronger.' I hate myself for even thinking it. I don't want to get drunk. But a swift shot to calm my tattered nerves wouldn't go amiss.

Dad rises. 'I'll get a bottle from our cottage, shall I?' he says, heading for the door.

'No, don't be daft. I'm not that bothered,' I say. It's a complete lie. 'Alcohol's not the answer.'

'Well, I've forgotten the question,' he says, and I wish for a moment he wouldn't encourage me.

Thomas makes the drumming sound people make at the end of a joke, which feels inappropriate somehow. But then what is appropriate? There's hardly a guide on the ways to behave when you find a dead body.

'The old ones are the best,' Dad says dully, pulling his winter gear back on.

'No, Dad, don't go. I'm totally fine,' I insist. 'There's no reason to go out there on your own. I'm not bothered. Truly.'

'If I'm honest, I could do with a shot myself,' he says, and before I can argue further, he's gone. Slamming the door behind him.

'You shouldn't rely on drink so much, sis,' Thomas says, tugging at my fear that I'm skirting around the edge of alcoholism. 'If I can give it up, you can.'

'You had a good reason to,' I say. Words crowd my head. It's a chance to talk about his accident – the reason he stopped drinking, and I want to grab it, despite my brain being already overcrowded. 'And you're stronger than me, Thomas,' I say, hoping he'll respond.

'Are you one hundred per cent sure Ruth's dead, Amelia?' Maddie has broken the spell. She's moved into the seat Dad vacated, next to me.

I nod and look up at her. 'Dad said she had no pulse.'

'But what if he's wrong? Should we check, do you think?'

'If you'd seen her injuries, Maddie.' I gulp down a surge of anxiety. 'You wouldn't have doubts.'

She shakes her head, her glossy hair falling about her face. 'Poor woman – Finn will be devastated. I know I didn't cope at all well when my mother died. I still have so many moments where I go to call her on the phone, or want to tell her something.'

I feel for her. 'I know exactly what you mean,' I say, avoiding eye contact.

'Of course you do,' she says. 'Sorry, I'm not thinking straight.'

We are silent once more. The clock on the wall ticks into the quiet spaces between us – telling us it's eight o'clock. It feels much later.

'So, have either of you got any life on your phones?' I say, finally, trying to be practical.

Thomas and Maddie pull their mobiles from their pockets.

'My cell's at forty per cent,' Maddie says, looking at the screen. 'No signal though.'

'Not much, I'm almost out of juice.' Thomas shoves his back into his pocket.

'Maybe turn yours off for now, Maddie,' I suggest. 'Between us we'll then have enough battery to call the police tomorrow.'

'OK,' she says, pressing the button on the side of the phone, and swiping the screen.

'I still think someone should try calling the police tonight,' Thomas says. 'Maybe a couple of you could go for a walk, try and get a signal?'

'I don't mind going,' Maddie says. 'Maybe we could go together, Amelia. We really should try to get hold of the cops. I mean I've seen enough TV shows to know if Ruth's left out all night in this weather, it will mess with forensics. We may even get in trouble for not reporting it.'

'It's not exactly normal circumstances.' I instantly regret my snippy tone. I doubt Maddie will ever be a friend – but I know right now we must pull together, and she's trying her best to help. 'I'm sure the police will understand,' I say softening.

There's a knock on the door, and Maddie jumps to her feet, dashes to open it.

Rosamund stumbles into the cottage, pale and shocked. 'I've lost Finn,' she cries, teeth chattering. 'He didn't wait for me. Said he was going to get his quad bike, but I couldn't keep up with him. And then I thought I heard a scream. Thought it was Elise, and took off in the other direction, but the cold got too much.'

'And the scream?'

She shakes her head. 'I don't know.'

Maddie is leading her by the elbow towards the wood burner, and once there, Rosamund crouches down in front of it and rubs her hands together.

'Where is she? Where's Elise?' she says, tears in her eyes. She's visibly shaken. 'Where the hell is she?'

Maddie finds a blanket and wraps it around Rosamund's shoulders, before disappearing into the kitchen.

Over the next few moments, Thomas breaks the horrific news about Ruth.

'Murdered?' Rosamund's eyes are wide in her pale face, her voice soft and quivering. She rises and perches on the edge of the sofa.

'We think so,' I say. It's lame. Of course someone killed her.

Maddie appears from the kitchen, and hands Rosamund a steaming mug of tea.

'But it makes no sense.' Rosamund blows on the liquid, takes a sip, and swallows. 'Why would anyone want to kill Ruth?'

We do a collective shrug, and I feel my heart picking up speed once more.

After the awful shock of seeing Ruth's body, and all the things that have happened over the last year, I would have expected to be a little desensitised by now, but if anything I'm worse.

'She's the most harmless woman I've ever met,' Maddie says. 'Such a sweet, gentle person.'

'Was she?' I say. 'I mean I'm not saying she wasn't, of course, but, how well did any of us know her?' I'm aware I'm speaking ill of the dead – that it's meant to be unlucky, and is far from kind – but I can't help thinking how overprotective and controlling she was of Finn. Nobody is without secrets.

135

'I'm sure you don't want to talk about Lark going missing, guys,' Rosamund says, 'but I can't help but compare.'

I open my mouth, about to say how different this is to when Lark vanished, when someone knocks on the door. I jump up and race to answer it. It's Dad brandishing a bottle of gin. 'Thank God,' I say, taking it from him. I head into the kitchen to search for some glasses. Whatever we decide to do now – and I know we've got to do something – I'm going to need a double to get through tonight.

Chapter 30

Present Day

Amelia

I sit on the edge of the sofa, lean forward, and splash gin into three glasses, screw the lid back on the bottle, and stand it by my feet like a crutch.

I pick up one of the glasses and take a large gulp, enjoying the warming sensation as it makes its way down my throat. Rosamund knocks back her gin in one, and I widen my eyes. I'm not thinking straight. She's pregnant. She shouldn't be drinking. I make a mental note not to give her any more.

I take another gulp, and say, 'I'm worried about Finn.'

'Finn knows these woods,' Rosamund says, banging her glass down on the table. 'It's Elise you should be concerned about. She's been out there for hours.'

'Of course I'm worried about Elise. I just meant—'

'We need to think logically,' Thomas cuts in. 'We know Elise isn't in your cottage, Rosamund. But maybe she's in Amelia and Dad's cottage, or Ruth's.'

'Or the farmhouse,' I say.

'Well, she's not in mine,' Dad says. 'I checked over the place when I picked up the phone adaptors, and again when I collected the gin.'

'What if someone took her? The same person who took Lark?' Rosamund says, still tearful.

'You mean Jackson?' Dad says.

'But even if Jackson was here at Drummondale House, where would he take her?' Thomas says.

'OK,' I say, raising my index finger. 'For one, we don't know for sure that Jackson took Lark a year ago. And two, if Elise has been taken; surely whoever took her couldn't have gone far. They certainly haven't gone anywhere by car. Maybe she's hiding somewhere, afraid.'

'Afraid?' Rosamund says, looking up at me.

'Of whoever killed Ruth,' I say. 'If she witnessed what happened, she could be hiding anywhere.'

'Of course, yes. Oh God, the poor child.' Rosamund shoves her face into her hands and lets out a painful cry. 'Whatever is Neil going to say?'

I look at everyone in turn as Rosamund continues to sob, shadows flickering across their faces. Did one of them kill Ruth? Am I in a room with a killer?

I splash more gin into Dad's glass, and another for me.

'Jeez, Amelia, this isn't Friday night at the local pub,' Thomas says, rubbing his forehead. 'You need to keep your wits about you.'

I put down the bottle, guilt rising.

'We need to do something, for Christ's sake,' Thomas goes on. 'Why aren't we checking Ruth's cottage? The farmhouse? Trying to get a signal so we can call the cops? This is bloody ridiculous.'

'I had to walk as far as the gate before I could get through to the cops earlier,' Dad says. 'The signal is awful around here at the best of times, but with this weather it's almost impossible.'

'Yeah, well someone needs to try again,' Thomas says.

'You're right.' I rise. 'We must do something.'

'OK, then shall we start by checking Ruth's cottage?' Maddie's eyes are on me. 'And then walk towards the gate until we get a signal. Use my phone to call for help?'

'OK.' I would much rather go with my dad, but she's up and clambering into her ski suit before I can suggest it. I pick up my phone and shove it into my pocket.

'Dad, why don't you build some sort of fire outside,' Thomas says. 'Elise or Finn will spot the flames if they're lost in the forest.'

'Finn knows these woods, Thomas,' I say. I'm tetchy. It's not only everything that's happened, or even thoughts of being alone with Maddie. I just feel we should all stay together to be safe. 'And you really think wood will burn in this weather?'

Rosamund's on her feet too, dashing her sleeves over her eyes. 'You stay here, Thomas; Robert, you light a fire; and I'll go with Maddie and Amelia.'

'No.' I shake my head. Despite wanting her with us as extra security, I'm worried about her unborn child. 'Stay. You've been in the cold far too long already. You need to think of your baby.'

She rubs her stomach. 'OK,' she agrees. 'Maybe you're right.'

Maddie's now in her super-warm ski suit, and I notice, as I shuffle into my not-so-warm padded jacket, Dad grab a box of matches, some dry logs from next to the wood burner, and a pile of magazines from the coffee table. I pull my woolly hat down over my ears, wrap my scarf around my face, and flick on my phone torch. 'Let's go,' I say, opening the door.

Heads down, Maddie and I battle against the weather, stomping through the deep snow towards Ruth's cottage. The squally wind makes it almost impossible to talk, for which I'm thankful. Although Maddie's and my differences seem minuscule compared to what is going on right now.

We reach Ruth's cottage, and I try the conservatory door. It's open, as I hoped it would be.

'Elise!' I call, stepping inside. I flash the torch around the room, the light bouncing off the windows, and onto the pine table where we sat this morning.

Maddie sniffs the air, as she steps in behind me and closes the door. 'Something's burning.'

She's right. We head across the conservatory, the torchlight guiding our way, and through into the main house. As we creep down a narrow hallway, the throat-cutting smell gets stronger.

Once in an old-fashioned kitchen, I turn off the oven where a beef Wellington has been charcoaled, feeling a jolt of sadness that Ruth always took such pride in her cooking, imagining how upset she would be.

I flash my phone torch around the room, picking out the sparklingly clean butler sink, the double fridge, and the floor-to-ceiling pale-green tiles. I step towards the window, lean my head close to the glass, and peer out into the darkness. Outside is Finn's quad bike, parked up against a wooden shed. I could have sworn Rosamund said he'd gone to get it.

Maddie flings open the door of a larder, and I turn to see inside tins stacked high, and more vegetables than I could eat in a lifetime. But there's no Elise crumpled in the corner scared for her life, or worse.

Back in the hallway, I call Elise's name again. Maddie does the same as we step into the lounge. It's small. Cosy. I peer behind the sofa, behind the curtains, before leaving the room and leading the way up the staircase.

There are photos on the walls – two or three of Drummondale House at varying angles, at different times of year, and several of a wide-eyed young boy. There's no doubting it's Finn.

Two bedrooms and a bathroom lead from the small landing. The bathroom seems empty – a shower curtain pulled across the bath. I step into the room, as Maddie hovers on the landing, take a deep breath, and yank the shower curtain back. I sigh with relief to find it empty.

'Elise?' I call again, as I leave the bathroom and we enter the first bedroom.

There's a TV and a single bed, a wardrobe and a chest of drawers. This is Finn's room. It feels bare. There's nothing here that tells us who he is – nothing to reveal his true personality. It's as though he doesn't plan to stay – that he's waiting for the right moment to break the news to Ruth that he's leaving. A wave of anxiety I can't quite explain clouds my thoughts, followed by a tug of sadness at the thought of him discovering his mother's been murdered.

We check the room thoroughly, before entering Ruth's bedroom.

'Elise,' we continue to call, but it's useless. She's not here.

I flick the torch around. It's a pretty room, decorated mainly in yellow, with pine furniture, and duck-blue curtains at the window. The bedspread is duck-blue too, with tiny lemon flowers. We check the wardrobe and under the bed. The curtains are open, and there's a perfect view of the snow-covered ruins. I shiver, my heart racing too fast.

'Hey, look at these.'

I turn. Maddie sits on the edge of the bed, Ruth's bedside cabinet open beside her.

'What are you doing? You won't find Elise in there.' I'm cross she's invading the dead woman's privacy, but I admit I'm curious about the photo album she's looking through with the aid of her phone torch. 'And I thought you'd turned that off to save the battery.'

I sit down beside her, and look over her shoulder, as she goes back to the beginning. The photos on the first page are of a young and beautiful Ruth, holding a baby in a lemon blanket.

'It's Finn, I should think,' I say.

Maddie turns the page. What follows are photos of a pretty blonde girl, a sprinkling of freckles across her nose. She grows as Maddie turns the pages. The final image in the album is of the girl at about fifteen years old.

'A friend's daughter, maybe?' But a spark of memory invades

of Finn mentioning last time I was here that he'd had a sister who'd died. I rise. 'Put the album back, Maddie. This isn't finding Elise. And please turn off your phone to conserve the battery.'

We head out into the cold once more, closing the conservatory door behind us, and make our way up towards the main gate. It feels as though we've been walking for miles, and I stop for a moment to catch my breath, my whole body aching.

'Still no signal,' I say, looking at my phone screen as she stomps on ahead of me.

The gate is still another fifty yards away, and I'm not sure I can make it.

Maddie peers at me over her shoulder. 'You OK, Amelia?'

I'm not. My legs below the knee seem to have turned to jelly and suddenly collapse from under me. I smash knee-first into the snow, and sink into the cold.

'Oh God!' Maddie hurries back to me, and attempts to lift me from behind, her hands under my arms, her fingers pushing into the fabric of my jacket. 'We're never going to get a signal,' she says, making little progress in hauling me up. 'We should get back to the cottage.'

'Hang on!' I cry. 'Just give me a minute.' She releases me, and I fall back down. After several deep breaths, I attempt to rub life back into my legs.

'Who's that?' There's a tremble in Maddie's voice, as she stares across the snow towards the forest.

I look to where she's pointing. Someone is standing there, partly shielded by trees.

'It could be the killer.' She's stepping backwards, away from me – away from the figure.

'Maddie. Wait. Help me up.' But she's spun round, scrambling to turn on her phone, and switching on the torch, her boots thudding the snow as she attempts to run. 'Maddie. Please,' I call after her, frantically rubbing my legs, hoping to bring them back to life. 'Christ!' I can't believe she's taken off and left me – only thinking to save herself.

I look back to where we saw the figure, but can no longer see anyone. I glance about me, shivering. Whoever it was could be anywhere. There's nothing else for it, I'll have to crawl back to the cottage.

I realise as I crawl like a baby through the deep snow that every part of me that isn't numb aches. If I pass out, I'll smash face first into the snow. I'm going to die.

I hear heavy footfalls thudding on the snow behind me. Oh God, I'm seriously going to die. I keep on going, crying now, so close to sobbing – tears freezing on my cheeks.

The footfalls get closer.

And closer.

Strong hands lift me to my feet.

'Jesus! Finn!'

He's injured – there's blood on his forehead. He picks me up and throws me over his shoulder, and as I moan and groan, tears plopping onto the snow below, he carries me towards the fire – a frenzy of flames whipped by the wind – outside Maddie and Thomas's cottage.

It's as we approach the front door a pungent smell, like burning paper, wafts in the air. I turn to see a piece of clothing in the fire, almost turned to ash.

*

'You left me to die,' I cry at Maddie as Finn carries me across the lounge and lays me on the sofa like a wounded soldier.

Maddie, who is standing by the wood burner, looks over at me as I shuffle from my wet jacket, then back at Finn who is taking off his coat and hanging it by the door.

'Finn. What a relief,' she says, ignoring me. 'Are you hurt?'

'You left me, Maddie,' I say again.

143

Her eyes are back on me. 'I went to get help.'

'I don't see any help.'

'Well, Rosamund is upstairs asleep, so I was waiting for your dad to return from finding more wood.'

'I could have frozen to death out there.'

'Yes, but you didn't. And I knew it was Finn anyway.'

'No you didn't. You thought it was the bloody killer.'

'Killer?' Finn says, puzzled. 'What are you on about?'

Oh God.

'Hey!' It's Thomas coming from his bedroom. 'What's the racket?'

'Your sister thinks I abandoned her,' Maddie says, kissing his head. 'When I was simply going for help.'

But suddenly I'm barely listening. Finn's eyes are wide, as he tries to follow what's being said. He drops down in the armchair, and tugs off his soaking socks, to reveal bright red feet. He has no idea his mother is dead.

'What happened to you, Finn?' I say, delaying the awful news.

'The quad bike wouldn't start, so I set out on foot.' He touches his head. 'A hunk of wood hit me; trees are losing limbs out there. I was out of it for a bit. Disorientated. Then I saw the fire. Good thinking whoever started it.'

Thomas grins. 'My idea,' he says like a proud child.

'Talking of the fire,' I say. 'Did anyone notice there's a piece of clothing burning on the fire? The remains of a top or maybe a jacket, I think.'

Everyone shakes their head, none of them seeming to see what I could see – that it could belong to the killer. I open my mouth to suggest it, then catch Finn's eye. It's more important that I tell him what's happened to his mum.

I rise from the sofa, my legs feeling less numb, and crouch at Finn's knees. I rest my arm on the armrest and twiddle a strand of my hair around my finger. 'There's something you need to know,' I say, placing my other hand over his. 'It's awful news. I'm so sorry.'

'What is it?' A shadow crosses his eyes. 'You're freaking me out, Amelia.'

'It's your mum—'

'Mum?' He covers his mouth as though he knows already what I'm about to say.

'She's dead, Finn,' I say, and squeeze his hand. 'Someone killed her.'

Chapter 31

Present Day

Amelia

Finn is in bits, his eyes wild, his body shaking, as he struggles to take off his coat. Dad arrived back moments after I told Finn about his mum. And at Finn's insistence, he took him to see Ruth's body.

'What the hell was she wearing?' Finn says now, as though that's important.

I jump to my feet and take his arm, lead him to the sofa, and sit down beside him. 'I'm so sorry, Finn,' I say, as he thrusts his head into his hands and sobs. 'I'm so, so sorry.'

Eventually, like a lost child, his sobs slow to small jolts of sadness, and he lays his head on my shoulder.

Tears burn my eyes. I'm devastated for Finn. But I'm afraid for us all.

*

It's gone midnight, and the wind howls around the cottage, rattling windows. There's still no power, and the wood burner and candles have almost burned out. The silence is unbearable. We have no answers to Elise's disappearance or Ruth's death. The only comfort I hold on to is that we are together – safe, for now.

Dad is sitting on the floor, his back to the wall. 'Tomorrow we'll start again,' he whispers into the silent room.

We haven't seen Rosamund since she went up to bed earlier. She must have been exhausted, and I remember how tiring pregnancy can be. Better she sleeps, than lie awake, her mind whirring with worry about Elise, when there's nothing any of us can do.

'Goodnight,' Thomas says, raising his hand, as Maddie pushes his wheelchair into the downstairs bedroom. She closes the door on him, and heads upstairs to her own room without a word.

Finn is sleeping next to me on the sofa, and I rise, grab a blanket from a pile Maddie got from the airing cupboard earlier, and move to one of the armchairs. Dad gets to his feet and drops into the chair Maddie vacated. 'I'm knackered,' he says, closing his eyes.

I wonder, once we are all settled, whether I will actually sleep. My head feels thick and heavy, as though I'm carrying rocks inside my skull. They bump against my thoughts and worries, bruising them.

The candles snuff out one by one, and eventually the fire is nothing more than red embers. Dad and Finn snuffle and snore, and as the wind cries, whipping around the cottage like a phantom, my eyelids finally fall heavy over my eyes.

Chapter 32

A Year Ago

Amelia

Despite the long day at the beach, and feeling so tired at dinner, Amelia struggled to sleep, her mind whirring with thoughts of the ridiculous game of Truth or Lie, followed by Elise's outburst, and Rosamund calling her stepdaughter a liar.

She tossed and turned for several hours, before rising and padding towards the window, gripping her Kindle in her mitts, intent on reading the night away.

She pulled back the curtain, and sat down in the wing-backed chair positioned so she could take in the view of the ruins and forest, the full moon lighting the area.

It was around midnight a flash of white in the forest disturbed her reading. Had she imagined it? Someone dressed in white flitting through the trees? A child perhaps? A shudder ran down her spine, as she peered closer to the window, the memory of Finn claiming ghosts wandered there – his dead sister – fresh in her mind. She swallowed. She was being ridiculous, and being spooked wasn't going to help her already overactive mind. She pulled the curtain across, and continued reading.

It was almost 2 a.m. when she heard a distant scream. Heart beating way too fast, she leaned forward and peered through the gap in the curtain like a nosy neighbour. The sky was clear of clouds, the moon high above the ruins. She shuddered, her eyes flitting to and fro. But all was silent and still. It must have been an animal. The other cottages were in darkness. Everyone was sleeping. She returned to the bed, propped her body against the headboard and began reading once more.

Before she'd even finished a chapter, she fell into a deep sleep. Within the midst of a strange dream, she heard a squeaking sound. It was real – outside the realms of sleep – she felt sure of it, but however much she tried, she couldn't break free of the dream.

It was a car engine starting up that finally woke her, followed by a squeal of car tyres. She glanced at her phone: 2.30 a.m. She leapt from the bed and raced towards the window.

Outside, red tail-lights disappeared into the distance. Someone was leaving Drummondale House.

When the car was out of sight, she returned to bed once more, and squeezed her eyes closed. Trying to forget the scream, the squeaking, and the disappearing car, she pulled the duvet over her head, burying herself in it, as though it was a cocoon. One thing was certain: Drummondale House was making her increasingly uneasy.

*

Amelia was on the sofa, cradling a cup of tea when an urgent hammering on the cottage door broke her from her trancelike state.

She opened the door to see her mum in her dressing gown and beanie, a look of panic etched on her face. 'Amelia—'

'Whatever's wrong?' Amelia said, ushering her inside. 'Are you feeling OK?'

'Robert,' her mum said, looking up at him on the stairs in his pyjamas, his hair standing on end.

'What's wrong, Caroline?' He dashed down towards her, took her arm, and lowered her onto the sofa.

'It's Jackson and Lark,' she said, grabbing a tissue from the box on the table, and pressing it to her nose. 'They've gone. Disappeared.'

He lowered himself onto the edge of the armchair. 'What do you mean gone?'

'Jackson wasn't in bed this morning when I woke.' Her eyes avoid his, the words clearly difficult to say. 'And Lark's bed hasn't been slept in. I've tried calling them both, but their phones go to voicemail.'

Amelia's forehead furrowed. 'Should we call the police?'

'Bit of an overreaction, sis.' It was Thomas, wearing his boxers and a Marvel T-shirt, holding a copy of Lord of the Flies, Maddie pushing him from the downstairs bedroom. 'They've probably gone for an early morning walk. Why the panic, Mum?'

She shook her head, shrugged. 'I don't know,' she said, her eyes filling with tears once more. 'You're probably right, Thomas. I guess I felt so alone when I woke up to find them not there, and had a bit of a meltdown. I'm being foolish.'

'I'll put the kettle on,' Maddie said. She was already dressed in an emerald green jumper and black jeans, her hair in a sleek, high ponytail. She made her way into the kitchen, always so helpful – so practical.

'Don't worry, Mum,' Amelia said, trying to force down the events in the night. 'I'm sure they won't be long.' She stroked her mum's back, watching her dad rise and head towards the window.

'Breakfast is at eight,' he announced. 'They'll be back for that – you'll see.'

Chapter 33

Present Day

Amelia

I wake at 5 a.m. pretty sure five hours' sleep isn't the recommended amount needed to track down Ruth's killer. My mouth is dry, and although the wood burner is flickering once more, I'm cold. I pull the blanket up around my neck, shivering.

Dad and Finn are no longer in the room, and I hear the clink of mugs and spoons in the kitchen, the kettle bubbling before reaching a crescendo. The light is on. The power is back.

'Dad?' I call towards the open kitchen door.

Finn appears, hair standing on end, eyes bloodshot. 'Tea? Coffee?' he says with a sad smile that doesn't reach his eyes.

'Coffee please – three sugars.'

'Three?'

'It's a one-off; I need the sugar rush.'

He sticks his thumb up, and disappears.

Soon he's back with two mugs of steaming coffee.

'You OK?' I ask. Stupid question.

'Feel a bit numb, if I'm honest.'

'I'm so sor—'

'Yeah. Thanks. I get that. You don't have to keep saying it.'

'Been up long?' I ask after a beat, as he puts the mugs on the table, and sits on the sofa.

'About twenty minutes.' He rubs his temples. 'Your dad's upstairs getting a shower while there's power.'

'Ah ... right.' I nod, pick up the coffee, take a sip.

'We need to call the police as early as possible,' he says. 'We'll try and get a signal when it's light. It's stopped snowing, at least.'

'Sounds like a good plan.'

'Morning, Amelia.' It's Dad heading down the stairs two at a time. He looks fresh, his damp hair combed back from his face. 'How did you sleep?'

'Not great,' I say. 'You?'

'Same.'

'Do you want some tea or coffee, Robert?' Finn offers, half-rising.

Dad lowers himself down into an armchair. 'I'm fine, son.'

There's a noise at the top of the stairs and Rosamund appears. She's dressed in a black polo-neck jumper and black jeans that show off her baby bump, her hair swept up in a high ponytail.

'How are you this morning, Rosamund?' Finn asks, as she stretches her arms above her head, before making her way down.

She shakes her head. 'Awful,' she says. 'I've barely slept. Is there any news?'

We all shake our heads. 'We're planning to call the police as soon as it's light,' Finn says.

'A few of us can head towards the gate,' I add. 'Hopefully we'll get a signal.'

'I'm coming this time,' she says, her voice rising.

'Is that a good idea?'

'I don't care if it's a ruddy good idea or not, Amelia. My step-daughter is missing, and I'll go mad if I don't do something.' She

152

covers her face with her hands, and I get up and put my arm around her. 'This is torture,' she cries. 'I need to call Neil. He needs to know.' She turns from my embrace, and heads into the kitchen.

I glance at my watch, and up at my dad. 'What time is sunrise?'

'About seven.'

'Well I need to pop back to our cottage and grab a change of clothes.'

'You really shouldn't go wandering off alone.'

I know he's right. 'But I need clean underwear,' I say, and when Finn's cheeks flush, I instantly wish I hadn't shared my intentions with the room.

Dad looks deep into my eyes. 'Don't go alone, Amelia,' he says. 'I mean it. We have to be sensible – there's a killer out there. I'll come with you.'

*

It's just after 7 a.m., and the sun rises in the pale sky. The wind has dropped, and it doesn't feel as cold out as yesterday. The snow is keeping off.

Maddie and Rosamund still have power on their phones, and Dad's and mine are being charged. We've agreed to divide into groups of three, without actually admitting we don't trust each other. Dad and Maddie will stay at the cottage with Thomas. Rosamund, Finn and I will head off towards the main gate.

We exchange phone numbers, just in case we lose each other, and make our way across the snow. I'm glad not to be freezing to death. Dad and I picked up my holdall from our cottage earlier, and I'm now wearing an extra pair of socks and three pairs of leggings. I don't want repeats of the last time I ventured out with Maddie.

Finn takes the lead, and is several yards in front of Rosamund and me.

'Christ,' he yells, as he reaches the ruins.

We hurry to catch up. A mask of a boy covers the face of one of the crumbling angel statues. I grab my chest. It looks so creepy, and is just like one of the masks the police found hanging in the woods the day after Lark disappeared.

Rosamund bursts into tears, and I freeze, unable to move.

'Who? Who would put …?' I stutter, looking at Rosamund. 'Elise said someone looked in her window with a mask on, didn't she?'

'I know,' she says through tears. 'I was sure she was making it up – like last time – or it was her imagination.'

Finn lifts his hand to touch the mask.

'Don't touch it,' I say. 'It could have fingerprints.'

'Seriously?' Finn narrows his eyes. 'You think someone is going gloveless in this weather?' He lowers his hand all the same, and turns on the spot, his eyes flitting across the area.

I do the same. It's far too quiet. Not even the rustle of trees.

'There's someone else here,' he says, snow absorbing his words. 'Can you feel it?'

My eyes are back on the mask. 'We should turn back,' I say, a tremble in my voice. 'All stay together.'

'We can't,' Rosamund says. 'We must call the police, and Neil. We have to find Elise.'

*

We trudge onwards, silent but on high alert, Rosamund and Finn checking their phones every few minutes, in the hope of getting a signal.

The gate to the estate is now in view. Surely if Dad got a signal when he was this far out, one of our phones should soon spring into life.

We take another twenty or so steps, before Finn calls over his shoulder that he's got a few bars. 'It's not much, but I'll give it a go.'

He taps his screen, and presses his phone to his ear. 'Hello … hello … sorry, this is a terrible line. Police please.'

We wait and watch.

'Finn Kinnaird,' he goes on. 'We're stranded at Drummondale House in Dunlaig. My mother—' his voice cracks '—my mother has been murdered.' He pauses. 'Ruth Kinnaird … yes, that's right.' Another pause. 'And a young girl has disappeared – Elise Green – we don't know where she is.' He takes a deep breath, holding his chest. 'And the weather conditions are awful. We need help. Fast.' He looks at us, and pulls the phone from his ear, whispering, 'I'm not even sure they can hear me properly.'

'Shall we try walking a bit further?' I suggest. 'Maybe Rosamund will get a better signal.'

'Yes, I'm still here.' Finn presses the phone back against his ear, and then he's silent. Listening. 'OK. Yes. There are … six of us, but we think someone else is here.' He screws up his face. 'Right.'

'Tell them to contact Neil,' Rosamund calls. 'Neil Green, he needs to know what's happened to Elise.'

'There's one more thing,' Finn says into the phone. 'Can you contact the girl's father, Neil Green …' He looks at Rosamund, as she reels off a mobile number, and repeats it into the phone, before finally ending the call.

'What did they say?' My words are weak; my teeth chatter.

'They said they can't get to us by road at the moment, and for all of us to stay together, until they can get us help.'

'When will that be?'

'How long is a piece of string?' He shrugs. 'As soon as possible, they said.'

'Maybe they'll send a helicopter,' Rosamund says.

'Maybe,' he agrees. 'But for now we should head back, don't you think? Stay in one cottage, like before.'

'I'm not going back without Elise,' Rosamund says, her cheeks red raw from the cold. 'There's one place we haven't checked yet, and I'm going there, even if I have to go alone.'

Chapter 34

Present Day

Amelia

By the time we reach the bottom of Vine Hill we are exhausted, and drop down like skittles hit by a bowling ball onto the bench dedicated to Kyla.

'Are you OK?' I ask Rosamund, who is holding her stomach, and looking down at her baby bump. 'You're not in pain, are you?'

'I'm fine,' she says through deep breaths, cold air clouding her lips as words leave her mouth. 'The baby's kicking, that's all. Exercising his little limbs.'

'You're having a boy?' I feel a twist in my belly. I found out my baby was a girl early on. Not that I minded what I had – I just felt by knowing I may bond even more with my unborn child. But, as things turned out, knowing seemed to make it even harder when I lost her.

'Yes, a little boy,' Rosamund says, tears filling her eyes. 'Neil so wants a boy.'

I place my gloved hand on hers, and swallow my sadness. 'We will find Elise, Rosamund.'

My neck tingles. It's as though someone else is here, sharing our airspace. Trees move behind us. A clump of snow thuds to the ground.

'Good God!' I hold my chest, as I look over my shoulder to see Dad appearing through the bushes, cheeks flushed.

'I saw you heading down here, from the cottage window,' he says. 'There's not much I can do back there. Maddie is reading in her room, and Thomas is asleep on the sofa.'

'But we're meant to stay in groups of three,' Finn says.

'Maddie and Thomas aren't killers, mate.' Dad rests his hand on Finn's shoulder and squeezes. 'Try to relax.'

'Relax!' He shrugs away from Dad, his eyed firing. 'My mum is dead, mate, and Elise is missing, and you tell me to fucking relax.'

'Enough!' I yell. 'Jesus! Fighting among ourselves isn't going to solve anything.' I glare at Finn then fix my eyes on Dad. 'We're heading to the farmhouse to check Elise isn't there. You coming?'

He gives Finn a long cold look, before heading away towards the farmhouse, his coat flapping around his calves, his scarf waving in the breeze.

*

As we get closer, the splendour of the farmhouse hits me. I count seven windows across the second floor, and three bay windows at ground level. In the middle of the building is a stunning double-fronted door, with a pitched porch.

I pick up speed, aware my toes and fingertips are growing numb despite my extra layers. Once there, I peer through one of the windows, my hand making a bridge over my eyes to block out the brightness of the day.

I take in the lounge with its three sofas, expensive units lining the walls, and open fireplace. I never came to the farmhouse last time I was here, only ever saw the place from a distance, was comforted in the knowledge that the police had searched the house at the time.

'I'll ring the bell,' Rosamund says. She's on the doorstep, glancing my way.

'I don't think anyone's here, but it's worth a try.' I step away from the window and join her on the doorstep. Dad and Finn are a few yards back, as though worried the house might blow up.

Rosamund rings the bell several times, before trying the handle. 'It's locked,' she says.

'Let's look round the back.' I take the initiative, and head across the snow and through a gate leading to the back of the house. I stand for a long moment. A five-foot wall surrounds the garden, behind which snow-covered public land seems to go on forever. I glance over my shoulder. Only Rosamund is with me. 'Where are Dad and Finn?'

'They said they'll go the other way, try to cover more area.' She heads towards a Victorian-style conservatory that stretches along half of the house, but I've spotted a stunning summerhouse halfway down the garden. It's green, and hexagonal in shape. Not the kind you find in a DIY store. In fact, it's big enough to live in.

'It's open,' Rosamund calls, and I glance over my shoulder once more to see her stepping into the conservatory.

I look back at the summerhouse and make my way towards it. The door is locked, so I step towards one of the windows and peer through the grubby glass. It's difficult to see inside, but I make out the shape of wicker furniture stacked up ready for sunnier days. I circle the building, but blinds are pulled down at most of the windows.

I head back to the house. I'm not keen on being alone out here, and I'm so cold. I step into the conservatory, knowing I shouldn't be here, invading someone's home, but I have no choice – we need to find Elise.

Embroidered pictures of flowers line the main wall of the

conservatory. At the far end, a circular table with a lace tablecloth, and four chairs around it, looks as though it's never used. A shelf laden with books, jigsaw puzzles, and board games is closer to me, next to a sofa that would seat six, with expensive throws covering worn upholstery. My eyes fall on a grey cat curled up on an armchair, silently sleeping. Someone must be here. Michael? His daughter Julia, perhaps?

Flashes of memory of Julia arriving in her yellow sports car at the same time as the police the day after Lark and Jackson disappeared invade my mind as I continue through the door into the main house.

'Rosamund,' I call. 'Rosamund?'

The hallway has several doors leading from it, and there's a staircase to the first floor. I pull off my woolly hat and scarf. It's warm in here – the central heating pumping out dry heat. 'Hello!'

I make my way into a dual-aspect room. It's the room I saw through the window at the front of the house.

I'm drawn to a heavy oak unit where framed photographs are on display.

There are pictures of Julia in her graduation gown, and several of Michael Collis. I know it's him. I looked him up online after Lark disappeared – though I never met him. He'd inherited the Drummondale House estate from his parents when he was in his thirties, almost thirty years ago. He's an attractive man with grey hair and ice-blue eyes, and there's a confidence about the way he stands, shoulders back, a crystal glass in his hand in almost every photo.

My eyes skitter over the faces in the pictures, landing on a large photo of a young girl of around fifteen. I pick it up. I've seen this girl before.

I go to place the photo back on the dresser, but something distracts me. There's movement outside, and I step towards the back window.

I gasp, and the photo slips through my fingers and lands with a thud on the patterned carpet. Someone, wearing the mask we saw earlier, is peering over the high garden wall. A chill runs down my spine as I step backwards, my heart racing. My stomach tight with fear, I spin round and race towards the door and fling it open. But before I leave I take a deep breath and turn back towards the window. Whoever it was out there in the snow has gone.

'Rosamund,' I cry, once I'm back in the hallway. 'Rosamund, where are you?'

Seconds later, the door to another downstairs room opens and Julia Collis appears, removing ear buds from her ears. She's dressed in a beige leotard and thick black tights. Looks slimmer than the last time I saw her.

'What the hell are you doing in my father's house? You totally messed up my meditation.'

'Julia, let me explain,' I say, taking in that her plaited hair is a shade lighter than the last time I saw her. Not that I'd got to know her when she appeared that day, telling Detective Inspector Beynon that she'd been staying at the farmhouse looking after the cat and working on her graphic novel, while her father was away. I hadn't had the headspace to properly take her in at the time.

She narrows her eyes. 'I remember you,' she says. 'Amelia Taylor, isn't it?' Her words are clipped. Sharp.

'We're looking for a teenage girl,' I say. As though it's perfectly OK to have entered the house uninvited. God it's hot in here. 'She's missing from the holiday site.'

She widens her eyes. 'Are you sure? It was only a year ago that your sister went missing wasn't it?'

'It was, yes.' I'm miffed by her flippancy.

'Have you any idea how much damage that did to my father's business? People stopped coming here for months.'

I'm fuming. 'Well, have you any idea how devastating it is to lose a sister? To have no idea where she is? To walk down a street and imagine you see her everywhere?' I'm close to tears – cold, scared, desperate.

Julia stares at me for a long moment. 'You know nothing about me,' she says, and drags her plait over her shoulder. 'I'm sorry for your loss, really I am, but it's unlikely another girl has disappeared. She's probably just gone walkabout. And didn't the police decide they'd taken off together – Lark and that good-looking chap dating the woman with cancer?'

Anger bubbles. 'My mother you mean—'

'Oh yes, that's right. Sorry. Totally forgot.'

'The police left the case open,' I spit. 'And it's not only Elise who's missing, Ruth is dead – murdered.'

'Christ! Ruth? Murdered?' She covers her mouth, and her flippancy drains away, as her eyes fill with tears. 'Oh God, are you sure?'

'Yes, there's no doubt,' I say, my voice calmer. 'I'm sorry, I shouldn't have blurted it out like that.'

Julia shakes her head. 'The poor woman – and Finn, how is Finn?'

'Not good, as you can imagine.' A beat. 'He's about somewhere. Is your father here?'

'He's away.' She flicks a tear from the corner of her eye. 'As you probably recall, I stay here when he's abroad. Funny, I hated living here as a child. It was so lonely, but now I crave peace.' She seems lost in her words, her voice low. 'Although I love living in Eyemouth, it's good—'

'You live in Eyemouth? My father lives near there.'

She nods. 'Quite a trek up here,' she says, turning, and I follow her into what appears to be another lounge. As well as two more sofas, there's a computer on a desk laden with graphic drawings, a piano by the window, and a huge TV paused on an episode of Fleabag. There's a cushion in the middle of the floor, which I guess is for Julia's meditation. But there's no sign of Elise having been here.

I walk towards the window and look out. 'Did you see the man in the mask?' I ask.

161

'Is it on Netflix?'

I turn and stare at her, wondering if she's joking, though knowing she can't be. 'Someone wearing a mask looked over the wall about five minutes ago.'

'Good God, that is creepy. Are you sure?'

I nod, catching sight of Dad through the window, coming out of the summerhouse. He looks about him before pulling the door closed and heading for the house. He must have found a key.

'Did you walk to the bench yesterday, Julia?' I say, spinning round.

'Kyla's bench?'

I nod. 'It's just there were footprints leading from the farmhouse?'

She shakes her head. 'That would have been Finn. He—'

'Amelia!' I look behind me to see Rosamund heading into the room. 'I've been all over the house. There's no sign of Elise.'

'Do you remember Julia, Rosamund? She was here when Lark and Jackson disappeared.'

'Not really,' she says, barely looking at Julia. 'Where are the others?'

'I've looked around the summerhouse and garden.' It's Dad appearing in the doorway, his cheeks red from the cold.

'Did you find a key?' I say.

'Yes, under the plant pot. There's no sign of Elise.'

'We should get back,' I say, pulling on my hat. 'Where's Finn?' I hate that I'm growing suspicious of everyone. 'Has anyone seen him?'

They shake their heads.

'Come with us to the holiday cottages, Julia,' I say. 'You really shouldn't be here alone.'

She's silent for a moment, as though her mind is processing my words. 'I'm not afraid,' she says.

'Well you should be. There's a killer out there.'

'I would rather stay. I feel safe here. Anyway, I need to care for the cat.'

I think about my little cat at home, hoping the woman with the pink hair isn't spoiling her too much and she'll still love me on my return. But, if I'm honest, being in London feels like a lifetime ago.

'Amelia?' It's Finn voice, and I know by the way it echoes he's heading through the conservatory. 'Robert?'

'In here,' Dad calls, and Finn appears, his eyes darting to each of us in turn.

'Where have you been?' I say.

'I thought I saw someone, so headed into the copse, but I must have been mistaken.' He looks over at Julia. 'Hey,' he says.

Julia walks over to him, and touches his arm. 'I'm so sorry about your mum.'

'Yeah. Thanks.' He looks down at the floor, his teeth pressing into his bottom lip. 'When I find whoever did that to her, I'll rip their head off.'

There's a connection between them I hadn't noticed a year ago – too full of finding Lark – and my heart, which seems to have forgotten for a moment the distress it's in, sinks. Under all this mess and sadness, I like Finn. I like him a lot. I straighten up, knowing my thoughts are random, stupid. I would have to be some kind of idiot to think of romance when things are so awful.

'Let's get back,' Finn says, and Dad and Rosamund follow him from the room.

'Are you sure you won't come with us?' I ask Julia.

She shakes her head. 'I'll be fine here.'

'Well make sure you lock all the doors, including the conservatory.'

'I will. Thanks.' She smiles. 'You take care too, Amelia,' she says.

I go to leave, but I have to ask her. 'I saw a photo in your father's lounge just now,' I begin.

She folds her arms across her chest. 'There are lots of photos in the lounge.'

'There's one of a pretty blonde teenage girl.'

'What of it?'

'I wondered who she is.'

'My sister,' she says, and I'm thrown. She just said she was lonely growing up.

'Your sister? But I saw the same photo in Ruth's cottage.'

'Can we leave it, please,' she says. 'This is really none of your business, and hardly the time to be discussing family histories.'

'No, you're right, sorry.' I leave the room, but I'm curious. My mum had remembered Ruth from when she came to Drummondale House as a teenager. I wish I'd asked her more questions. Discovered what went on when she camped here with my grandparents.

We congregate in the conservatory. 'Where's Julia?' Finn says, eyes on the door we've just come through.

'She's not coming,' I say.

'But there's a killer out there.'

'She's determined to stay, Finn. You won't change her mind.'

'Then I'll stay too,' he says. 'I can't leave her.'

Julia walks into the conservatory and glances at us gathered by the exit. She thumps down on the sofa, and the cat looks up at her, rises and stretches, releasing her claws as Julia tickles her ear. 'I'll be fine,' she says.

'I'm not leaving you, Julia.' Finn sits down next to her. 'Not after what happened to my mum.'

'OK. Fine. Whatever you say,' she agrees. 'I'm guessing you're not the killer,' she adds with a small laugh.

His smile is grim. 'Mum annoyed me at times, but I'd never—'

'Of course you wouldn't.' Julia takes his hand. 'You're the kindest person I know.'

We head through the door, and the cold takes my breath away. I look towards the summerhouse in the garden, desperate to see inside.

'I've already checked in there, love,' Dad says, seeing where I'm looking. He puts his arm around my shoulders. 'Let's get back, shall we? Before we all freeze to death.'

Chapter 35

A Year Ago

Amelia

Amelia broke free from the family as they made their way towards the conservatory for breakfast, making a detour towards the car park. And she knew as soon as she stepped onto the cobbled area that Jackson's car was missing. The only cars were Rosamund's Mercedes, and Dad's Ford Freedom. Jackson had gone. Had he taken Lark with him?

Her heart thumped as she ran to the conservatory.

'Jackson's car's not there,' she cried, breathless as she entered to see everyone taking a seat at the table.

'Oh God,' her mum said. 'Where could he have gone?'

'The thing is,' Amelia continued, 'I saw a car leave in the middle of the night. I thought it was a visitor leaving, but now I'm thinking it must have been Jackson. Do you think Lark's with him?'

Her mum shook her head. 'I'm sure Jackson leaving has nothing to do with Lark.' She was close to tears. 'Lark has probably wandered off somewhere, like before. It's a coincidence that's all. Let's just concentrate on finding Lark.'

The door swung open, and Rosamund, Neil and Elise entered. 'What's wrong?' Rosamund said. 'You all look as though you've seen a ghost.'

'Lark and Jackson have disappeared,' Amelia said.

'Have you seen Jackson, Rosamund?' her mum said, her tone suddenly cold as she met Rosamund's eye.

'No, why?' Rosamund folded her arms, averted her eyes.

'Well I still think we need to get help,' Amelia said.

'I agree,' her dad said. 'I'll call the police.' And as he pulled his phone from his pocket, Amelia's neck prickled.

Something was wrong.

Something was very wrong.

Chapter 36

Present Day

Amelia

It feels like hours since we left Finn and Julia at the farmhouse, and by the time the cottages are back in view we can barely see in front of us for heavy snowfall.

It's 2 p.m. when Dad, Rosamund and I step through the door of Bluebell Cottage, and once again I feel as though my feet and fingers no longer belong to me, they're so numb.

Inside, Dad leads the way into the lounge, where we shed our wet outer layers, and hurry towards the burner to get warm.

'You're back then,' Thomas says, opening his eyes. He's sprawled on the sofa, his hair loose to his shoulders, giving him a hippy air. He pulls himself to a sitting position, his socked feet sticking out from under the blanket that covers him from the neck downwards. I blink, feeling sure I see his toe move again, and open my mouth to speak. But I know my eyes must be deceiving me once more, blurring due to sheer cold outside. Anyway, he would have said if there were any signs of improvement, wouldn't he?

'Where have you been?' he says. 'You've been ages.'

'Down to Michael Collis's farmhouse,' Dad says. 'We saw his daughter.'

'Julia?' Thomas says.

'That's right.' I rub my hands together. 'I suggested she came back with us, but she wouldn't.'

'She's on her own down there?'

'No, Finn stayed.'

Maddie appears at the top of the stairs, holding her Kindle. 'You're back then,' she says, making her way down. And suddenly the room feels too full, too claustrophobic – though better we're all together, I tell myself, safety in numbers.

'I'll put the kettle on, shall I?' I say, disappearing into the kitchen.

'Finn got through to the police,' I hear Dad telling Thomas and Maddie, as I pull mugs from the cupboard. And as I cock my ear to listen, my concentration dips, and I catch my thumb on a sharp knife that stands blade up on the dryer next to the sink. I put down the mug. Blood oozes through my flesh, and I shove my thumb into my mouth – it tastes metallic. With my free hand I lift the knife, run it under the hot tap for some time, before putting it in one of the empty slots in the knife rack.

'And we saw a terrifying mask.' It's Rosamund, her voice high-pitched. 'It was on a statue, at the ruins.'

I pad across the kitchen and stand in the doorway, my thumb still wedged in my mouth, like a child. Thomas is on the sofa, now sitting upright next to Maddie. Rosamund is in the armchair looking exhausted.

I pull my thumb from my mouth. 'Where's Dad?'

'Gone to the loo, I think,' Thomas offers, and everyone turns to look my way.

I take a breath. 'I saw someone at the farmhouse,' I say, a wobble in my voice. 'Behind the garden wall – they looked right at me through the window.'

'A man?' Maddie's eyes widen.

I cough, clearing my throat. 'I think so,' I go on, as the kettle rumbles behind me. 'Though I can't be sure. They were wearing a mask.' My stomach tips as I recall the eerie sight. 'The same mask we saw on the statue.'

'This is far too freaky,' Thomas says, running his hand over his beard.

I turn back to the kitchen, leaving them with my revelation, my thumb stinging like crazy, and move closer to the window. Outside, trees are almost masked by the heavy snowfall, and I lift onto my toes and lean over the counter, my nose touching the glass. I see faces everywhere; faces I know aren't there, but still scare me. I drag down the blind, my whole body trembling.

It takes a while before I'm still, and calm enough to make hot drinks. But once I've managed it, I bring the tray through to the lounge with a bowl of sugar and a jug of milk, and place it on the coffee table. And as everyone thanks me, I kneel down on the floor close to the burner.

We sip our drinks in silence, all deep in our own thoughts, until the shrill sound of a phone ringing pierces the quiet. It's coming from Rosamund's pocket. She pulls it out, eyes wide with shock as she looks at the screen. 'It's Neil,' she whispers. 'How the hell have I got a signal?' She presses the phone to her ear, and takes a breath. 'Neil?' A beat. 'Calm down, please, we'll find her, I know we will.'

'Put him on speaker,' Dad says, his tone assertive, and Rosamund does as he says, and places her phone on the table.

'The police said you're stuck up there,' Neil is saying through a crackle on the line, talking fast, his voice tense.

My mind darts back to just before Mum died, when she gave me a letter to post to him, but the thought evaporates as he goes on.

'They said Elise is missing, and Ruth's been murdered.' We all stare down at the phone, and even though we can barely make out his words, I hear he's close to tears.

'We'll find her, Neil,' Rosamund says. 'We think she could be hiding …'

Silence drags on the line for a moment, before he continues. 'What are you doing in the highlands of Scotland, anyway, Rosamund? Elise should be at school. Christ!'

Rosamund leans forward, her arm embracing her stomach, tears rolling down her face. 'I had to come, Neil. And I didn't tell you, because I knew you wouldn't understand. But Elise did. She said she wanted to come too.'

'But she loves school, Rosamund.' The line buzzes and crackles. 'Why the hell didn't you tell me?'

'I don't know. I'm so sorry.'

'I can't hear you – speak up,' he says, raising his voice. 'The line's dreadful.'

'Elise understood I wanted closure, Neil.' Rosamund turns, her eyes meeting mine, as she dashes tears from her cheeks with the back of her hand. 'She knew I needed to see Robert and Amelia and Thomas. How I needed their forgiveness.'

'Neil,' Dad cuts in. 'Robert Taylor here. Listen, what are the cops going to do? Are they coming up here anytime soon?'

'Robert.' Neil sounds wrong-footed, and I suspect he hadn't realised he was on speakerphone – that others could hear the conversation. 'Inspector Beynon said they are having difficulty reaching you. The roads are treacherous, but the ploughs are out, and the coastland rescue helicopter will be heading up there once it's stopped snowing.'

'They need to get up here as soon as possible.' Dad's voice is calm, but his eyes are red, his knees bouncing.

'Don't you think I know that?' Neil yells.

'All right, mate. Calm down.'

'Yeah, that's easy for you to say, your daughter isn't missing.'

Dad lowers his head, and covers his mouth, as though holding in the words he wants to say.

'Christ,' Neil says. 'Sorry, Robert, I didn't think, it's just—'

'Every second is important when a child goes missing,' Dad goes on, and I know he's struggling. 'Get on to Inspector Beynon again. Get help, Neil. We're depending on you.'

The line goes dead, and Rosamund picks up her phone, looks at the screen. 'I've got a text as well,' she says, furrowing her forehead as she presses the screen. 'Oh God.'

'What?' I ask, and she hands me the phone:

I told you you shouldn't have brought Elise to Drummondale House, but you didn't listen.

*

After a long spell of quiet, Rosamund rises, and places her empty cup on the table. 'I don't really want to go back to my cottage,' she says. 'But I need to collect my holdall. I'm lost without it.'

'I'll come with you,' I say, rising too. Any excuse to get away from the confines of this overcrowded lounge.

'Me too.' Maddie is up and putting on her ski suit before we can say anything. But I'm pleased she's coming. I want to trust Rosamund, trust everyone here, but one of them could be a killer.

The three of us walk across the untrodden snow towards Honeysuckle Cottage, and as we get closer, the thought of going back inside seems like a dreadful idea.

'Are you sure you can't get by without your holdall?' I say to Rosamund, who is ahead now, taking long strides.

She glances back. 'I need my iron tablets, and my moisturising cream for my stomach – I dread getting stretch marks.'

I'm taken aback that she can even think about stretch marks at a time like this, but I stay quiet.

Once inside the cottage, Rosamund heads up the stairs at quite a speed, as though she's forgotten about the blood, about what happened up there.

Maddie and I stay near the door. 'Is there a lot of blood?' she says, her eyes skittering around the room.

171

'A fair bit, yes. It's OK, there's none down here.'

'It's so awful isn't it?' Her voice is shaky, her eyes shimmering, and it hits me how young she is, how far away from her home in America. She might not be my favourite person, but I feel desperately sorry for her. I touch her arm, and she tries to smile.

'We'll be OK, Maddie,' I say, but they're words I don't really believe. 'We just need to stay together, that's all. Whoever is doing this can't touch us then.'

We stand for some time in suffocating silence. Waiting. 'Rosamund's been a while, hasn't she?' I say, looking up the stairs, and Maddie gives a nervous nod. 'Maybe I should check on her.'

My heartbeat quickens as I move across the room, and stop at the foot of the stairs. I open my mouth to call Rosamund's name, but something stops me. What if someone's up there? I look about me, spotting two walking sticks propped against the wall. I grab one.

'Should we get the others?' Maddie asks, but I'm already gingerly climbing the stairs. 'Amelia, you just said we should stick together,' she calls after me.

Once on the landing, I try not to let my eyes stray, but the sweet metallic smell of Ruth's blood makes me gag.

Rosamund's bedroom door stands open, and I step towards it and peer around the door. I grab my chest. 'Thank God,' I say, letting out a breath when I see Rosamund's sitting on the edge of the bed. She's holding something in her hand. It looks like the scan of her baby, and I see she's crying.

'Rosamund,' I say, approaching, and she looks up. 'Are you OK?' She shoves the photo in the holdall beside her.

'Yes. I'm fine.' She dries her cheeks on her sleeve. 'I was just thinking about Elise, that's all.' She rises, takes a deep breath, and looks around her. 'That's odd,' she says. 'My bed jacket is missing.'

'Is it in your case?'

Her forehead furrows. 'No, it was at the bottom of my bed.'

'Do you need it?'

She shrugs. 'I guess not.' She zips up her holdall, and pushes past me, heading onto the landing.

I follow, and as we head down the stairs, I notice Maddie is standing by the coffee table, staring down at the half-played Monopoly game. She leans over and picks up a counter. By the time I reach her side, she's rolling the token around in her hand, trancelike.

'Are you OK?' I ask her, as Rosamund approaches.

She slips the counter into her pocket.

'Maddie?' I say.

'Sorry, yes, yes, I'm fine.' She heads towards the door. 'We should get back,' she says opening the door, and we step into the snow once more.

'Actually, I desperately need a cigarette,' Maddie says as we reach Bluebell Cottage.

'I'll stay out here with you, if you like,' Rosamund says.

'No. No, it's fine.' She fumbles in her pocket for her cigarettes, her hands shaking. 'I just need some space. Thanks though.'

'But you can't be out here on your own,' I say. 'I'll stay with you. Remember what we said about sticking together.'

'For God's sake,' she snaps, and glares at me. 'I'll be five minutes, is all. Just let me be. I'll be in shortly.'

Rosamund and I exchange looks as we head inside, and I slam the door to make a point.

'She shouldn't be on her own,' I say, as I pull off my boots. 'We're meant to be looking out for each other.'

'Where's Maddie?' Dad says, looking up from the armchair.

'Outside, having a cigarette.'

'Alone?'

'Mmm, she didn't want us to stay with her.'

'I'll go out there.' He rises.

'She wants space, Dad. That's what she said.'

'Well, tough.' He throws on his coat and scarf and disappears outside.

'We should stay in threes,' I say, hanging up my coat, my head spinning. 'That's what we agreed, wasn't it?'

'Dad isn't a killer, Amelia.' Thomas glares at me from the sofa, as though he can't believe I would think it.

'I know, but …'

He narrows his eyes. 'I know you've never liked her much, but Maddie's no killer either.'

'Well someone fucking is,' I cry, surprised how angry my words sound. Tears are close, and my stomach aches with tension. I flop down in the armchair Dad vacated, and bury my head in my hands.

Nobody speaks for some time. It's as though there's a bomb in the room, and any movement will set it off.

'Maybe I'll go back out there,' Rosamund says eventually, and I look up to see her standing by the door. She's still in her boots and coat, her hand on the doorknob.

'No, Rosamund, I'll go.' But she's through the door before I can scramble to my feet.

'And then there were two,' Thomas says in a silly, creepy voice, as she closes the door behind her.

I turn to meet his eye. 'I'm afraid, Thomas,' I say simply.

He stares at me, his face so pale. 'Me too, sis. Death is a fearful thing.'

I have the beginnings of a headache, and I'm hungry too; my sugar level has dipped to silly levels.

'I might go to Ruth's cottage and grab some food in a bit,' I say to Thomas, after we'd sat in silence for ten minutes. I point the remote at the TV, and flick through the channels, until I reach the weather, which looks as grim as ever.

'Don't go out there alone,' Thomas says. 'Wait for Dad.'

I turn to look at him. 'OK. I'll wait.' I'm glad he cares. And I mean it. I won't be going out there alone, because in all honesty I haven't got the courage.

'I would have thought the others would have come back inside by now,' I say. 'How long does it take to smoke a cigarette?' I pause for a moment. 'We should be brainstorming. There must be something we can do. We can't just wait around for the police, or worse the killer. In fact, maybe between us we can clear the snow enough for one of us to attempt to drive out of here.' I rise, and begin pacing the room.

'You know what that hill was like on the way in,' Thomas says. 'There's no way anyone can drive.'

'Well what if we walk?'

'And leave me with a killer?' He pulls a fake sad face, but I see by his eyes he's worried that's exactly what we might do.

'Of course not – we'd never leave you alone, you idiot. But maybe two of us could attempt to get out of here.' I know as I say the words it's impossible. It's too cold and already dark. 'We must do something,' I say, knowing I'm getting worked up, fidgety, close to tears. 'It's really getting to me.'

'It's getting to us all, sis.'

'Yes. Yes. Sorry.' I look at my watch, continuing to pace. 'Maybe I ought to check on the others. Do you think Maddie's smoking the whole box?'

'My guess is the three of them are huddled on the porch discussing our plan of attack.'

'I suppose so.' I stop pacing.

'On the plus side to all of this ...'

I turn. 'There's a plus side?'

Thomas raises his arms above his head and stretches. 'Yep. For once I'm not the only one who feels bloody helpless.'

I smile, but I'm sorry. Sorry my brother, who was once so full of life, will never walk again. Sorry he feels so negative and helpless. Sorry he got in that bloody sports car two years ago when he'd been drinking.

I head back to the sofa, and perch down next to him. 'Talk to me,' I say.

'About what?' He picks up a hairband and ties his hair into a ponytail.

'Talk to me about Maddie.'

'What about her?'

'Are you in love with her, Thomas? Because …'

He shakes his head. 'God, no. I depend on her; she's my friend, but no, I'm not in love with her.' He lowers his head. 'Truth is, and I'm only telling you this because we're all going to die …'

'That's not funny, Thomas,' I say, feeling a shudder run down my back.

'Truth is …' he repeats, 'any chance of love went when I had my accident.'

'You were in love? When you were in the US?' A memory of hearing about his accident filters in – the call from Mum saying he may never walk again.

He nods. 'It was pretty serious. Almost meet the parents time.'

'Really?' I feel a lump rise in my throat. My little brother in love, and it all slipped away from him. 'So where is she now?'

'Back in the US. She was a TV presenter, doing well.' He smiles. 'I follow her on Twitter with a fake name, in a non-stalker kind of way.'

'Sounds pretty stalker-like to me.' I half smile. 'So you're not in touch?'

He shakes his head, and looks down at his hands. 'The course of true love never did run smooth.'

'It was true love then?'

He shrugs. 'I never told her about the accident.'

'What? Why not?'

'She would have stood by me, and it would have ruined her life, or worse, she may have taken off – deserted me. I couldn't live with either scenario. I called her from the hospital, told her it was over, that I was heading back to the UK.'

I grab his hand and squeeze it. 'Oh, Thomas, I'm so sorry.'

'I didn't deserve her, sis. I was drunk at that party, and I took a bloody car out on a racing track.'

'But those idiot so-called friends encouraged you – handed you the keys to the car, let you into the racetrack.'

'And I got behind the wheel and turned the key,' he says. 'I can only blame myself.'

I sigh deeply. 'Still. You should call her.'

'That's what Maddie says.'

I ignore a pang of envy that he told Maddie before me.

'Maybe I will if we get out of here. These kinds of things have a habit of making you evaluate your life.'

The front door slams open, and we look up.

It's Dad. He's carrying Maddie in his arms, and, leaving the door wide open, he limps across the room, his face distorted. He lays her on the floor by the fire. 'She's alive – just about. Concussed, I think.'

'Jeez, what happened?' Thomas cries, and makes an automatic attempt to rise, and I see the frustration in his face when he can't.

'All I know is there's blood on her head,' Dad says. 'Finn said earlier branches are falling. It could be what's happened, but with everything else … well, I just don't know.'

'You think someone attacked her?' I drop to my knees, and put a cushion under Maddie's head, blood from an open wound coating my fingers.

Dad shrugs. 'I couldn't find her when I went out there. I was worried she could have been taken, you know, like Elise, so I took off looking for her.'

'You should have told us,' I say. 'You shouldn't have gone off on your own.'

'You're an idiot, Dad.' Thomas is angry – upset. 'There's a bloody killer out there. What the hell were you thinking?'

'I wasn't. All I could think was another young girl wasn't where we thought she was.' He pauses and takes a deep breath.

'Is she going to be all right?' Thomas says, and I feel his frustration that he can't get close to her.

'I don't know. She's in a bad way.' Dad reaches for a blanket, and as he attempts to cover Maddie, he lets out a cry of agony, and grabs his calf. There's a six-inch rip in his trousers, blood oozing from a deep gash.

'Jesus! What the hell happened to you?' I meet his glassy eyes. There's no doubting his pain.

'Caught it on a branch when I was searching for Maddie. I'll be fine.'

But colour drains from his cheeks. 'You don't look fine, Dad.'

At that moment, Maddie's clenched fist falls open, and a Monopoly top hat tumbles to the floor.

I pick up the tiny silver top hat and roll it around in the palm of my hand. It must be the piece Maddie picked up from Rosamund's cottage.

'Maddie, can you hear me?' I whisper, close to her ear, hoping my darkest fear is wrong. That she hasn't been attacked. She doesn't stir. 'Maddie, what happened?'

I see a dark stain on her ski suit. The fabric is torn.

'Oh my God,' I cry. I gingerly place my hand on her stomach. Blood coats my fingers.

'Shit!' Thomas drags himself onto the floor, and takes her hand. 'Maddie! Maddie, wake up!' But she doesn't stir. She's far too still. 'Oh God, she's dead isn't she?' he cries.

As the cold truth sinks in I sob. Crushed. Broken. Scared. I turn to Thomas who sobs too, and we fall into each other's arms.

'No! No, she'll be OK, you'll see,' Dad cries.

But I know she won't be. I know because she looks as Mum did the day we lost her.

After a few moments, Dad accepts Maddie's no longer with us, and covers her face with the blanket, and I rise, and dash into the kitchen. Who would kill her? Who? Who would do this? My mind races, and suddenly everyone's a suspect – Finn, Rosamund, Julia – even my dad. I hate how distrusting this has made me, but two people are dead, and Elise is still missing. I breathe deeply, trying to gather my thoughts.

A stranger did this, I tell myself. It's got to be. I refuse to believe anyone here is capable of murder.

I rummage in the kitchen cupboards on the off chance there's a first-aid kit for Dad's leg, but there's nothing. So I fill a bowl with warm water, and grab a couple of clean tea towels and some scissors from a drawer, returning to the lounge ready to cut the bottom off Dad's trousers and do my best to stop the bleeding.

The wound is deep, and jagged, about two inches long, and as I clean it he winces in pain. 'You'll need stitches,' I say, placing one of the tea towels across the wound, trying to avoid the sight of Maddie's body, and cutting the other to hold it there. 'For now, hold this against your leg.'

'You should have been a nurse, love,' he says, with a strangled smile, tears on his cheeks.

After a few moments I ask him, 'Where did you find Maddie?'

'At the edge of the forest, near the top of Vine Hill.' A pause. 'She was just lying there.'

Thomas thrusts his head into his hands. 'Oh God, this can't be happening.'

I brush away my tears with my sleeve, and sniff. 'Did you see Rosamund out there?'

'Christ! She's not out there too, is she?'

I nod. 'She went out to be with you and Maddie, and didn't return. We thought you were all together. You're sure you didn't see her?'

He shakes his head.

'Do you think Rosamund did this to Maddie?' Thomas asks. He hasn't taken his eyes off Maddie's lifeless body for a moment.

'Why would she? In fact, why would anyone do this to Maddie? Why would anyone kill Ruth? Abduct Elise? None of it makes any sense.'

Dad shrugs, and shakes his head once more.

And through the silence come unwanted memories of how I treated Maddie – how angry I was with her. The fact she'd said

179

those words on her vlog, that rang in my ears after Lark disappeared.

Lark's sister, Amelia, raced back to London to be with her partner, William, a week after the disappearance, leaving her father and disabled brother to take care of their terminally ill mother.

Maddie's words had hit hard at the time, bringing my guilt into focus – haunting me. I should have stayed longer, helped my family cope.

'Such a sad day,' Maddie had said at my mum's funeral, the first time I'd seen her since she'd posted the vlog, and I'd turned, met her red-rimmed eyes.

'I'm so sorry, Amelia,' she said.

'Are you?' I said far too loud.

She reached out to touch me, but I jolted away, spilling wine over my black jumper.

'You OK, sis?' Thomas had appeared by her side in his wheelchair.

'I'm on top of the world. Mum's dead, and our sister is still missing – life's just peachy. But it's OK because I'll take off to London soon, and leave my disabled brother and Dad to take care of everything.'

As soon as I'd spat out the words, the room fell silent.

'I'm so sorry, Amelia,' Maddie repeated. 'I realise my vlog post wasn't one of my best.'

My cheeks burned with anger and alcohol. 'You can say that again.'

'I'm not sure what I was thinking.' Her eyes glistened. 'Do you want me to take it down?'

'What's the point? The world's already seen what an uncaring sister and daughter I am,' I said, lowering my voice a little.

Two women from Dad's am-dram society watched as I scuttled

away, tears rolling down my cheeks. 'What?' I snapped at them, and they both looked down.

I dashed towards Dad alone in the kitchen. He took me into his arms and I sobbed. But I wasn't crying about Maddie's vlog post, not really. It was the thought that Mum died without knowing where Lark vanished to. That they never said goodbye.

And now Maddie is dead, and I wish I hadn't confronted her that day – wish I hadn't rejected her apologies when we first arrived at Drummondale House.

I rise, and head towards the front door to close it. The temperature in the cottage has dropped several degrees while it has stood open.

'Where are you going, love?' Dad's voice is full of anxiety.

'Just closing the door, that's all.'

'Good,' he says. 'Listen, I'm going to take a couple of painkillers and lie down for a while. I'm drained of energy, I need to recharge.'

'Use my room,' Thomas offers, and Dad limps through the door, closing it behind him.

I stand in the doorway, and stare out into the cold silence. 'Whoever did this to Maddie and Ruth is out there somewhere,' I whisper to myself, stepping onto the snow-covered porch. The clouds are heavy and dark – but the snow is easing. My eyes flit from the ruins, to Ruth's cottage, and then to the forest.

I'm about to step back inside, when a piercing scream echoes in the trees, and my heart races. There's nothing to see, but when another scream rings out, I'm sure it's female. Rosamund? Elise?

'Did you hear that?' I cry, racing inside, and grabbing my coat, a surge of strength I can't quite explain rising inside me.

'Hear what?' Thomas says.

'The scream – outside – someone's in danger.'

'Yeah, and that's one good reason to stay inside, sis. Close the door and lock it. Don't leave. Please.'

But I ignore him, and pull on my boots and coat, then race

into the kitchen. I grab a knife from the rack and shove it into my pocket.

Back in the lounge, Thomas is fretting. 'Please don't go out there on your own, Amelia. Wait.'

'For what? Nobody's coming to help us, Thomas,' I yell as I fly past him and out of the door, determined to find out who screamed. Knowing I have to do everything I can to stop whoever killed Ruth and Maddie from killing again.

Chapter 37

Present Day

Amelia

I zip up my jacket, and hurry across the snow, brandishing my phone torch as I head for the trees, surging adrenalin keeping me warm.

A recent track of footprints leads from the area near the top of Vine Hill towards Bluebell Cottage, droplets of blood telling me they are Dad's heavy boot prints from when he carried Maddie. I use his imprints to help me walk faster.

I reach the trees, and glance back over my shoulder at the sheets of snow stretching behind me, deadening sound. The silence rings in my ears. The cottages are all in darkness, except the one I've just come from, and I feel desperate, sad, confused, my blood pumping too fast. This is such a beautiful yet tragic place.

I beat back tears, turn, and take a deep breath. 'Rosamund?' I call, disappearing into the wood, trees covering me, making visibility difficult. Panic surges through me, as I spiral deeper and deeper into the wood. 'Elise?' Memories of the ghost walk that Finn, in his top hat and cloak, had taken us on a year ago touch my thoughts. But I'm not afraid of ghosts – I'm afraid of real life.

Finally I emerge beside Kyla's bench, and walk up behind it, gripping it to steady myself, to catch my breath. It takes a moment before I see a phone lying on the snow-covered wooden slats. I've seen it before. It belongs to Elise. The pink case with a glittery "E" is distinctive. I pick it up, and look at the screen. The phone is on, and I look at the screen, before looking about me. 'Elise!' I call. 'Elise?'

My eyes back on the phone, I find myself searching the address book. She hasn't many friends, but I recognise her dad, and Rosamund.

There's no password, and I search her text messages. Two sent recently – to Rosamund:

Why bring your stepdaughter to Drummondale House? You know what happened to Lark.
I told you you shouldn't have brought Elise to Drummondale House, but you didn't listen.

The freezing air suddenly buzzes with the presence of another person.

The snapping of branches startles me.

I drop the phone with a clatter.

Before I can turn, someone presses up against my back. So close I hear their raspy breathing. I try to turn, but my coat rips. Something sharp touches my spine.

I want to cry out, but the blade silences me for a moment, before words bubble up. 'What do you want?' My voice shakes, a sob so close. 'What have I done? What have any of us done?'

A gloved hand grabs my arm, and with a jolt I'm thrown against a tree.

My head bounces painfully against the bark.

184

My head swims.

My vision blurs.

A masked figure looks down at me, silently, a knife glinting in their hand.

A crunch of footsteps in the snow close by gives me sudden hope.

'Help me,' I whimper, heart thudding against my ribcage. And as I shake with fear and cold, my vision dips out. Everything goes black.

*

When I come round my surroundings are a blur. Someone is crouching down in front of me, features distorted. My survival instincts kick in, and I fumble the knife from my pocket. If I want to live I have to do the impossible. With a deep breath I pull my arm back, and with a jerk I plunge the blade into their stomach. I heave, sick, bile rising in my throat.

He cries in agony. A male. Yes, I'm sure it's a man.

But the forest spins as if I'm drunk, and within seconds everything goes black once more.

Chapter 38

Present Day

Amelia

My eyes are gritty and sore. My head and ears throb. My bones and teeth ache.

I'm propped against a tree in the solid darkness, unable to see in front of me. Afraid to move in case the killer is still here.

Did I really push the knife into his flesh? Or did I dream that?

I listen. The wood is silent. No screams. No footsteps. No masked killer.

The moon creeps out from behind a cloud, and I see my phone lying abandoned nearby. I reach for it, and close my gloved fingers around it. I flick on the torch.

The moon and my torch give out enough light for me to see in front of me. There's blood on the ground, but no sign of whoever attacked me – the person I stabbed.

I look up Vine Hill; memories of Finn pushing me down it on the sled invading my head, as my eyes skitter across to the farmhouse. The downstairs windows glow orange, and I imagine Julia and Finn inside, unaware of Maddie's death. But they know of the dangers. They know there's a killer on the grounds of Drummondale House estate. They know to keep the doors locked.

The moon disappears once more, and I move my torchlight towards Kyla's bench, but before I can take it in, my phone dies. Now, apart from the faraway glow of the farmhouse, everything is black. I can't see a thing.

I pull myself up, and lean against the tree, squinting into the darkness. I have to move soon or I'll die of exposure.

There's a rumble in the sky – a helicopter overhead, getting closer, beams of light searching the area, rotary blades stirring treetops. Snow falls to the ground in heavy clumps.

But something else stirs in the cold air – closer, much closer – and my heart leaps as the beam from the helicopter highlights a figure sitting on Kyla's bench. Whoever it is wears the mask of the young boy with the bright pink face and the too wide smile – the dead eyes.

I'm shaking with cold and terror, when whoever is sitting there raises their arm and reaches out to me through the darkness. Their arm drops down; their head slumps to one side.

Within seconds, adrenalin pumps through me. I'm running. Stumbling. Tripping. Falling. I scramble back to my feet, the bright lights of the helicopter guiding my way. My pulse thumps in my ears, as I head for the farmhouse. Finally, I glance behind me. But there's nobody there. Nobody is chasing me.

I'm almost at the farmhouse, and haven't dared look back again for fear of slowing my pace. The helicopter, after appearing to land on higher ground, has gone, taken off towards the coast. I desperately hope it's the police.

When I finally reach the front door of the farmhouse, I bang my fists against it. 'Help!' I cry. 'Help me! Julia! Finn! Let me in. Please!'

I steel myself, and glance back once more, but there's still nobody behind me, only a vast expanse of muffling snow, the perfect sheen ruined by my anxious footprints.

It seems like an age before the door swings open. It's Julia in her pyjamas, hugging the cat. She tilts her head. 'Amelia. What is it? I was about to watch TV.'

'Let me in,' I cry, and she steps back startled. I storm into the house out of breath, and she closes the door. 'Lock it,' I yell. 'Lock it for Christ's sake!'

She puts down the cat, and turns the key slowly. 'What the devil's the matter with you?'

'Where's Finn?' I call after her as she heads away, my voice husky. 'Where the hell is Finn?'

'He's not here, Amelia,' she says over her shoulder. 'He went out about an hour ago,' she goes on, disappearing into the lounge, where I hear the TV blaring out. 'What's this about?'

I stand in the dimly lit hallway, trying to catch my breath and make sense of everything, when I notice blood on my jacket, my gloves. It wasn't a dream. I stabbed someone. A man.

The masked killer is a man, and I stabbed him.

Yes.

Yes.

And there are only three men here at Drummondale House.

But it can't be Thomas, or Dad – it can't be my lovely dad, and anyway he's hurt his leg.

There's only one person it can be, and I desperately pray I'm wrong.

'You're covered in blood,' Julia says, as I step into the light of the lounge. 'Oh God, are you hurt?'

I shake my head. 'No, but someone attacked me. There's someone out there, Julia.' I'm talking too fast. 'And someone's killed Maddie.' Oh God, none of this feels real.

'Maddie?' She sits on the edge of the sofa, and points the remote at the TV. Turns it off. Looks back at me.

'Thomas's carer.'

'The pretty American? Oh God, that's awful.'

'You don't sound remotely shocked.' I'm still out of breath, and press my bloodied glove against my chest.

She narrows her eyes. 'Of course I'm shocked, Amelia. I'm practising my calming techniques, is all. It won't do any of us any good if we all act like crazy people.'

'Like me, you mean?'

'I never said that.'

I bite down on my bottom lip hard, determined not to lose it with her. Knowing it won't help. 'Someone was sitting on the bench,' I say, trying for calm. 'Wearing a mask.'

'Kyla's bench?'

'Yes.'

She splashes red wine into a glass in front of her. 'Who was it?'

Finn. Finn. I think it was Finn. 'Christ, Julia, I don't know – but whoever it was is the killer.'

'Do you know who Kyla was, Amelia?' she says, taking a gulp of her wine, and I realise she's trembling, nowhere near as calm as she pretends.

'Christ sake, Julia, is that important right now?' I say, heading for the window. I pull back the curtains to reveal snow stretching towards a copse.

'She was Finn's half-sister.' A pause. 'My half-sister.'

'What?' I turn. 'I don't understand.'

The lights dip, and chills run down my back.

'She died twenty-six years ago.'

'Kyla?'

She nods. 'She was only fifteen, and her death had a dreadful effect on Ruth, left her mentally scarred – unstable. Poor Finn had a hard time of it as a kid.' She takes a sip of her wine. 'Ruth became possessive of him – scared she might lose him too.' She pauses. 'Of course this was before I was born, but I saw the outcome, what it did to poor Finn.'

189

My eyes flash from Julia to the window and back to Julia. 'But you said she was your half-sister too.'

A bang on the French windows startles us, and Julia's glass slips through her fingers and shatters on the floor.

It's Finn, his bloody palms pressed against the glass, his eyes wide.

'Don't let him in,' I yell.

'Don't be silly, Amelia. It's only Finn. We can't leave him out there.' She heads over to the French doors.

But I see the mask sticking out of his pocket. 'Wait. No!' I cry.

'But he'll freeze to death out there,' she says, ignoring my plea – unlocking the door.

Finn stares in, not moving, his pupils dilated in bloodshot eyes, his skin red raw from the cold.

As he finally steps forward, teeth chattering, one hand on his stomach, his other loose by his side, my heart thuds, and I step backwards.

'Julia,' he says, his voice barely audible as he reaches out his hand towards her, in the same way the figure on the bench had – there's no doubting he was sitting there earlier, wearing the mask.

'Oh God, Finn.' Julia steps forward, and I want to yell at her to be careful, that she has no idea what he's done, but my throat swells. Words won't form.

Julia moves outside, almost toppling on the ice, and allows him to put his arm around her shoulders. She's helping him into the house, when I see the blood on his clothes, the drops of blood on the snow, leading to the door.

'What happened?' she's saying to him, as she guides him into the lounge. 'You're bleeding.'

Should I run? Would I be safer out there?

'Christ sake, Amelia,' Julia cries, glaring at me. 'Can I have a bit of help here?'

I stare, as she hobbles onwards, almost collapsing under Finn's weight.

'Amelia, please!' she yells.

I catch up, and shudder as Finn drapes his free arm around my shoulders. We manage to get him to the sofa, where he flops down hard.

'What happened to you?' Julia asks him again, but his eyes have receded into his head. 'Finn! Finn, can you hear me? Oh God, he's been stabbed. Oh God!' She grabs a throw from the back of the sofa, and presses it against his stomach, her hands shaking. 'Who would do this?'

My mind drifts again to the moment before I passed out. I'd rammed the knife into him, hadn't I? Heard him cry out in pain. But I had to do it. He would have killed me if I hadn't. Wouldn't he? It was him or me, and it wasn't going to be me.

An urgent hammering on the front door brings me out of my thoughts, and I race towards it. I don't care who it is. We've caught the killer. It will be help. I know it will.

I throw the door open, and breathe a sigh of relief. It's Detective Inspector Beynon. I remember her from when Lark vanished. 'Thank God you're here,' I cry, beckoning her and DS McKay inside.

DI Beynon looks exactly as she had a year ago, strength oozing from her five-foot frame. 'Amelia,' she says.

She remembers me: The young woman with the red hair who traipsed the woods in tears on the Drummondale House estate a year ago, searching for her lost sister until her legs went from under her with exhaustion.

I'd found an inner strength back then, and I thought I'd found it again as I'd set out earlier, but now I'm beaten once more – anxious, frightened.

'What's happened?' she asks. 'You're covered in blood.'

'Oh. Yes. It's Finn's blood.' I'm aware my voice is shaky – that I'm avoiding eye contact. 'We just helped him into the house. He's been attacked.' I'm lying. I hate lying.

As Beynon turns to close the door, she looks into the distance, where two police cars are slowly moving across the snow. 'Backup,' she says, and smiles, before pulling the door ajar.

I lead Beynon and McKay across the hall. 'Finn killed Ruth and Maddie,' I say, before heading into the lounge where Julia is kneeling in front of him.

'He's been stabbed. I think he's dead,' Julia cries, tears in her eyes.

'An air ambulance will be here soon,' Beynon says moving closer. She places her fingertips on his neck for several seconds. 'There's a pulse. Just keep pressure on that wound. Do we know who stabbed him?' Her eyes flick over his body.

Julia shakes her head.

'Maybe someone who knew he was the killer,' I say, looking at Beynon. 'He's got the weird mask, see.' I point to his pocket.

Beynon pulls it out with gloved hands. 'That's fucking freaky,' she says, and I shudder at the sight of it. 'It's the same as the ones in the trees when Lark disappeared. Finn was about then too.'

'But I've known Finn a long time,' Julia says. 'He'd never hurt anyone.'

Four uniformed officers enter the room, and Beynon looks up. 'It seems we may have our killer,' she says. 'We may even have our connection to Lark's disappearance.'

'No! Didn't you hear me? Finn isn't a killer,' Julia says through tears. She's holding his hand, squeezing. 'He wouldn't hurt anyone. You've got it wrong.'

'We need to do a search of the property for the missing girl, Elise Green.' Beynon looks around her, glancing out through the French doors. 'Let's get that summerhouse checked out too.'

'Yes, ma'am.'

'She's not here,' Julia says. 'You're wasting your time. You need to be out there finding out who did this to Finn.'

I stare down at Finn, beating back tears. Was he a killer? Had he taken Lark too? I'm so close to sobbing right now.

Finn groans, and Beynon looks up at McKay who is hovering close by. 'Chase up the air ambulance,' she says. 'Before this man takes his last breath.'

Chapter 39

Present Day

Me

I barely know my own thoughts anymore. Can barely keep awake. I often cry like a small child. Bury my head in the pillow and sob.

Some days I lie here and imagine my mother by my side. She tells me to be strong. Brave. Take the pain, like she did.

Now those tears roll down my face, but Misty is still here. He knows I'm in pain. Scared my life will soon be over. I take long deep breaths, and look through the window. It's getting dark, but nobody is coming to save me. Not tonight. Not ever.

I sob so loud that Misty jumps from the bed, gives me a daggering look before licking his fur.

'Help!' I cry out. 'Somebody. Please, help me.'

Chapter 40

A Year Ago

Detective Inspector Kate Beynon

The steep hill towards Drummondale House felt never-ending.

'Christ, it's like travelling up a rollercoaster,' DI Kate Beynon said, pressing down on the throttle. They were at least ten miles from civilisation, and God knows how far from the nearest McDonald's.

'I hate rollercoasters,' DS Gavin McKay said from the passenger seat. 'Never liked bumper cars much either. It's the sparks – they smell like singed flesh. And don't get me started on the ghost train.'

Kate laughed, but it was forced. Lark Taylor – just seventeen – was missing. Taken? This was a case she needed to solve. Quick!

Kate eased her foot off the accelerator as she drove through open, wrought-iron gates.

'This whole place is fucking freaky,' she said as they passed the ruined part of Drummondale House, before veering off towards the car park. 'Why would anyone want to holiday here? Give me Benidorm any day of the week.'

She came to a stop, and pulled on the handbrake. 'Looks like they're waiting for us, Gav.' The brightness of the sun silhouetted the group of ten, all statue-still on the grass – some sitting, some standing.

Gavin nodded, opened the car door, and dragged his six-foot, heavily built self out of the car and onto the cobbles, where he stretched his arms into the air.

Kate took a deep breath. She'd wasted no time after getting the call from Robert Taylor. A wee lass disappearing in the middle of the night, possibly with a man in his mid-thirties, had to be investigated. Totally out of character, her father had said on the phone. I've never trusted Jackson Cromwell.

Kate took another deep breath – her daughter had just turned seventeen. Thought she was so grown-up, yet …

She climbed from the car. At five foot, and tiny-framed, she'd often been told she looked younger than her forty-eight years. But she was strong. With cropped black hair, Doc Martens, and a fierce Glaswegian accent, she knew she could take on anyone.

They crossed the car park, cobbles crunching under their feet, and onto the grass.

'I'm Detective Inspector Kate Beynon,' she said on reaching the gathered group, brandishing her badge, before shoving it back into her jacket pocket. 'And this is Detective Sergeant Gavin McKay.'

Gavin's silver-threaded ponytail and bushy grey beard gave him an ageing rock-star look. He was older than Kate – late fifties – and her opposite in many ways, with his gentle persona and kindly face.

'Which of you is Robert Taylor?' Kate said, scanning their bewildered faces.

'Me.' A tall man in a long black coat raised his hand.

'You called in?'

He nodded. 'Lark, my daughter – she's missing.' He blinked. Anxious? 'Jackson took her.'

'We don't know that, Robert.' A woman with a pale-blue scarf around her head and wearing a parka, despite the warm day, met Kate's eye. 'I'm Lark's mother. Caroline Taylor.' Her voice cracked. 'My partner, Jackson Cromwell, is missing too, but I'm not convinced it's connected.'

'OK,' Kate said. 'So, I understand from your call that Jackson's car was driven away in the middle of the night. Is it possible they would they have gone away together?' She had to ask the question.

'Never,' Caroline said without hesitation. 'I just said, it's not connected.'

'And one of you heard a scream?' Kate's eyes cruised the worried faces.

'Me.' A pretty redhead, who looked as though she hadn't slept in a month, raised her hand. 'Though I can't be sure. It could have been an animal … I don't know … but with her disappearance I assume it was …'

Kate narrowed her eyes. 'We can't assume anything … and you are?'

'Amelia Taylor. Lark's sister.'

'Well, if one of you could give DS McKay here the registration number and make of Jackson's car, we can then check CCTV and get the number plate out to traffic police.'

A car drove onto the cobbles, and came to a stop. Kate turned to see a young woman climb from the driver's side of a yellow sports car.

'Who's that?' Kate asked.

'Julia Collis,' a scruffy young man with an attractive face said, rising from where he'd been sitting on the grass fiddling with a blade of grass. 'Julia!' he called to her, raising his hand. 'She's Michael Collis's daughter. He owns Drummondale estate.'

'We'll need to speak to them both.'

'Michael's abroad at the moment; Julia stays at the farmhouse while he's away.'

Julia was in her twenties, overweight, and wearing a long, patterned skirt, high boots, and a mustard-yellow fake-fur jacket.

197

'What's happening, Finn?' she called to the man, as she headed towards him, her fair hair twisted into a long plait down her back. 'I heard sirens.'

'Two guests have gone missing,' Finn called back.

Kate turned and eyed the guests once more. 'I'll need to speak to you all individually,' she said. 'Is there somewhere we could set up? We need to know more about Lark.'

Was she a happy teenager? Taking any medication? When did you last see her? How did she seem?

'Oh God,' Caroline said, turning to Robert, who wrapped his arms around her.

Two police cars appeared and pulled up next to Julia's car.

'Ah, good, uniform.' Kate took a deep breath and addressed the gathered guests, 'Even though the car's gone, we can't rule out that one of them could still be on site,' she said. 'I'll organise an immediate search of the area.'

*

They were called into the conservatory one by one. They'd all seen Lark the night before at dinner, and Caroline told Kate that her daughter went straight to bed when they got back to their cottage.

Once the final guest had been questioned, Kate's mind skittered over what they'd told her – breaking down the main points:

'It was the man in the mask. I've seen him lots of times since I've been here. He took Lark.' Elise Green

'I've never really trusted Jackson. Not the kind of person I'd chum up with, if you know what I mean. He has a look about him, you know.' Neil Green

'Lark hasn't been herself lately. She's been taking Diazepam. It worries me. And she took off the day before when we were on the beach. She worried us all. I can't believe Jackson would take her. But then why would she take off? She knows how ill I am.' Caroline Taylor

'She isn't herself – that much is true. But I've never trusted him. I would catch him staring at my daughter. And then there was the night of the ghost walk. He led her off the path. She seemed upset.' Robert Taylor

'He's a type, you know. Thought he could have any woman – or girl in this case – he wanted.' Rosamund Green

'I heard the scream first, about two in the morning. The squeaking was weird, but I can't be sure it wasn't a dream. It was later I heard the car roar away. Saw the tail-lights of Jackson's car disappearing.' Amelia Taylor

'Such a pretty girl, but sullen – I put it down to her mother's impending death – an awful thing for her to have to cope with.' Ruth Kinnaird

'Lark has an attitude, a stroppy teenager. But she has a lot on her plate with her mum dying.' Finn Kinnaird

'No, I never met either of them. I was in the farmhouse, working on my graphic novel.' Julia Collis

'I can't believe my sister would go off with Jackson voluntarily.' Thomas Taylor

'He's an extremely good-looking man. I wouldn't be surprised if he tempted her away.' Maddie Jenkins

*

It was mid-afternoon when Kate and Gavin were called into the forest. There were five in all – hanging from trees closest to the site – masks depicting the face of a young boy, swaying hauntingly in the light breeze.

Kate swallowed. 'Christ. Who the fuck put these up?'

'There's blood on the bark of a tree, ma'am,' said a young constable. 'And wheel marks in soil nearby.'

But there was no sign of Lark or Jackson.

Later, Kate gathered everyone back in the conservatory.

'You can leave Drummondale House,' she said, dragging her

fingers through her short hair. 'But don't leave the country. We may need to talk to some of you again, so leave contact details.'

'Get the cases, Neil,' Rosamund said, jumping up. 'We need to get away from here, for Elise's sake.'

The girl looked up from her Kindle. And within seconds she was on her feet and following Rosamund through the door.

'Sorry,' Neil said to the room, rising too. He leaned in, and kissed Caroline's cheek. 'Keep in touch, won't you? And if there's anything we can do, just shout. I hope to God you find them soon.'

Once the Green family had left, Kate drifted outside to take a call from traffic police.

'Jackson's car has appeared twice on CCTV,' the officer told her. 'Once on the A9 at Aviemore, and later on the M90 heading south, and there's something else.'

'Go on.'

'There was nobody in the passenger seat.' A beat. 'And the driver had shoulder-length brown hair and was wearing a mask.'

*

'We'll do a wider search at first light,' Kate said; now back in the conservatory, beating down thoughts that the lass may already be dead. She took a deep breath. 'We'll grab the locals to help, and get the dogs up here, plus coastal rescue.'

'I'd like to stay and help,' Amelia said.

'Me too,' Robert said with a sad nod. It was clear the man had been crying.

'Good.' Kate rose, and doing her best to sound positive, she added, 'We'll do everything in our power to find her.'

Chapter 41

A Year Ago

Amelia

The blood on the bark of the tree was human, but untraceable. The masks had no fingerprints. Neither Ruth's trolley nor Thomas's wheelchair had matched the wheel imprints. The wider search had revealed nothing either, and a TV appeal several days later only attracted a few dead ends. Things weren't looking hopeful.

Amelia returned to London a week later, unable to cope with seeing her parents and Thomas fall apart.

But the irony was, being in London was no easier. The months that followed dragged her down. Pulled her so far under, she could barely breathe.

*

'She only has a few more weeks,' her dad said down the phone. 'That's what the nurses have said. If you want to visit, now would be a good time.'

Amelia had packed an overnight bag and headed straight there.

Her heart had constricted as she stepped into her mum's bedroom. Seeing her so washed out, her eyes so heavy, broke her heart.

'I'm so glad you're here, Amelia,' her mum said. Whether it was the cancer or Lark's disappearance that had caused her mum's light to fade so fast, Amelia couldn't be sure.

After kissing her mum's cheek, Amelia looked about her. This room was where Caroline had worked on flower arrangements after Rosamund's florist closed. She'd set up a small business, all those years ago – not that it had been particularly successful – and there were still boxes of ribbons, silk flowers and rolls of cellophane piled high on a pine table.

A pale-blue journal and gold pen lay on the bedside cabinet, and rows of photo albums she'd made over the years lined a pine shelf. Watercolours of flowers – bluebells, daffodils and roses – hung on the walls. Her dad had left everything as it was when she moved out with Jackson.

The single bed, where Caroline had spent most of the time over the last few weeks, was new. Robert bought it when she moved back in. 'Stay,' he'd said to her. 'Stay, until Lark and Jackson are found.'

It was a sunny bedroom – cheery, the open window letting in a warm breeze that gently moved the pretty lilac curtains. It was a nice place to spend her final days.

Amelia gripped her mother's hand, the feel of her skin against hers comforting, yet at the same time tearing her apart to see her mother so ill.

They talked about anything and everything, but avoided any mention of how little time they had left to share those precious words.

'Could you look in my bag? There's a letter inside.'

Amelia leaned over and picked up the bag. Handed it over.

'I need you to post it for me,' her mum said, pulling out a sealed envelope and handing it over.

Amelia turned the envelope over in her hands. It was addressed to Neil Green. 'What's it about, Mum?'

'Just do this one thing for me, Amelia. Neil needs to get this letter. Don't ask me why, please. Just post it.'

Amelia knew her mum was getting a little confused due to the morphine, but today, although she was growing tired now, she felt sure her mum knew what she was doing.

'It's important.' Her mum closed her eyes, sighed, and with a voice barely audible, added, 'That's all you need to know.'

Amelia had fought down tears in all the time they'd been talking, but now they burned against her eyes.

'I'm not afraid of death.' It was as though her mum sensed her daughter's tears hiding there. 'I'm so, so tired,' she said.

*

Rosamund didn't come to the funeral, but Neil was there, sitting at the back of the crematorium, as Amelia, Thomas and their dad took turns reading poems.

Amelia sat at the front with her family. William hadn't been able to take time off work to be with her, and once again it hurt that he hadn't supported her.

As they listened to the celebrant talking about her mum's life, Amelia glanced over her shoulder at the door, hoping it would open and Lark, like a miracle, would appear in her flowing black dress, and lace-up boots. She even hoped Jackson would turn up, with his perfect features and sandy-blond hair, but neither came.

Outside the crematorium she gripped her dad's arm as they looked at the flowers.

'I can't believe she's gone,' he said. He was wearing his long black coat, despite the warm weather, and perspiration coated his forehead. He hadn't cried during the service, but his eyes filled with tears now.

'We'll get through this, Dad,' she said, squeezing his arm,

moving in closer. But, truth was, she didn't know how they would.

She kept thinking she saw Lark that day, as the sun glinted on surrounding trees. Her presence was so strong, like an angel sent to take their mum.

Later, back at the family home, she laid out the sandwiches she'd ordered from Waitrose, and tipped crisps into bowls. She put French Fancies – Mum's favourites – onto her best china plates. Everyone knocked back cheap white wine, as though it might help with the awkwardness of it all.

Amelia's grandparents had died a long time ago, and her mum had no brothers and sisters. She'd lost touch with most of her friends when she moved in with Jackson, but there was still a good turnout – mostly Robert's colleagues from the museum, and a few friends from the am-dram society.

Following an argument with Maddie, Amelia left the gathering, and after a brief hug with her dad, she climbed the stairs to bed, burying herself under the duvet, and crying until she fell into a restless sleep.

*

After the funeral, Amelia returned to London to attempt to get her life back on track. Her dad and Thomas insisted they would be OK without her. But the truth was, she wasn't sure she would be OK without them.

Chapter 42

Present Day

Amelia

Still reeling from believing Finn is the masked killer, and almost killing him, I struggle to sleep – tossing and turning, jolting in and out of terrifying nightmares.

At DI Kate Beynon's suggestion, Dad, Thomas and I are staying at a B & B in Inverness overnight. We're to stay in the area until the search of the estate is complete. Rosamund and Neil are here too, though I haven't seen them.

By 5 a.m. I'm wide awake, staring at the ceiling, trying to piece everything together.

And then it hits me.

There were two people there the night I was attacked. Yes, I heard two people. I'd called to the other for help. Had the second person been Finn?

I throw back the duvet and head into the shower. The piercing water on my flesh goes some way to making me feel human again, but I can't rid myself of a dull headache, despite taking strong painkillers.

It's 9 a.m. when Beynon rings my mobile. 'I'd like you to come down to the station, Amelia,' she says, and my stomach twists. 'We need to take formal statements from everyone, and I'd like to begin with you.'

*

Dad drives me to the police station, and agrees to wait for me outside.

Once in the building, I head for reception, my skin prickling.

'Amelia.' It's Beynon, appearing through a side door. 'This way, please.'

Once sitting in the kind of room I'd only ever seen in crime dramas, Beynon and DS McKay opposite me, I say, 'Do I need a solicitor? This is all a bit formal, isn't it?'

'It's just a few questions, Amelia.' She smiles. 'You're not under arrest. We just need a statement from you, that's all.'

'OK.'

'And also to see if you've remembered anything new since we last spoke.'

'Like what?' Should I mention the second person?

'Anything at all that might help us with our enquiries.'

'Well, someone attacked me,' I say.

She nods. I've told her this before.

'And when I came round I saw a figure on the bench ... wearing that awful mask. Finn.'

She nods. 'We know that was Finn. His blood was all over the bench. But we know he wasn't stabbed there. Someone moved him. Do you know anything about that?'

I shake my head. 'I've no idea.' At least that much is true.

'If you know anything at all, Amelia, now would be a good time to say.'

There was something about Beynon that reminded me of a girl I knew at my senior school – a girl I never wanted to cross. And part of me wants to yell that it had all been a huge mistake. That I thought, when Finn crouched down in front of me, that he was the masked killer. I stabbed him.

'He isn't the killer,' I say in a rush. 'I remembered this morning. There were two people there that night, I'm sure of it.'

Beynon bites down hard on her lower lip, her dark eyes boring into me. 'Really?' she says. 'Well, we're just waiting on forensics, and once Finn comes round from the coma and we can interview him, things will be a lot clearer.' She leans back in her chair.

'Is that it?' I say. 'Can I go now?'

'Once you've signed your statement, yes.'

'Inspector Beynon,' I say. 'Do you think Jackson had anything to do with this?'

'Whoever did this violently killed two people, Amelia. There are similarities – the masks – the fact they are both young girls – but differences too. Rest assured, Amelia,' she says, rubbing a hand across the back of her neck, 'we haven't ruled out a connection.'

*

Two days later I take a taxi to the hospital. I'm not sure why I've come. Maybe I just need to see Finn – I've been so worried about him.

Once outside his hospital room, I can see through the glass panel that he's awake. My relief that he's no longer in a coma is tainted by fear and guilt. Has he told the police what happened that night?

I push open the door, and step inside. He looks vacant, his skin raw from ice burns, his lips cracked and sore. A lump rises in my throat. I did this to him.

A rosy-cheeked nurse with tight blonde curls looks round and smiles. 'He's doing well,' she says.

Julia is by his bed, holding his hand. 'I don't mean to be rude, Amelia,' she says, catching my eye, 'but you look ruddy awful.' She doesn't look much better herself – her round face stony pale.

'I haven't slept since ...' I begin. The sounds of the machine whirring – beeping Finn's vitals, making sure he stays with us – make me shudder. I did this to him.

Julia looks at Finn, who closes his eyes without a word. 'He's still in a poorly way,' she says. 'The police are on their way.'

'They haven't interviewed him yet?' My heartbeat quickens. What will Finn tell them?

She shakes her head.

'Will he be OK?' I ask.

The nurse, who is monitoring his drip, nods. 'It's looking that way.' There's hope in her voice.

'The police have given up their search of Drummondale House estate,' Julia tells me, and I'm selfishly relieved I can finally leave Scotland. 'They're convinced Elise has been taken from the area. Like Lark was.'

'But that doesn't ring true, does it?' I say. 'How could anyone have got her away from there?' I'm still convinced Elise was murdered on site, just as Maddie and Ruth were. That it was only a matter of time before her body turns up.

The door swings opens and DI Beynon, and DS McKay enter.

'Finn,' Beynon says, unzipping her tartan jacket, seemingly unaware of anyone else in the room. She drags up a chair, and Finn opens his eyes. 'Do you remember me?'

'Inspector Beynon,' he says, his voice husky.

'That's right. It's good to see you're improving, Finn. Listen, we'd like to talk to you, if you feel up to it. Is that OK?'

He nods.

'So let's begin at the beginning, shall we? You were out alone? Even though you knew there was a killer about.'

'Looking for Maddie,' he mumbles.

'But you didn't find her.'

He shakes his head.

'Do you remember who hurt you?'

Finn moves his eyes to look at Julia, who is still clasping his hand.

This is it. This is the moment I've been dreading.

'Someone attacked Amelia,' he says, turning his eyes to me. I step backwards, hoping the wall will absorb me.

'Someone?' Beynon glances at me briefly.

He swallows hard, and lifts his eyes to the ceiling. 'Whoever it was wore that awful mask.' His voice fades.

'Take your time, Finn. No rush.'

'I cried out to them to stop,' Finn went on. 'And they took off. But when I bent to help Amelia, she ... she ...' He blinks several times.

Please don't say the words. Please, Finn, I didn't mean to hurt you.

'Did Amelia stab you, Finn?' Beynon is leaning forward, as close as she can get to him without climbing onto the bed.

'She was in a dreadful state – confused.' Finn's voice quivers. He lifts his hand. 'I'm so thirsty.'

Julia jumps up, and pours water from a jug into a glass, then helps Finn take a sip. 'Amelia thought I was going to hurt her,' he says.

I tense. I shouldn't be here listening to this. But Beynon seems unaware of her surroundings, her focus fully on Finn.

'And then what, Finn?' she goes on, insistent.

He pauses for a long moment. 'Someone stuck the knife in me.' He closes his eyes, and winces as though feeling the blade going in again, his face ashen.

'Someone?'

'Someone in a mask.' There's a beat before he continues. 'The next thing I know, I'm on the bench, wearing the mask, bleeding out, and Amelia is there too, propped up against a tree.' He's becoming breathless.

'You really should leave him alone now,' Julia says. 'He's been through so much.'

'Do you know who it was in the mask, Finn?' Beynon persists, ignoring Julia. 'Who stabbed you?'

He shakes his head.

'Can we go back to why you were you out there in the first place, pal?' McKay chips in, rubbing a hand over his bearded chin.

'I got a text message from Maddie saying she knew who the killer was, that she needed to see me.'

'I thought you couldn't get a signal up there,' Beynon says.

'It was erratic, yes. But sometimes there was a signal.'

'Rosamund got a call from Neil while we were up there, and a couple of text messages,' I say.

'So Maddie got lucky, aye?' Beynon says. 'So what did it say? This message.'

'I can't remember exactly. It will be on my phone.' Finn furrows his forehead. 'She said something about Elise would have wanted the dog. Said I was the only person she could trust.'

'But you never saw her.'

He shakes his head again, and closes his eyes once more. 'Julia told me Maddie's dead,' he whispers, a single tear rolling down his cheek. 'Why would anyone kill her? Why would anyone kill my mum?' His voice fades to nothing, and I stare at him for a long moment, relieved he's going to be OK, and relieved too that he's kept quiet about me stabbing him – though, in truth, I'm not sure I can live with the guilt.

'Enough now,' the nurse says. 'Let him rest.'

'You should go, Inspector,' Julia rises, firmness in her voice. She grabs a pink padded jacket from the back of her chair, and puts it on.

Beynon rises too, and looks up at her. 'Is he your boyfriend?' she asks her.

'No,' she says. 'Not that it's any of your business.'

'Everything is my business in a murder enquiry, Miss Collis.'

210

'Well he's a good friend, is all,' Julia says, as the police leave, followed by the nurse, and the door clicks closed behind them.

'I'm so glad he's OK,' I say, about to leave too.

'Well, you would be, wouldn't you?' Julia sounds suddenly bitter.

'Sorry?'

'It would have been murder if he'd died, Amelia. I saw the blood on you when you arrived at the farmhouse that night. It was his blood, wasn't it?'

'Julia.' It's Finn. 'I need more water.'

She picks up the glass once more, and I make a dash for the door, my heart thumping.

She knows. She knows it was me.

Chapter 43

Present Day

Amelia

'Are you sure you don't mind?' I say down the phone, relieved the girl with the pink hair who lives next door to me back in London – I so wish I knew her name – has agreed to look after my cat for a bit longer so I can stay with Dad and Thomas.

We returned from Scotland five days ago, and I'm staying at Dad's for now. I feel safer here. Despite fears that Julia knows what I've done, I haven't heard anything from her or Finn.

Dad called DI Beynon yesterday, and was told Finn is out of hospital, but, for now, no arrests have been made. They are still looking for Elise.

'I feel awful putting on you like this,' I go on down the phone to the girl with the pink hair. 'Is she OK? You're sure she's no trouble.' God I miss my cat.

'She's absolutely fine,' the girl says. 'Been an angel, in fact. Stay as long as you need. No worries at all.'

'Thanks so much, I appreciate it.' I end the call, and look over at Thomas, who has his back to me. He's busy on his laptop at the dining-room table, working on the screenplay of a book that a film director he knew in the US has sent him. It's good to see him trying to get back into something that resembles normal.

'Your cat's still OK then?' he says, clearly having eavesdropped on my call.

'Uh-huh.' I move across the room towards him. 'A tiny ray of sunshine, at least.'

'Pretty sure you need to find out what that woman's name is though,' he says with a half-laugh, not looking up, his fingers dancing on the keyboard.

'Yeah, it's getting kind of embarrassing.' I smile, and he mirrors it, but our smiles are weak and half-hearted. I go to turn away, and he stops typing, and grabs my hand.

'Are you OK, sis? This has been total hell for you.'

'For all of us, Thomas – you haven't exactly come out of it unscathed.' I pause for a moment, before saying again for the umpteenth time, 'I'm so sorry about Maddie. I know I wasn't her biggest fan, but she was so young, so full of life.'

Thomas releases my hand, and dashes fingers across his eyes, and I realise he's changed recently – more open with his emotions.

'I keep going over and over everything,' he says. 'I mean why would Maddie turn to Finn and not me? I realise I'm pretty lacking in the superhero department, but ...'

'I think she had a bit of a thing for him.'

'Really? I didn't notice.'

I shrug. 'I could be wrong, of course.'

'But who killed her and Ruth, Amelia? And who took Elise?'

'I wish I knew.' A beat. 'If I'm honest, I'm still not convinced Elise was taken.' I don't say: I think someone killed her in the same way they killed Ruth and Maddie. 'The thing is, we couldn't get off the estate, could we? So how could anyone abduct her? It doesn't make sense.'

'Well, let's hope the police do a better job of finding her, than they did finding Lark.' He pauses for a moment, as though allowing the thought of our sister to seep in. 'You know what? I still dream we'll find Lark one day,' he says. 'Haven't given up hope.'

'Nor me,' I say. But it's a lie. Truth is, I have given up hope, and it breaks my heart.

'And I still think Finn took Elise,' he says, his breath catching on his words. 'I don't want to believe it, but—'

'No,' I say, wanting to defend Finn. He lied for me. 'He's a good man, Thomas. I know he had issues with his mother …' I rub my hands over my face. 'Anyway, how can you tell if someone is a killer? They don't exactly wear a T-shirt saying "I kill people".' I shudder at my stupid words. 'And Finn is kind and cute.' Cute? I wonder at my choice of word.

'Kind and cute, aye?' Thomas smiles. 'I won't suggest you google Ted Bundy.'

'Oh shut up!' But I'm glad he's lightened things a little. 'I'll put the kettle on, shall I?' I go to walk away. 'I think there are some custard creams in the tin.'

'No wait.' He wheels his chair away from the table. 'There's something I need to tell you.'

'Do I need to sit down?' I say, picking up on his sudden serious tone.

He nods, and I perch on the edge of the sofa, my body tensing.

'It's not bad news,' he says.

I relax my shoulders, reassured. 'That's a relief. I'm not sure I could take any more.'

'In fact,' he says, moving closer and taking my hands in his. 'It's good news.'

I look into his eyes, and it's as though whatever he's about to tell me has ignited a light there I haven't seen for a long time.

'The thing is,' he begins, 'before we went away, I saw another specialist.' He pauses for a moment, and takes a breath. 'I'd been having sensations in my toes, Amelia. I can even move my feet sometimes.'

214

'Oh, Thomas.' I fling my arms around his neck. 'That's amazing.'

'Hang on,' he says, as I release him. 'It could be nothing, but he says there's hope.'

A memory of seeing his toe twitch and his foot move when we were at Drummondale House filters in – how I thought it was my imagination playing tricks.

'Oh, Thomas,' I repeat, wrapping my arms around his neck once more, and kissing his forehead three times. 'This is the best news ever. Why didn't you tell me before? Does Dad know?'

He shakes his head. 'I didn't tell either of you. I didn't want you to get hopeful, for it to turn out to be nothing. But now – well we need something, don't we?'

'We do. We do.' I kiss his cheek.

'Hey that's enough kisses for one day,' he says with a laugh. 'I've got my tough image to think of.'

'I love you, Thomas,' I say.

'I love you too, sis.'

Moments later Dad appears in the doorway, shoving his arms into his coat sleeves. 'Ready, Thomas?'

Thomas looks up at him blankly.

'The cinema? Dinner at the Foundry Arms? Have you forgotten?'

'Of course not.' He looks at me and winks, closes down his laptop, and heads over to where Dad hands him his coat.

'You forgot, didn't you?' Dad says.

'Yep!' They both laugh, as they head for the door.

'I didn't want to come anyway,' I call after them, playfully.

'You hate Marvel,' Dad calls back.

'I like Chris Hemsworth,' I say, as they close the door behind them. 'And Tom Hiddleston's not bad either.' The words feel too frivolous on my tongue. And I don't hate Marvel. In fact, Dad mentioned earlier that they were going, but I haven't got room in my head for films, or TV or anything much at all right now – every thought consumed by everything that happened at

Drummondale House. But I get why they need to go. Why they need to act as if life is normal – because that's all it is. An act.

It's almost six o'clock, when I make my way into the kitchen, and pour myself a glass of gin, adding ice and tonic. I grab a half-empty tub of Pringles from the cupboard, and head back into the lounge. The only light is from the fire, but I like it this way – flopped on the sofa, taking short sips of my drink, munching on the crispy snacks.

After a while, I rise and head for the front window, where I take in the wide road, and the grass verge opposite that leads to the river. Berwick-upon-Tweed hasn't had anywhere near as much snow as Scotland, but still people are huddled in warm coats and knitted hats as they scurry home, trying to stay upright on slippery pavements.

I squeeze my eyes together, and move closer to the window, peering through the glass. I loved living here when I was young. I was happy then.

Someone is standing across the road in the shadows. They seem to be looking straight at the house. My heart leaps into my throat. The young woman looks so much like Lark, and my eyes fill with tears. I know it can't be her, but I so wish it was.

I place my hand on the window, as though touching her.

I've seen my sister often since she disappeared. On the street, her voice in a shop, even when I'm alone I think I can smell her musky perfume. I accepted a long time ago, it's just my imagination.

But still, I race to the front door, and throw it open; almost slipping over as I hurry down the path in my slippers. But as I expected, the girl has gone – if she was ever there in the first place.

Back in the lounge I pull across the curtains, and bash away tears. I take another sip of my drink, my heart thudding. It's post-traumatic stress – that's what Dad said, when I told him I've barely slept since we returned from Drummondale House. Maybe see the GP.

216

When I do sleep, the nightmares are vivid. Just last night I felt sure I was awake as I staggered through the house, dragged down by snow, ears numb from the cold, calling out for Mum and Lark, begging them to show themselves, but I was locked in a dream, and when I finally woke, gasping for breath, tears came.

I flick on all the lamps, and head for the back window. I'm about to close the curtains when something catches my eye. Something's hanging in the tree at the foot of the garden. My heart picks up speed once more. I should close the curtains, but my curiosity won't let me. Instead I grab my coat, and gingerly open the back door.

The garden sensor-light springs to life as I step onto the patio, and my stomach lurches. It looks like a face in the tree. The mask?

I step closer, looking about me.

A bang, and my heart jumps into my throat. I grab my chest, realising within seconds it's the next-door neighbour putting something into their wheelie bin.

As I move closer to the tree, I see it's only a plastic carrier bag caught in the branches, waving in the wind. I turn and race back into the house, and slam the door, my body alive with pulses, and wrap my arms around myself. My stomach is a tight knot; my chest fizzes. I need to calm down. Finally freeing myself from my frozen position by the back door, I dash into the lounge and take a gulp of gin.

*

It's some time later that the doorbell rings and kick-starts my out-of-control pulses once more.

I creep, trembling to the front door. 'Who is it?' I call.

'Hi, Amelia, it's only me – Rosamund. Can I talk with you?'

'Rosamund?' I open up to see her eyes shimmering with tears. 'What's wrong?'

'I'm so sorry to bother you. I didn't know who else to turn

to. Neil's still in Scotland, and, well ...' She rummages in her bag and brings out a mask like the one the masked killer wore.

'Oh God.' I step backwards.

'It was on my doorstep. I don't know who put it there.' Her eyes fill with tears.

'Come in,' I say.

She pushes the mask into her bag, and steps in. She shuffles free from her coat, hangs it up, and sniffs.

I don't know whether to hug her. Truth is, I barely know the woman, and although I've forgiven her for deserting my mum – some people can't deal with other people's grief and sadness – I can't say she's somebody I wanted to see again.

She bends to take off her boots, and stands them against the wall. 'I have this horrible fear that it was Finn who left the mask on my step,' she says.

'Finn?'

'Yes. Apparently he's just come out of hospital, which seems more than a coincidence, don't you think?'

I lead the way into the kitchen, saying nothing until I reach the fridge. I turn. 'But why would he?'

'I'm convinced he killed Ruth and Maddie, took Elise, and Lark,' she says. 'I mean he lived up there on that lonely estate with an overprotective, strange mother. He's textbook psychopath.'

'The police don't seem to think so.' I sound defensive.

'I'm sure it's only a matter of time before they catch him out. Apparently he's staying with Julia in Eyemouth. It makes me uneasy that he's so close.'

I shudder. Have I got it wrong? Had he tried to kill me that night after all? 'I just don't think it was him,' I say.

She touches my arm again. 'Well let's agree to disagree, shall we?'

I nod, deciding not to enter into a debate. 'Listen, I was about to have a glass of wine.' I open the fridge, and grab a bottle of sauvignon blanc. 'Oh God, sorry,' I say, remembering she's pregnant.

She smiles, and lifts her hand, as though to say, don't worry. 'I'd love a cup of coffee, though.'

I reach for the kettle, and shove it under the streaming tap. 'You've got over your hatred for the demon coffee beans then?'

'Sorry?'

'You went off coffee.' I turn and tilt my head. 'Didn't you?'

'Yes. Yes, that's right.' Her cheeks flush, and she squeezes her hands into fists. 'Well, that's all passed now thank goodness.'

We stand. Waiting for the kettle to boil. Awkward. And I find myself making small talk. 'I'm having a makeover tomorrow.'

'Makeover?'

I laugh. 'Well, I'm getting my hair cut in town – that's as adventurous as it gets for me.'

Another awkward silence follows, and I feel I have to fill it. 'Does it help you get through this awful nightmare, knowing you have to stay strong for your baby?' Her face crumples, and I instantly wish I'd kept my mouth shut. But I remember that warm feeling inside me when I was carrying my own baby. It was as though I had permission to be happy.

'I can't imagine life without Elise, if that's what you mean,' she says. 'I know she's not my daughter, and we've had our differences in the past, but when I fell pregnant we bonded. Though I think I know what you're trying to say.' She pulls her phone from her bag, and taps the screen. 'Here,' she says, thrusting it towards me. 'It's the latest scan of baby Green. It was taken yesterday.'

I gulp back tears as I take in the tiny image.

'If you look closely,' she says. 'You can make out his toes.'

I make a weird noise, as I force back invading tears.

'Are you OK?' she says, pressing her hand on my arm. 'I'm so sorry if I've upset you.'

'No, no you haven't. I'm fine.' I hand the phone back, and turn away from her, fumble a spoonful of coffee into a mug. I pour on boiling water. Add a splash of milk. 'Sugar?' I say, glancing over my shoulder.

219

She shakes her head.

I take a breath and hand her the mug, before splashing wine into a large glass.

And then it hits me.

The scan she just showed me. The one she said was taken yesterday. It was dated 10th October. 'Did you say you had the scan yesterday?' I ask, to be sure.

'Yes, why?'

Is she lying? Or perhaps she showed me the wrong photo. But I recall her reaction when I mentioned the coffee – it was as though she'd been caught out. And now a memory invades of her at Drummondale House, tears rolling down her cheeks as she looked at a photograph of a scan of her baby.

I stare at her. It's as though I can see into her soul, sense a terrible loss, feel her suffering as though it's mine. She's lost her baby.

But that can't be right. Her body tells me otherwise.

'Do you want to talk?' I say. It's a gamble. If, and only if, she's lost her baby, she's pretending she hasn't – going as far as wearing a fake pregnancy bump – a good one too. She doesn't want to be found out. 'I understand.'

She shoots me a startled look, and I take a deep breath.

'I lost my baby too,' I say, my voice cracking. 'I know how painful it is to lose your unborn child.'

'I don't know what you're talking about.' She's flushed, and tears fill her eyes.

Mentioning my baby has left me vulnerable – exposed. Rosamund is the first person I've told, and I hadn't factored in my own need for comfort.

And what if I'm wrong about Rosamund?

No. I'm right. I'm sure I'm right.

I move towards her, but she steps away from me, banging her back on the worktop, spilling her coffee, wincing in pain. Her tears come faster now.

'I'm so sorry,' I say, my voice cracking, as I realise I'm crying too.

She takes a tissue from her pocket, and dabs her cheeks. 'OK,' she says. 'You've got me, governor,' she adds in a silly cockney accent that's at odds with how distressed she is. She raises the white tissue in surrender.

We make our way into the lounge, and sit silently at opposite ends of the sofa. I've unearthed something I'm now struggling to deal with.

'How did you know?' she says finally.

'The coffee, the scan dated October, but most of all it was when I thought back to you crying at Drummondale House, when you were looking at the scan of your baby. At the time I thought you were crying over Elise, but looking back I recognise that pain.'

She nods.

'But why lie, Rosamund? Why pretend?'

'I wanted to stay pregnant,' she says, her voice intense. 'Is that so awful? I wanted to believe my baby was still inside me.'

'I get that,' I say, and I do, I really do.

'And I couldn't bear the thought of telling Neil.' She leans forward and grabs tissues from a box on the table, presses them against her nose.

'He still believes you're pregnant?'

She nods. 'He's been working away for the last two months.' She shakes her head. 'He's always away.'

'But you'll have to tell him sometime.'

She nods again. 'Don't you think I know that?'

A painful silence falls once more, as all the questions I have lined up in my head feel invasive, unsupportive, wrong.

'Listen, could I have a glass of wine?'

'Of course.' I wander into the kitchen, grab another glass and the bottle, and return.

As I pour, she goes on. 'I fell. Stumbled backwards, hitting my back against the coffee table. That's how it happened. That's how I lost him.'

'I'm so sorry,' I say, sitting down once more.

'Me too.' She turned watery eyes on me. 'Does it get any easier?'

I look down, and run my hand over my stomach. 'You learn to live with the loss, but it will always be there. It's grief, after all.'

She touches my cheek, looks deep into my eyes. 'You know you have your mum's caring nature, Amelia. You may not be able to play tennis like Lark, or be academic like Thomas, but you have the best quality of all – kindness and understanding.'

'Thanks,' I say, feeling myself blush.

'You've had far too much loss, Amelia,' she says, squeezing my hand. 'I pray you find Lark one day.'

I force back tears. 'I hope so too.' There's a beat before I add, 'I thought I saw her earlier.' I look over at a photo of my sister on the dresser.

Rosamund looks to where I'm staring, and her eyes widen. 'Really?'

'Mmm. It wasn't her, of course. But I sometimes think I see her, you know.'

She shuffles closer, and rests her hand on my knee. 'I know exactly what you mean,' she says. 'I see Elise all the time.'

*

'It makes no sense. Why would Finn kill Maddie?' I say to Rosamund, combing my fingers through my hair, a half-drunk glass of wine cradled in my mitts. I hadn't meant to stray back onto the subject, but drinking on an empty stomach has loosened my tongue, and I'm now flopped in a relaxed state, my legs curled up under me on the sofa, twittering on. 'And you know what else? I keep thinking about the Monopoly counter.' I lean forward and splash more wine into both our glasses, knowing I'm being an idiot.

'Monopoly counter? What Monopoly counter?'

222

'The top hat.' I curl my legs back under me. 'Maddie picked it up when she left your cottage the night she died.'

'Did she? Whatever for?' She leans back in the chair, and takes a gulp of wine.

'Oh, I'm sure it's nothing. It's just she was holding it when Dad brought her back to the cottage, as though it meant something to her. It was from the game you and Elise were playing before she went missing.'

'Sounds like something and nothing,' she says. She knocks back the last of her wine. 'Anyway,' she says rising to her feet. 'I should probably make a move. It's getting late.' She pauses. 'You won't say anything to anyone about the baby?' she says. 'Not until I can find the right moment to tell Neil. He's in Scotland, hoping he'll find something that will lead to Elise, so I can't tell him until the weekend.'

'But you will tell him?'

'Of course, I just dread it, that's all. This news on top of Elise's disappearance will break him.'

She turns and heads for her coat. And as she slips slender arms into the sleeves, she adds, 'There's going to be an appeal soon. I just can't see what good it will do, but I guess the police know best, and Neil is desperate.'

'It will keep Elise in the public's mind,' I say.

'Well it didn't do any good in the search for Lark and Jackson, did it?'

I feel her comment like a slap.

'And all the publicity there's been around Elise makes me feel violated, as though everyone's staring and gossiping.'

'It won't go on forever, Rosamund,' I say. 'Make the most of the press while you can.'

But I understand how she feels. The national papers have connected Lark and Elise's disappearances. Put their photos together on the front page. Two pretty blonde teenagers disappearing without trace sold papers. And there was a feature on

Jackson's past almost identical to one that had appeared when he and Lark disappeared. It told of how he left home at eighteen, went to live in America right up until his parents' death three years ago. Told of how he'd moved in with my mum. How he'd split up her marriage. But this time they'd tracked down an old girlfriend over in the US, who'd talked freely about how he'd used her, slept with other women, and left her broken-hearted.

I wasn't surprised they described Jackson as a womaniser, though I was unsure of the relevance. And the media had simply joined the dots between Lark and Elise, and made a wiggly line.

After pulling on her boots, Rosamund leans in and kisses my cheek. 'Take care, Amelia,' she says, and with a waft of expensive perfume, she's gone.

Chapter 44

Present Day

Amelia

'Let me treat you to your cut and blow-dry, or whatever you young women do to your hair these days.' Dad grabs his wallet and hands me a wad of ten-pound notes.

'You don't need to do this, Dad.' I'm not even sure I want to go into Berwick. I look dreadful, and feel more than a bit dodgy after drinking too much last night. Quite frankly, having my hair cut really doesn't feature highly on my life plan right now.

'Take the money, Amelia,' Dad says. 'Do whatever you want with it. Buy some new clothes, perhaps. A bit of retail therapy might do you good. Do it for me, love. I'm worried about you.'

'I'm worried about you too, Dad,' I say.

'Then go into town, treat yourself, and that will make me feel much better.' He smiles. 'Tell you what, let's meet for lunch at Molly's Café after my museum stint.' He walks away, leaving the money on the table, and grabs his coat from the hook by

225

the door. 'I'd quite enjoy a heart-to-heart with my beautiful daughter.'

*

I retrieve my old bike from the garage, dust off the cobwebs and pump up the tyres, and begin my ride into town, careful to miss any icy patches as I go. It's a bright chilly day, and the sight of open fields stretching for miles either side of me, and a clear blue sky, is uplifting. By the time I lock up my bike outside the Berwick Advertiser, my head has cleared and endorphins waken from what feels like a hundred-year sleep.

I stroll along the snow-free pavements of Marygate, heading for the salon I used to go to in my teens. Yes, I definitely feel lighter. Perhaps Dad was right: I needed to get out, do something for me.

It's almost eleven when I push open the door of the salon. Sandy, the owner, who's in her fifties, and sports short white hair and trendy red-framed glasses raises her hand. 'Amelia,' she calls. 'I thought I saw your name in the appointment book. How lovely to see you.' She doesn't wait for a reply, goes on talking to her customer, whilst tonging the man's blond tresses.

'Take a seat,' a young girl with a ready smile says, and I remove my jacket, and sit down next to the window. 'Would you like some tea or coffee while you wait?' The girl takes my jacket and hangs it on a hook near the door, 'Sandy shouldn't be long.'

'I'm OK, but thank you.'

I take out my phone, and thumb through Facebook, then Instagram, though I'm barely taking in the posts, my mind far away. I'm finding the smell of hairspray, and perculating coffee; the sound of dryers humming, calming – normal; and the sun warming my face through the glass, comforting.

A sudden thump on the window shatters my peace, and my heart goes into overdrive. I'm clearly not as relaxed as I thought!

'Hey, Mum,' calls the young girl, waving at a woman in her forties who has pressed her nose against the window.

Oh God, my heartbeat won't slow down and a fizz of anxiety pumps through my veins. I need to get out of here.

'Right, what can we do for you today, Amelia?' It's Sandy, now beside me brandishing a comb and a pair of scissors, and I realise it's too late to escape.

'Just a trim, please,' I say, my voice squeaky.

'I was so sorry to hear about your mum,' Sandy says, once the young girl has washed my hair. 'And your sister too. Terrible. Terrible.' She shakes her head. 'I don't know how you're coping.'

I'm not.

I should have known Sandy would mention them; but it's too late. I'm here now, trapped beneath a hairdressing cape, frozen. Thank God she doesn't know about the murders, Elise's disappearance.

'And I read about the murders too,' she goes on. 'What a nightmare.'

'It's been a difficult time,' I say.

She sighs deeply, and takes hold of my shoulders, her eyes meeting mine in the mirror. 'I can imagine,' she says, her voice syrupy smooth.

I want to tell her to stop. Stop or I'll cry. I want to tell her this isn't what I came here for – that I came here to forget.

As she combs through my wet hair, I take a deep breath, and let it out slowly, counting backwards in my head. But something's taken over. Something I can't control.

'Listen, I'm not feeling too well,' I say, pulling the towel from around my neck, and fumbling to untie the cape. I rise, the cape and towel falling to the floor, and race across the salon. I grab my jacket from the hook by the door. 'I'm so sorry, Sandy. I've got to go.'

I rush out into the cool air, and hurry down the road, where I lean against a wall some distance away, unable to catch my breath.

'Are you all right, dear?' It's an elderly woman, with a cute Yorkshire terrier tucked under her arm. It stares at me with brown velvet eyes, much like its owner's. 'You don't look well.'

I gather my wits. 'I'm fine, thank you. Honestly. It's been a long day, that's all, and it's not even lunchtime.' I try to laugh, and she chuckles.

'Well as long as you're all right, dear,' she says, and goes on her way.

I look at my watch. I'm not meeting Dad for an hour. It's not enough time to cycle home and come back, so I wander into Boots.

Feeling a little disorientated, my heart thumping far too fast, I meander up and down the aisles, breathing in the perfumes, scanning the shelves, buying nothing.

Managing to lose almost an hour in the store without getting accused of loitering, I finally step back out onto the pavement with a few minutes to kill before I meet Dad. I go to move away from the store when I see Julia – her long, patterned skirt flapping her ankles, her phone pinned to her ear.

I look about me, remembering Rosamund saying Finn was staying with her. But it seems she's alone.

She takes quick steps down the other side of the road. Then, as though seeming to sense me here, glances my way. I duck back into the shop doorway. I don't want to talk to her – fear what she might say.

'It would have been murder if he'd died, Amelia. I saw the blood on you when you arrived at the farmhouse that night. It was his blood, wasn't it?'

She slows her pace, and shuffles her brightly patterned bag further onto her shoulder, before picking up speed once more.

I exhale a sigh of relief as she disappears from view, and I head for Molly's Café.

Through the window I spot Dad already settled at the back, a mug of tea in front of him.

'Amelia,' he says, as I enter to a waft of tempting smells. He pats the seat beside him. 'Come and sit down, love.'

A young chap approaches and I order some coffee. He thrusts a menu into my hands, and disappears.

'What do you fancy?' Dad says.

'Give me a sec,' I say, shuffling out of my jacket, before sitting down.

'Your hair looks nice.'

'No it doesn't. I didn't have it done.'

'Well I've always liked it when you don't drag out your natural curls.'

I smile, and we look at the menus. 'I think I'll go for the prawn salad sandwich in granary,' I say.

Dad's eyes flit across the choices. 'It's amazing news about Thomas, isn't it?' he says. 'I'm trying not to get my hopes up, but yes, definitely something to keep us buoyant in a sea that's intent on dragging us under.'

'Very poetic.' I smile at him.

'I try my best.'

'And yes, it's great news. We certainly need it.'

'We do indeed.'

'I saw Rosamund yesterday, Dad.' I avoided telling him last night and this morning, but to not mention her visit now feels deceitful. 'She came round when you were at the cinema.' I pause for a moment. 'Someone left a mask on her doorstep.'

'Well she needs to tell the police, not you.' Something shifts in his eyes, and he shakes his head. 'That bloody woman.'

'I know you don't like her but—'

'I think I'll have poached egg on toast.' He puts down his menu.

'Dad?'

'She's a thoroughly dislikeable woman.'

'Mum liked her.'

229

'Mum didn't know her. Not really.'

'And you did?'

'Are you ready to order?' The young man is back with my coffee. He puts it down in front of me, as I reel off our order in a monotone.

Once he's gone, I continue. 'I know she let Mum down but she's sorry, Dad. Why do you hate her so much?'

'Not hate, Amelia. Hate is too strong a word. Let's leave it, shall we?'

'But you promised me a heart-to-heart.'

'Not about bloody Rosamund Green.'

I lean forward. There's something else. I know it. 'Dad?'

'OK, if you really want to know.' He breathes in a sigh. 'She made a pass at me, a very long time ago.'

'Rosamund?'

'Don't sound so surprised. Your dad wasn't always a dusty historian.'

I smile, remembering how Mum described him that way.

'As I say, it was a long time ago, when your mum worked in Rosamund's flower shop. There was a party.' A long pause fills the air, and the sounds of chatter and clanking cutlery fill my senses. 'She flirted with me during the evening, but your mum couldn't see it, kept telling me how friendly she was. That she hoped I liked her. And then—'

'You turned her down, I hope.'

'Of course – what do you take me for?' He looks hurt, as though he can't believe I would think otherwise. 'But she didn't like being turned down. Was used to getting her own way, a product of parents who spoilt her rotten, apparently. And of course she was – and still is – a beautiful woman. Anyway, it was after that party that she sold the shop, and never contacted your mother again. Until—'

'Mum left you for Jackson?'

He nods. Takes a gulp of his tea.

'So she got in touch with Mum because you'd broken up?'

'It seemed that way.'

'Why didn't you tell Mum when she made the pass?'

'At the time, I thought it would make things worse. Your mum was already low from losing her job and her supposed friend. Later, when I realised Rosamund was back in touch, I didn't think your mum would believe me. Our relationship was fragile by then; I didn't want to damage it beyond repair.'

'It was a long time ago, Dad.'

Our food arrives, but I've lost my appetite. I glance out of the window, onto the street. 'Do you ever think you see Lark, Dad?'

'Do you?'

I look back at him tucking into poached egg, and say, 'I know it's wishful thinking, but I sense her sometimes. Like at Mum's funeral. It was as though she was with us.'

He puts down his cutlery, reaches across the table, and takes hold of my hand. 'We'll find her one day.'

'No, Dad, we won't.' I pull my hand away. 'We have to stop believing that. We wouldn't have ended up trapped in the middle of nowhere with two people murdered and another girl missing, if we'd let Lark go. We have to let her go, Dad.'

He looks down. I've hurt him and instantly regret my choice of words. 'I'll never let her go, Amelia. Not until someone proves to me she's dead.'

I gulp back tears. Dead. It's so final. Like poor Ruth and Maddie. 'Sorry,' I say. 'I didn't mean—'

'I know you didn't. We're all so volatile at the moment. But then it's not surprising, is it?'

I shake my head. 'I'm just not sure how much more any of us can take,' I say, burying my head in my hands.

Chapter 45

Present Day

Amelia

Outside Molly's Café I kiss Dad goodbye, and watch as he limps up the road. With a brief wave, he turns the corner towards the museum. Gone.

I feel suddenly lost, as I loop my bag over my shoulder. I need to head back down Marygate, to where I've locked up my bike. I need to get home.

I'm not sure what makes me turn to look in the window of the antique shop next door to Molly's. But I see it. Propped in the corner of the window by the door, a horrifying contrast to the china teapots and vases, fob watches and red brandy glasses: the mask.

The ground moves beneath me, and my legs give way as everything spins.

The mask.

I open my mouth to cry out, unsure if I say the words out loud, or in my head. It's the mask the killer wore.

*

The next thing I know I'm lying on my back on the pavement with something soft under my head. A woman crouches down beside me; others look on, their faces full of concern.

'I'm fine,' I say, attempting to pull myself up to a sitting position, and despite feeling weak and woozy, I glance over my shoulder at the antique shop. There's no mask in the window. Had I imagined it?

'We've called an ambulance,' the woman says. 'Lie back down, sweetie. Everything's going to be OK.'

*

Once I've convinced paramedics I fainted due to not eating, and they've checked me over, and ordered me to eat something before I attempt to cycle home, I open the door to the antique shop. A bell rings out. 'Hello!'

Inside, the air is musty, and high shelves are crammed with ornaments, jewellery, and pictures from past lives. I make my way towards the back of the shop to where a man in his forties is doing a crossword puzzle in a folded newspaper. He doesn't look up. 'Strange – connected to death, seven letters, beginning with "M".'

'Macabre?'

'Spot on!' He scribbles the word, and jolts his face upwards. 'Can I help?'

'There was a mask in the window a little while ago. I wondered if you remember who brought it in, or maybe who bought it?'

He screws up his nose. 'Do you mean the rather lovely Chinese opera mask?' He points to the wall, where a Chinese mask with a creepy smile hangs.

'No.' I shake my head. 'This was a modern mask of a young boy's face, made of plastic.'

His forehead furrows. 'I'm afraid we only sell antiques. You must be mistaken.'

'Maybe.' Had I imagined it? 'Has anyone been in here in the last half an hour?'

'Only a man picking up a 1950s sewing machine, I'd put by for him. Are you OK? You seem a little agitated.'

'And that's it. Nobody else. Nothing?' I'm lost for words, and turn to leave.

'Hang on!' he says. 'Now I think about it the bell above the door rang out a couple of times this morning, but whoever it was must have changed their mind – never came in.'

'So they could have put a mask in your window?'

'I guess so. But it's a rather odd thing to do, don't you think?'

'Yes,' I say, retreating. 'Yes it is.'

Chapter 46

Present Day

Amelia

My eyes flick over the lounge where I spent so much of my childhood. Sometimes it's painful transporting myself back there, but today I feel lucky that I can lose myself in the memories. Today I want to go there.

Dad and Thomas went out about half an hour ago. I didn't tell them what happened in town today. That I thought I saw the mask in the antique shop window; that I collapsed, an emotional wreck, on the pavement. They've got enough to contend with. And I'm OK now, really I am.

I head over to the CD player and put on my parents' Fleetwood Mac CD, and as the music blares from the speakers, I can almost see Mum dancing around the room in her own world, a glass of wine in her hand, while Dad sits at the table, lost in his museum research, barely seeing her. Maybe they were never as suited as I always dreamed they were.

I drift around the lounge cupping a glass of wine with both

hands, as I follow my family's journey in pictures that grace the walls – from Mum and Dad's wedding day, through the baby years, the teen years and beyond. There are so many studies, put up by Mum long before she took off with Jackson. Dad hadn't taken them down when she left. In fact, he changed very little – even the fake sweet peas she made into a beautiful display more than ten years ago still stand on the windowsill.

'Why were you so flattered by Jackson's stupid boyish charm, Mum?' I say into the silence, a bubble of anger rising, then dissipating. 'You were so lucky Dad was there for you at the end to pick up the pieces.'

I put down my glass, and bend down to pull an old photo album from the dresser, and flop down on the sofa. The album smells musty. Black-and-white photos are held on greying cardboard pages with photo mounts. I've seen these photos before over the years, but now they are painful to see. I take in a study of Mum in platform shoes, and a fake-fur jacket. There's no conservatory but there's no doubting it was taken outside Ruth and Finn's cottage, and the other teenagers in the picture are Ruth and Michael Collis.

I look at their young faces, at the way Ruth holds hands with Michael, staring up at him adoringly, and the tragedy that both Mum and Ruth are now gone hits me once more.

I'm far from drunk, but the booze is fuelling my emotions. I desperately want – no, need – to see more photos from the past. I rise. Most of the family albums are in Mum's old workroom. I make my way upstairs.

Within moments of stepping into her room, I know I shouldn't be here, encased in this shrine to Mum. The neatly made bed where she spent her final weeks; the boxes of brightly coloured ribbons, silk flowers, and rolls of cellophane that are piled high on a pine table, the pretty curtains at the window, all nudge at my already fragile state.

I take a breath, kneel down, and pull out an album, then

another, flicking through the pages at speed, as though searching for something I can't find, my emotions chaotic.

It's as I give up my search and thrust the albums back onto the shelf that I see it: a thick, pale-blue notebook, with the words Caroline's Journey written on the cover in Mum's swirling, curling handwriting. I've seen it before on her bedside table a few days before she died.

I pick it up, clasp it tight against my chest, and leave the room.

Back on the sofa downstairs, tears stream my face as I read from the pages, all written in Mum's beautiful hand. Her thoughts and deepest fears all there in front of me, telling me how much she struggled through the awful disease, whilst putting on a brave face for the world – for us – for me.

It's when I come to the pages she wrote when we visited Drummondale House – the night Lark and Jackson disappeared – that my tears stop, and my anxiety heightens.

I woke. Jackson wasn't beside me. I don't know what made me get up and leave Bluebell Cottage to try to find him. Maybe I knew deep down. Maybe I'd always known.

But I wish I hadn't gone into the wood.

I didn't take a torch, as the moon was so bright that night. I saw the masks first – six of them, hanging in the trees. I'd shuddered, was tempted to turn back, but then I heard it – the sound of lust, betrayal – and my blood ran cold.

I continued towards the sound. I shouldn't have. The sight of Jackson and Rosamund – so crude, basic, like animals – will stay with me until I die.

I thought he loved me.

I thought she was my friend.

I close the book, my heart thudding. Jackson was having an affair with Rosamund. Jackson was having an affair with Rosamund. Oh God, my poor mum discovering them. My poor, poor mum.

But why hadn't she said anything?

I recall how certain Mum was that Lark and Jackson's disappearance weren't connected. Had she thought Jackson had walked out on her? Planned to be with Rosamund? Had she been too proud to tell us what she saw? A surge of anger threads through my veins. Why the hell had she kept quiet about something that could have helped find Lark?

I head to the kitchen and make some strong coffee. I need a boost of caffeine, and to feel totally sober. I sit for some time at the kitchen table, sipping the warm liquid, my mind whirring back to that night at Drummondale House, and I'm suddenly there, sitting in the wing-backed chair at the bedroom window, seeing the flash of white, the figure in the trees. Had it been someone hanging up the masks? Elise? She was certainly obsessed with them. What if she'd seen Rosamund betray her father? What if she'd decided, a year later – now older, taller, stronger – that it was time to take revenge on Rosamund?

Rosamund had said Elise was in her bedroom the night Ruth was murdered. Ruth had been wearing Rosamund's fur bed jacket. Had Elise mistaken Ruth for her stepmother? Sometimes revenge is the only way – that's what Elise had said when they'd played Truth or Lie.

Was Elise still out there waiting to take her revenge on Rosamund?

But why did Maddie have to die? Where was Elise now? How did she get away from Drummondale House?

OK, yes there are loose ends, but my main concern is for Rosamund's safety, even if she had betrayed my mum.

Had Elise left the mask on her stepmother's doorstep? If she'd tried to kill her at Drummondale House, what was to stop her trying again?

I reach for my phone. I need to call her. Warn her. Let her know she could be in danger.

Chapter 47

Present Day

Amelia

I go to grab my mobile as it vibrates on the coffee table.

'Thomas,' I say once my phone's pressed against my ear. Should I tell him my suspicions?

'I've met an old mate, so Dad is about to head home. He wants to know if you fancy fish and chips.' He sounds relaxed. Happy. I decide to say nothing.

'Some chips maybe.' I pray my brother doesn't twig there's something up.

'Cool,' he says, clearly not registering the wobble in my voice. 'See you later.' He ends the call, and I fumble with the phone, searching for Rosamund's number.

'Amelia, how lovely,' she says when the call goes through.

'Rosamund. Listen.' My stomach leapfrogs. 'I need to talk to you. It's really important.'

'Calm down, you sound like you might pop—'

'It's just—'

'Hang on, I'm on hands-free and keep losing you—'

'Pull over somewhere, Rosamund. This is really important—'

'Tell you what; I'm not far from you. I'll pop round. Be there in five.' The line goes dead.

I look down at my phone. Maybe her coming here is for the best. I can suggest she doesn't go home until she's spoken to the police. Maybe she can book into a B & B for the night.

I watch from the window, waiting. Hoping she won't think I'm over-reacting. In less than five minutes she pulls up, and I dash to open the front door.

'Amelia? Whatever's wrong?' she says, locking her car, as she races up the path towards me. She pulls me into her arms, and I feel the fake baby bump, and I pull away. She clearly hasn't broken the news to Neil yet. 'You've worried me,' she says. 'Is everything OK?'

'I'm so sorry.' I lead the way into the house. 'It's just I really need to talk to you. It's important.'

In the kitchen, I put the kettle on, and gesture for her to sit at the table. I take the seat opposite her, and twiddle a strand of my hair around my finger, arranging the words I want to say in my head so they make some sort of sense. 'The thing is,' I begin, 'I found a book, well a kind of diary really, that my mum wrote before she died.' I pause. 'Rosamund, she saw you and Jackson together in the woods.'

'What?' Her eyes widen.

'It was the night he and Lark disappeared. You were …' I scramble for the right words, but she knows exactly what I'm trying to say.

'That's just not true. Look at me. Do I look the type of woman who would have sex in a wood?' Her cheeks flush, and she avoids meeting my eye.

'But why would she make it up, Rosamund?' I narrow my eyes. 'Why would she write it in her diary if it wasn't true?'

There's a beat. 'OK, yes, yes—'

241

'Christ!' I lean back in my chair, cover my mouth with my hands. 'Why the hell didn't you say anything at the time?' Why didn't my mum?

She thrusts her head into her hands and begins to cry. 'Jackson and I were having an affair – a fling really. It meant nothing.'

'But you should have told the police you were one of the last people to see Jackson before he vanished.'

'I couldn't, OK.' She looks up. 'I couldn't bear the thought of Neil finding out. I didn't want to lose him. Is that why I'm here, Amelia? Are you going to rake it all up – ruin my marriage?'

I shake my head – no.

'Then what's so important that you needed to talk to me?'

'Well one,' I say, leaning forward and raising my index finger, 'I think Elise may have seen you with Jackson. And two, I think she may still be alive and—'

'Alive?' She widens her eyes.

'You need to be careful, Rosamund. She could be dangerous.'

'Elise? Dangerous?' She furrows her forehead. 'Oh, Amelia, why would you even think that?'

'OK. Right. The first thing is Ruth was wearing your bed jacket when she died. What if Elise thought it was you? And I'm pretty sure I saw her in the wood the night Lark went missing. I didn't realise at the time – my head so full of ghost stories – but now I'm pretty sure it was Elise hanging up those awful masks ready to scare you – us – when we went in the woods the following day. And now she wants revenge.'

'A whole year later?'

'I know. That part doesn't quite fit. But then she's bigger now, stronger.'

'Although the mask bit fits,' she says, her voice rising, her eyes flashing as though she can suddenly see what I see. 'She was obsessed with those stupid things, wasn't she? Maybe she is still alive and she left the mask on my doorstep. Put one in the antique shop for you to find.'

'Exactly,' I say. 'I don't think you should go back to your house alone, Rosamund.'

'Oh God,' she says, covering her face with her hands. 'No, no you're right. I can't go back there.'

There's a painful silence for some moments, before she removes her hands from her face, and clenches her fists. 'He ended it with me that night,' she says.

'Who? Jackson?'

She nods. 'He said he felt guilty.'

'Well, he bloody well should have.'

'I regret every moment, Amelia,' she says. 'Jackson was a terrible flirt – a handsome charmer. He took me to his caravan in Laurel Wood a few times, that's all. It was a short fling, nothing more. I loved Neil, always will. You have to believe me. It was over the night Lark vanished.'

'So that's why you took off, never spoke to my mum again?' I stare into her eyes, see them shimmering.

She nods. 'And I'm so, so sorry.'

The kettle boils, and I rise.

'Can I borrow your loo?' she says, rising too. She leaves the room, and as I make hot drinks, my mind buzzes. Mum had seen Rosamund and Jackson together. She'd known they were having an affair. Was that what the letter to Neil had said? Had Mum told him she'd seen them?

But no, that can't be right. Neil is still with Rosamund. So did he forgive her? Had he known all along?

As I put the drinks on the table something niggles at my thoughts, but I can't quite reach it. Frustrated I sit down; take a long sip of my coffee.

'Maybe you could get booked into a B & B in Berwick tonight,' I say as Rosamund returns.

She nods, sits too, picks up her mug. 'Good idea.'

I pull out my phone, about to look up a suitable place for her to stay, when it hits me.

243

I stare into her eyes. 'I never told you about the mask in the antique shop,' I say.

Fear floods in. I get to my feet. 'You should leave. Now.'

Something shifts in her eyes. She's on her feet too. Within moments she's grabbed a knife from the rack.

'Christ!' I cry. 'What the fuck?'

'I tried to veer you away from finding out the truth.' She leaps towards me, pins me against the wall, points the blade at my throat. 'Tried to lay the blame at Finn's door. I thought the mask in the antique shop was a nice touch.'

'Rosamund, please,' I say, trying to fight back tears.

'I hoped you'd recall Finn was in the area, put two and two together and make some absurd number. I never dreamed you'd think Elise was after me.' She laughs. 'God I wish I'd thought of that.' She grabs me, slams me against the wall with the same force as the masked figure in the wood. It was her. It was her that awful night.

She looks down at me crumpled in fear and pain, and tilts her head. With a jolt she crouches down, and presses the tip of the knife against my throat. I whimper, pathetic.

She lifts her manicured finger against her lips, and I yelp as the knife nicks my skin. Her face is so close to mine, I can smell stale coffee on her breath. 'It wasn't meant to turn out like this,' she says. 'But one domino fell, then another, then another.'

'Did you kill them?' My words catch on my breath. 'Maddie? Ruth?'

'Yes. Yes I did.' She's so calm, proud of herself.

'Please let me go. I promise I won't tell anyone.'

Blood pumps in my ears, as she shakes her head. 'No can do, I'm afraid. And you might as well know, because I'm going to kill you anyway, that Elise is dead. I killed her too.' She sounds triumphant.

'Oh God, no. Why? Why would you do that? She was just a child.'

She screws up her nose. 'In my defence, it was an accident. She's buried in a field not far from here, where nobody will ever look for her. Not when they think she was abducted or killed at Drummondale House. And if DI Kate Beynon makes as much of a hash of Elise's death as she did Lark's disappearance, she'll never work it out.' A beat. 'You look puzzled, Amelia. Do I have to spell it out for you?'

My head spins, my emotions in tatters. She's right. I can barely make sense of what she's saying.

'Elise. Was. Never. At. Drummondale House.'

'What? But I saw her.'

She shakes her head. 'Nobody saw her. How could they? She was never there. Although it was fun pretending she was.'

'But she phoned you. She saw someone in a mask at her window.'

She shakes her head. 'She wasn't on the other end of the phone line that day.'

'There was no intruder?'

'Exactly. No intruder that night. I made the footprints in the snow. I even set out the Monopoly game as though we were playing. I built the snowman, whilst wearing Elise's hat and coat – hoping you and Finn – both early risers would see me. And I walked to the top of Vine Hill when you were tobogganing, wearing Elise's coat and hat. I looked down at you – hoping you would think I was Elise. I even sent a couple of threatening text messages to myself from a phone much like Elise's, and left it on the bench for you to find. Though, if I'm honest, I got lucky with that one. The signal up there was pretty awful.'

She moves the blade from my throat, and brushes the flat side against my cheek.

'But why?' I manage.

'Elise died at my hands, Amelia. Neil would never have forgiven me for that. I couldn't let him find out. He was away, you see.

I was watching TV, when Elise appeared in the lounge. She was spiteful. Angry. She'd found a letter your mum sent to Neil.

'I got up, angry too, yelled at her for snooping in my things. But she was so vehement.' She lowers her head. 'God knows why I didn't destroy the bloody letter.' A beat, as she looks up and into my eyes, hers vacant and lifeless. 'We rowed and she pushed me hard. I fell against the corner of the coffee table. The pain was like nothing I'd felt before. I knew I was losing my baby.'

She's no longer brushing my face with the blade, and there are tears in her eyes. And despite the awful position I'm in, I feel her sadness, her pain at losing her child.

'I cried out to Elise,' she goes on. 'Told her I was losing my baby, but she spat that the baby deserved to die.'

'Oh God, Rosamund. That's awful,' I find myself saying, but she straightens her shoulders and the blade is back at my throat.

'I reached for a brass ornament,' she says. 'Struck Elise.'

'But you didn't mean to kill her.'

She smiles, and shrugs. 'When I heard on Maddie's video log that you were all having a little anniversary reunion at Drummondale House, I knew what I had to do. If I could convince everyone Elise vanished from the Scottish Highlands, at the hands of the same person who took Lark, Neil would never find out what really happened.'

'So you set it all up?'

She nods slowly. 'I knew Ruth would bring towels to the cottage and snoop about – she always did that – such an annoying woman. She totally deserved to die. I hid in Elise's bedroom with the door locked. I heard Ruth call out, and pretended to be Elise.

'When Ruth went into my room, the power finally came back on, so I dashed from Elise's room and turned on the shower, giving the illusion that Elise had gone into the shower, then hurried downstairs to put on the mask.

'My idea was for Ruth to think she'd witnessed the masked

intruder, before being knocked unconscious. When she came round, she was supposed to think Elise had been abducted, and tell everyone what happened.' She shakes her head. 'But my timing was out. Not helped by the loss of power. What can I say? I made a mess of things.

'When I came up the stairs in the mask, Ruth was already in the bathroom. She would have seen Elise wasn't there.'

'So you killed her.' Nausea rises. This woman is a monster.

'Yes. I killed her. I had no choice. If Ruth had told everyone Elise wasn't on the estate, the search for her would go wider. Neil would find out what I'd done.'

I'm aware if she stops talking, she will kill me, so continue with more questions, 'But why Maddie? Why her?'

'Maddie worked it all out, so I had to kill her too.' She pushes the knife into my flesh, pierces my skin once more, and I cry out, pain and fear building. 'She wasn't on the porch smoking when I went out to confront her that day, but I saw her about to disappear into the wooded area near Vine Hill.

'I caught up with her. She told me she was meeting Finn, and I knew by the look on her face, she was afraid of me.

'I told her I'd seen her take the Monopoly token from my cottage, asked her why, and she cried, and tried to hurry away, saying Elise wouldn't want to be the top hat. That she'd want to be the dog. She'd worked it out, you see.' She moves her head from side to side, staring into my eyes, a small smile on her face.

Blood trickles down my neck, the second nick in my skin so painful.

'It wasn't in the plan to kill either of them. In fact, I didn't want any of you to die – not even Elise. I'm not a murderer.'

A thought seeps into my head, like a black river drowning my hopes. 'Did you kill Lark and Jackson?'

'No.' She presses the knife against my neck once more. 'Why would you even think that?' She lays her hand against my chest. 'My, my, your heart is beating like a drum, Amelia.'

247

The back door opens. 'Amelia?' It's Dad, stepping in and bringing with him a waft of fish and chips.

Rosamund looks down at me, and places her finger against my lips. 'Shh,' she whispers.

'Amelia,' Dad calls again. 'Your chips are here, don't let them get cold.' Blissfully unaware I'm in the corner held at knifepoint he opens a cupboard, singing to himself as he pulls out a jar of pickles. 'Amelia!'

He finally turns, and the jar slips from his fingers, crashing to the floor, glass shattering.

'Dear God,' he cries, limping across the kitchen, but he stops when Rosamund pushes the knife deeper into my flesh, so close to cutting through the skin again. 'Christ, Rosamund, what the hell?'

I'm silent, the pulses in my head thumping. Knowing the trickles of blood on my throat is nothing to what Rosamund is capable of.

'Let her go,' Dad cries. He edges forward, blinking furiously, and Rosamund rises to her full height and before he can step away, she lunges at him, plunging the knife into his stomach, then pulling it free. He falls to the floor, yelling in agony.

I let out a scream. 'Dad,' I cry, trying to get up.

But Rosamund is quick. She has the knife back at my throat in an instant.

'You do know this means you both have to die,' she says.

'Why?' Dad whimpers, his body crumpled in pain.

'Oh, it's nothing to do with you, Robert. Don't give yourself any credit. That was a very long time ago.' She turns to me. 'It's OK; your father turned me down. You're a good man, aren't you, Robert? Such a shame Caroline couldn't see that. Even she couldn't resist Jackson.'

I want to hit out – she's going to kill me anyway – but I can't move. I'm frozen in fear.

Chapter 48

Present Day

Amelia

Rosamund closes her eyes for a brief moment, sucks in a sigh, and moves the knife away from me. I stay still. With one stroke she could slit my throat.

From her crouching position, she thumps down on the floor and, knees bent, she sits next to the half-open kitchen door, the knife dangling in one hand.

'It was your mum's letter to Neil that changed everything,' she says, her voice calmer. 'I knew it was from Caroline when I saw it lying on the doormat eighteen months ago, the swirling, elaborate handwriting so familiar. It was addressed to Neil and I knew that whatever she had to say wouldn't be good. But, when I opened it and read her words, those of a dying woman out for revenge, I couldn't believe how cruel she could be. Her spiteful decision to tell Neil that she saw Jackson and me in the wood the night Lark and Jackson disappeared, when she had only weeks to live, was wicked. I thanked God when she died.' She lifts the knife and presses her finger against the blade. She doesn't wince as it pierces her skin, or when a bubble of blood rises to the surfaces and drips to the floor.

There's so much I want to say, but I can't find the courage.

'If Neil had read that letter he would never have forgiven me. He'd forgiven me too many times before.' She leans forward and rubs her bloody finger across my cheek like war paint. 'If your mother hadn't sent that letter none of this would have happened, Amelia – it's her fault so many died.'

'So Neil didn't read it. You found it before he could?'

She nods. 'That's right.'

Dad lets out a groan, and I look over. He's holding his stomach, his eyes closed.

'Please call an ambulance.' Tears roll down my face. 'He's losing so much blood. Please, Rosamund. He's bleeding out. He's going to die.'

She laughs, long and hard. Hysterical, crazy laughter, that reminds me of a mechanical clown I once saw on a pleasure beach as a child, that gave me nightmares for weeks.

'Oh, Amelia.' She holds her chest, her laugh petering away, her face transforming to a look of disgust. 'Do you really think I'm going to pick up the phone and save his life?' She strokes my cheek once more with her bloody finger. 'You both have to die. Don't you see? You know too much.'

She's so absorbed in her own fantasy; she doesn't seem to hear the click of the front door opening. Thomas?

'When Neil holds his baby son, everything will be as it should be,' Rosamund continues, stroking her fake baby bump as though she still believes she's carrying a child. 'It's Neil I love. It's Neil I've always loved. Jackson and I would never have lasted. None of the other men meant anything.'

Rosamund has her back to the kitchen door seemingly unaware it's edging open an inch at a time. Thomas?

With a jolt, she presses the knife against my throat once more.

'I need to finish you off now,' she says. 'You and then your precious father.'

'She's got a knife,' I yell, and Rosamund swings round, but before she can speak, the door slams hard against her head, with the sheer force of something behind it. She slumps forwards, her head cracking against the corner of the kitchen unit, her eyes rolling.

I gulp back tears and confusion as I look up into my brother's dark eyes, as he moves into the room in his wheelchair. 'Thank God,' I say, breathless. 'Call 999. Dad needs an ambulance. Fast.'

Chapter 49

Present Day

Amelia

Someone knocking on a door some distance away wakes me from a fitful sleep. My neck is sore and bandaged. My head throbs in pain. Two nurses, talking in whispers as they hurry through the Intensive Care Unit waiting room, pay me no attention as I shuffle up in the fake leather chair.

I squint at the sun's rays shining through the high windows, dust particles raining down on the long, narrow room. I grab my bag, and rummage for a couple of painkillers.

Thomas is asleep in his chair, his mouth open, making a rumbling sound like a train.

We've been at the hospital since the ambulance brought Dad here at midnight. Earlier we'd taken it in turns to collect coffee, and chocolate and bags of crisps from the machines, trying to keep awake, just in case they brought news about Dad, but eventually our tiredness took over.

'Any news?' Thomas rubs sleep from his eyes, his voice croaky.

I shake my head. 'Not yet.'

He brushes his fingers over his dry lips.

'Do you want some water?' I rise and make my way to the water cooler, and fill two cups.

I hand Thomas one, as he jerks a sideways thumb towards the door. 'Should we ring the bell, do you think? Ask how Dad is?'

'They said they would let us know.' I swallow down the two tablets. 'I know it's hard being patient, but they are doing everything they can.'

It's 9.30 a.m. when we finally hear.

'Your dad's out of danger,' the doctor says as he approaches, and we let go of the tears we've been holding on to, and hug each other. 'He's going to be OK. He's sleeping now. Go home. Get some rest. You should be able to see him by early evening.'

Chapter 50

Present Day

Amelia

It's been three weeks since Rosamund's horrendous attack, and although Dad is home from hospital, he is far from well.

Now, it feels as though the whole experience happened to someone else, not me, as though I witnessed it from an outside viewpoint looking in, as though I was never there at all. Maybe it's my brain's way of trying to deal with it.

We say goodbye to Elise today, and I'm standing at the back of the crematorium, a sea of pink outfits – at Neil's request – in front of me, and so many more people spilling out of the door behind me. She was a popular girl.

Neil calls it a celebration of Elise's life, not a funeral – and I get that. However fleeting her time here, it should be celebrated. Though in equal measures I admit to struggling. How can you celebrate the murder of a teenage girl?

I read how Rosamund led the police to where she buried poor Elise in a field near her home. It hadn't taken the police long to find her. Or discover the bloodied jacket Rosamund wore when she killed Maddie, which she'd hidden in a hollowed tree trunk near Kyla's bench. They'd also found remains of the jacket she wore when she killed Ruth, on the fire that Dad had made outside the cottage at Drummondale House. She'd been arrested for the young girl's murder, and those of Ruth and Maddie, plus the attempted murder of Finn. The guilt that it was me who stabbed Finn still hangs heavy. In fact, it all feels surreal. A nightmare I can't wake up from.

Neil rises, approaches the lectern, and puts down a sheet of paper with shaking hands. He's lost weight, his face ashen. He clears his throat, and begins, 'There's got to be somewhere else.' A beat. 'I keep telling myself that. That somewhere, someday, I'll see you again, and we'll laugh and talk, and you can tell me about your day, and I will hold you in my arms, and tell you everything will be OK.' His voice cracks, and he takes a deep breath. 'Elise … Elise was my everything.'

He crumples, breaks down in tears – pushes his head into his hands. There's movement in the front row, and an older man with a shock of white hair rises, stands beside him, and takes Neil's arm.

Neil lifts his head from his hands, and goes on, 'Elise was a bright, intelligent young woman setting out on life, who was taken long before she should have been. They say the departed wouldn't want us to be sad, that they are at peace, but I know my Elise, and I'm pretty sure she'll be bloody fuming that she's up there too soon.' He raises watery eyes to the congregation, as a low ripple of laughter drifts around the room.

We all struggle through heart-wrenching poems, a hymn, and words from the celebrant telling us about Elise's short life. This is too much.

After the service, we are led out to the sound of Avril Lavigne singing 'Keep Holding On', and I look about me, witnessing so many tears. This tragedy will stay with me forever.

*

Outside, Neil stands some distance from the crematorium, surrounded by friends and family. Scattered across the grass are pools of weeping youngsters hugging each other. And some distance away in the car park DI Beynon, and DS McKay are getting into their car.

I go to leave, feeling as if I'm intruding on the family's grief.

'Amelia!'

I turn to see Julia, huddled into her pink padded jacket, her plait poking from a pink beret. Finn is walking beside her. He's taken the whole pink thing seriously, wearing a cerise jumper, and pale pink trousers. I should have made more effort, perhaps – but it felt right wearing Mum's pink scarf around my neck.

'How's your dad?' Finn asks, once we've agreed, not for the first time, how tragic Elise's death is.

'Improving,' I say. 'And you? How are you?'

'Getting there, slowly.'

'I think I owe you an apology, Amelia,' Julia says, reaching out and touching my arm.

'For what?' But I know. I know exactly what she'll say.

'I shouldn't have accused you of stabbing Finn. Finn's told me it wasn't you, and now we know it was Rosamund, so … well, I'm sorry. Can you forgive me?'

Her words echo in my ears. 'It's fine,' I say, looking up at Finn, knowing he lied for me, knowing I'll never be truly guilt-free. 'We've all been through so much.'

'Are you going back to the house?' Finn asks.

I shake my head – the thought of going to the house where Rosamund killed her stepdaughter gives me chills. 'I should get back.'

'Oh, come. We don't know anyone … safety in numbers?'

'OK,' I say, feeling I owe him. 'I guess I could go for a little while. I'll see you there.'

*

256

The house is full of people supporting each other, and every surface seems to have a photograph of Elise displayed on it.

Finn is with Neil and Neil's parents, wrestling a canapé into his mouth, and I find myself alone with Julia.

Despite her apology, I'm still uneasy around her, though I'm not sure why. She's giving me no reason to be.

We're sitting by the window in two armchairs. And however hard I try to avoid it, my eyes are drawn to the oak coffee table in the centre, surrounded by sofas where yet more guests sit. Was that where Rosamund fell? Where she lost her precious baby?

'I feel a bit intrusive being here,' Julia says, and I turn to face her. 'I never met Elise, and barely know Neil. I'm here to support Finn really.'

'I didn't know Elise very well myself,' I say. 'But I'm sure Neil appreciates our support.'

She nods, and pulls her plait over her shoulder, runs a finger over the intertwined strands. 'You like Finn, don't you?' she says.

I instinctively glance towards him, and he catches my eye and smiles. 'Yes,' I say, looking back at Julia. 'He's a good man. But you know that.'

She smiles. 'He is. I guess we're kindred spirits.'

'Did you play together when you were little?'

She shakes her head. 'No, Finn is older than me. But we have Kyla in common; she's the reason we bonded.'

I recall how she told me Kyla was her half-sister too.

'Kyla cast a shadow over both our lives when she died. We spent our childhoods in different decades, but both suffered the same gloomy darkness.'

I take a sip of my wine, hoping if I stay silent, she'll go on.

'My father, Michael Collis, fell in love with Ruth when they were seventeen. I guess their relationship was a bit like Romeo and Juliet – rivalling families. Ruth's father had won part of the Drummondale estate in a poker game with my grandfather. My grandmother, an awful woman by all accounts, bore a grudge against Ruth's parents. She certainly didn't think Ruth was good enough for my father.

'My dad got Ruth pregnant, but by the time Ruth realised, Dad had gone off to university.'

'And Ruth's baby was Kyla?' I ask, swallowing down more wine.

She nods. 'My grandmother found out Ruth was having Dad's baby, and told Ruth that my dad had got engaged to someone else while at university, that he didn't love her and didn't want a child.'

'That's so cruel. Ruth must have been broken-hearted.'

Julia nods. 'She was. As I say, my gran was cruel. Anyway, Ruth's mother forced her to marry a man who'd been giving Ruth the eye. She didn't care too much who he was, just that Ruth was married.

'The truth was, my father wasn't engaged, but when he discovered Ruth was married with a child, he married my mother.

'It was some years later that Finn was born. And then Ruth's husband left her.'

'And then Kyla died?'

Julia tosses her plait back over her shoulder, and nods. 'That was three years later on Vine Hill. It was after her death that Ruth told my father that Kyla was his daughter. Dad went to pieces. Mourning a child he didn't know he had. He couldn't believe Ruth had never told him.

'He put the bench in the grounds, and spent most of his time there. Even when I was born, his mind was always on Kyla, and what might have been. In the end my mother left him … and me.'

'I'm so sorry.'

'Neither Finn nor I could escape our lost half-sister – though the irony is, I would have loved an older sister. In fact, I often spend time just sitting on the bench, just like my dad and Finn do. It's as though I can reach her there. It's as though I almost know her. I wish I had.'

You were sitting on Kyla's bench the night of the ghost walk.

She turns and meets my eye. 'Do you believe there's something else?' She looks about her, then upwards, and it's as though she can see right through the ceiling and into the heavens. 'You know, after this?'

'I hope so,' I say, and I take hold of her hand and squeeze.

*

We've been at Neil's house for over an hour, and now, as often happens at funerals, family and friends are sharing memories, laughing, their tongues loosened by alcohol. I've overstayed.

'I'm going to make a move for home,' I say, and Finn and Julia nod enthusiastically, seeming desperate to leave themselves. In fact, they leave before me as I need the loo, and as I watch them go, Julia calls out that we must stay in touch. 'No reason not to,' she says, with a flourish. 'We live so close, and now Finn's feeling so much better he can travel down anytime.'

*

As I leave the bathroom, and head onto the landing, I hear voices. One of them is Neil, and it's coming from the master bedroom.

'Perhaps it was all my fault,' he's saying through tears, his voice sounding broken.

I move across the landing, and peer through the gap in the door. The white-haired man who stepped up when Neil crumbled at the funeral, who I now know is his father, sits with him on the edge of a king-sized bed.

'No, Neil,' he says. 'You mustn't think like that.'

'But if I'd been here more, done more to prevent the brewing anger in Elise about me replacing her mum, maybe Rosamund would never have lost the baby, and Elise would still be here.'

The man puts his hand over Neil's. 'I'm so sorry about the baby, son. But I can't see how you being here would have changed that.'

'But it might have.' A beat. 'I knew my Elise hated Rosamund.

259

How full of anger she was, and I did nothing.' He breaks off sobbing, his head in his hands, and I cover my mouth, tears springing to my eyes.

It's a while before Neil is calm enough to say, 'She confessed to having an affair with Jackson.'

His father shakes his head. 'Oh, Neil, I'm so sorry.'

'Me too, I was a fool, knew what she was like when I met her, but kidded myself we had something special. She used to sleep with him in his caravan in Laurel Wood. Can you believe that?'

'Can I help you?'

I startle, step away from the door. I recognise the woman staring at me from the top of the stairs as Neil's mother. 'I'm fine,' I say. 'Just a bit lost – it's such a big house.' I zip past her, and once downstairs, almost fall through the front door. The cold air tingles my cheeks and darkness swallows me as I head for the car.

And as I sit in the driver's seat, gripping the steering wheel, deep breathing in an effort to calm down, I realise the first domino fell long ago.

*

I'd borrowed Dad's car to go to Elise's funeral, and now, as I drive home through the darkness, my mind whirs. Rosamund mentioned Jackson's caravan in Laurel Wood. And then there was that day at Drummondale House when we played Truth and Lie, and Jackson told us he grew up in a caravan. And now Neil has mentioned it.

I pull over into a lay-by, and leave the engine running. My heart thuds as I get Google Maps up on my phone. With shaking hands, I key in the address of the apartment Jackson and my mum shared in Tweedmouth, and see as I expand the map, there's a wooded area nearby called Laurel Wood. It looks to be about a mile across.

Rain splatters the windscreen. I flick on the wipers.

Within seconds, I'm on the road once more.

Chapter 51

Present Day

Me

I haven't always been the best person I could have been. I've let people down. I let my mum down. I should have been there for her. I regret that now, and I'm so sorry for the things I've done. But it's too late for apologies. You have chosen to punish me, and there's nothing I can do.

Rain splatters the window behind me, and I hear your car approaching. The snapping and cracking of sticks under slow-moving tyres as you drive through Laurel Wood. You will be here soon. You said you would be – that it's almost time.

And I know, even if I beg and scream and cry, it will do no good: my life will soon be over.

But I'm not afraid. I can't take any more of this misery. I'm ready. I want to die.

I hear the key turn in the lock, and the door open. I try to lift my head, but the room spins and I can barely move.

Why are you doing this? But you've told me so many times it's almost a mantra. I know the answer – it's because you love me.

Chapter 52

Present Day

Amelia

Wipers thrash across my windscreen – thud, thud, thud, and I can barely see through the hammering rain, but I know I'm close. I have to keep going.

After trawling country roads for another ten minutes, I slow to an almost stop. I've found the entrance to Laurel Wood. I indicate, and take a left turn down a narrow track.

Overhanging trees block the night sky, as I weave my way deeper and deeper. Have I made a terrible mistake? But it's too late. There's no way of turning back.

The sound of my tyres breaking twigs and branches as I crawl along is as loud as the pulse in my ears. My eyes flick to my rear-view at the swirling shadows folding around the car. Why didn't I wait, come tomorrow in the daylight? Why didn't I contact DI Beynon? A chill prickles my neck, as I imagine someone watching from the dense trees. I was a wreck before this, so I'm pretty sure this will finish me off.

I stop the car, and pick up my phone from the driver's seat. I'll call Inspector Beynon now. Tell her where I am.

I get through to DS McKay, and explain in a garbled, panicked fashion where I am and where I'm heading, and he promises to inform DI Beynon immediately. 'Wait for us,' he says, before ending the call.

I notice a dim light burning through the trees, and my heart thuds a warning as I take a deep breath and open the car door. I flick on my phone torch and climb out into the hammering rain. With the quietest of footsteps, I move to where the track widens. It's as I take a bend I see the caravan. Its grubby, hanging baskets by the door hold nothing more than twigs. My torchlight picks out a wet cat climbing up the rusty metal steps. It leaps through a cat flap into the caravan.

Is this really where Rosamund came with Jackson to have sex behind Neil and Mum's back? But then women found him irresistible. I think back to how Maddie swooned over him when we were at Drummondale House. How Mum fell for him so quickly. How the media painted him as a heart-breaking womaniser.

Mizzling rain stings my cheeks as I move closer. An old Clio Campus is parked up, and another car by the caravan is covered with old blankets. I drag up my hood and make my way over to it, looking about me before lifting the cover and shining the torch on the number plate. It's Jackson's car.

I drop the blanket, frozen, unable to move. Fighting back fear, I look about me, spotting a branch, thick and sturdy, on the wet ground. I pick it up and approach the caravan.

I push open the door, surprised to find it unlocked, and step inside. In the lounge area there's a folded duvet and a pillow at the end of a sofa, and a closed laptop. A wheelchair is collapsed in the corner – Mum's wheelchair. The whole place smells awful, the pungent hum of pee overpowering.

I grip the branch in my fist, so hard my knuckles turn white. As I head through a narrow kitchen, the rain hammering on the roof sounds unsettling. The cat walks with precision over a sink loaded with dirty plates and cups, meowing urgently, trying to get my attention. I run my hand over its wet fur. It's thin, but seems healthy.

I hear crying, and every hair on my body lifts as I turn. Hanging ominously on the curtain pole is a mask.

Chapter 53

Present Day

Me

Tears spill down Lark's cheeks. I hate seeing her cry. That I've brought her to this. If I hadn't treated her the way I did, told her I loved her, it would never have come to this.

I recall how my mum used to cry when Dad slept with other women – when he knocked her about. Everyone thought they were such a happy couple – Indigo and Phoenix united in their traveller ways. But I felt her pain. Saw her cry. She told me once – I could only have been six – to never hurt a woman. But maybe I'm more like my father than I realise.

'Why, Jackson?' Lark says, not for the first time. But this time she's clenching a needle, and I know she will kill me soon. And I've accepted my fate. Living like this – trapped in a tiny world, one arm clamped to the metal headboard by a chain and padlock for over a year, has taken away my fight.

I hear movement, and although I can barely lift my head from the pillow, I see her standing in the doorway, her eyes wide with shock. 'Amelia,' I whisper. 'Thank God.'

Chapter 54

Present Day

Amelia

Lark wheels around to face me, clenching a needle, tears rolling down her face. 'Amelia?' she says, hands shaking. 'What the hell are you doing here?'

'Christ, Lark, what's going on?' I cry, taking in the sight in front of me: Jackson, looking horribly thin, Lark beside him, her cheekbones prominent, skin pallid, eyes cradled with dark cushions of flesh, her blonde hair cut short and uneven. Gone are her long tendrils. I barely recognise her.

'What have you done?' I cry, racing towards her. 'Oh God, what have you done, Lark?'

'It's heroin.' Jackson's voice is raspy, defeated, as though he doesn't care if he lives or dies. His once trendy hair touches his shoulders, messy and greasy, and a straggly beard covers his chin. His eyes are washed out and sallow, his pupils dilated.

Lark points the needle towards me. 'Stay away, Amelia. This has nothing to do with you.'

'Lark, please. We used to be friends, didn't we?' Jackson whispers, his voice barely audible.

Lark turns back to him. 'Never friends, Jackson. I love you. I've loved you since the first time you brought me here.'

'I'm sorry,' he says.

'Lark … please … give me the needle.' I hold out my hand.

'And then you said it had just been a bit of fun,' she says, ignoring my request. 'That we were both wrong, that we both let my mum down.'

'Sorry.' He tugs on the chain that's holding him to the bed, his wrist raw, covered in scabs and sores.

'Stop. Saying. Sorry,' she yells. 'Why the hell are you fucking sorry anyway? Because you led me on, left me consumed with so much love for you? Or sorry you lured me in and left me with so much guilt that I'd betrayed my mum? Guilt and love is a dangerous cocktail, Jackson.

'Then my mum got ill,' she continues. 'And my guilt was like my very own cancer – killing me. But I kept it all inside, until that night I saw you with Rosamund in Scotland.'

'I know sorry isn't enough,' he whispers.

'No it fucking isn't. This is your comeuppance, Jackson. Your punishment.' She walks towards him. Strokes his hair, his cheek. 'You're not as handsome as you once were,' she says. 'Far too thin – your muscles wasted.'

She kisses his dry, cracked lips. 'I love you, Jackson,' she says, and biting down on her bottom lip so it bleeds, she plunges the needle into his flesh.

'You're right, it's heroin,' she says, as his eyes linger on hers. 'It will kill you.'

I stare. Do nothing. My mind paralysed.

'Lark!' I finally scream, blaming shock for my delayed reaction, rather than a desire to see Jackson six foot under. I grab my phone from my pocket, but she bashes it from my hand. It crashes to the floor.

'He must pay for what he's done, Amelia.' Her voice is calm and low, but tears roll down her face. 'Can't you see that?'

'No, please, Lark. You can't let him die.'

Her eyes are wide, vacant, I barely know her. This should have been the best moment of my life – finding my sister alive after all this time – but as I look at Jackson, life draining from him, it's one of the worst.

'I attacked him that day at Drummondale House,' Lark says – she's still clenching the needle, pointing it my way. 'I saw him with Rosamund; I couldn't believe he would do that to me. I struck him with a branch across his head. A bit like the one you're holding now. Put it down, Amelia. Please.'

I know I won't use it, so prop it against the wall. 'Lark, listen to me, we need to get Jackson help.' I step closer. 'Keep with us,' I say to him, touching his arm. 'You need to keep with us.'

'I raced back to the cottage that night,' Lark goes on. She clearly wants me to know everything. Wants me to understand. 'Mum was crying in her room. She knew what he'd done – seen him too.

'I grabbed Jackson's car keys, some money and Mum's wig, then took her wheelchair from the car.'

I make a dive for my phone, but she kicks it across the room.

'When I got back to him he was woozy, confused. I crushed three of my Diazepam, and made him swallow them. In fact, I've been putting some of my old prescription in his food recently.

'I grabbed a mask from one of the trees, as I wheeled Jackson to the car in the chair. It squeaked and I was so afraid I might be heard.'

I heard – it hadn't been a dream.

'But nobody came, so I heaved him into the back of the car. I knew where I was heading – and took mainly back roads here – avoiding cameras – and wearing the wig and mask if a road had CCTV. Easy really.'

I can't believe my sister had been so calculating. All this time

I'd feared she was the helpless one. 'How have you survived?' I whisper.

'Working at a local farm, cash in hand.'

'They never recognised you?'

She shakes her head. 'Once I'd cropped off my hair, nobody would have thought I was the blonde-haired girl covered in make-up that they shared all over the media.'

Jackson's breathing is shallow. 'He's going to die, Lark,' I say. 'Please don't let him die. You're not a killer.'

'Aren't I?'

'Please. I don't want to lose you again. I'll be here for you. Please. Let's get Jackson to hospital.'

A tear rolls down her face. 'Do you miss Mum, Amelia?' she whispers.

'All the time.'

'I was at the crematorium. I was there. I said goodbye to her.' Tears stream down her face, and I reach for her hand. She lets me take it.

'I know. I felt you there,' I say. 'Please let me get my phone,' I go on, stepping forward and reaching for it. She doesn't stop me.

'I love Jackson. I love him so much it makes my insides ache,' she says. 'Why did he hurt me? Why did he break my heart?' She drops the needle to the floor and climbs onto the bed next to him. His lips are dry – his breathing raspy, but he's hanging on. She puts her arm around him, curls her body into him, like she's joined, growing there. 'I love you,' she whispers and closes her eyes.

I pick up the phone, but before I can dial, I hear sirens.

The police are on their way.

Epilogue

Three months later

Amelia

I've officially moved back in with Dad and Thomas, unable to face returning to London. After everything that happened, I need the security of my childhood home. And it's worked out well for Thomas too, as I've been caring for him, being there as he improves day by day. He can feel his legs now, and he's building up his muscles. It's a miracle – when everyone thought he would be in a wheelchair forever.

He's confided in me many times how much he misses Maddie, and he's talked about the woman he loves in America who he insists he doesn't stalk on Twitter. He hasn't contacted her, but says he will. One day.

I'm still coming to terms with everything. Attempting to move my life back into the normal zone, whatever that is. It isn't easy, as I'm battling through a mixture of insomnia, and traumatic dreams, whilst grieving for everyone we've lost – including the part of Lark we hopefully haven't lost forever.

My cat jumps onto my lap, startling me from my thoughts. 'Hello, Bella, my little furry ball of love,' I say as she nibbles my chin. She's a bit overweight from staying in London with the girl with the pink hair, but I'm working on cutting down her diet. It isn't easy, as Misty, who never stops purring, is rather thin. He's a stray that Jackson fed regularly when he went to the caravan in Laurel Wood – he'd even put in a cat flap for him, so he could get warm on cold nights. We've adopted him officially, as once the trial is over Jackson intends to return to the US.

I'm still reeling in shock at what Lark was capable of, and wonder now, if I'd had my eyes fully open on our first visit to Drummondale House if I'd seen how close to the edge she was. If I'd studied more closely the looks that passed between her and Jackson, would I have seen how besotted she was? But instead I was blinded by my own sadness.

Now Lark is going through a traumatic court case for the kidnapping and attempted murder of Jackson – but I'll be there for her, always. She told me only yesterday, how she would sit in the caravan and listen to Maddie's vlogs. She'd found out when Mum died that way. I try to understand how desperate she must have been to take Jackson. She'd fallen so deeply for him, and he'd messed with her young mind, fooling her into thinking he loved her.

Dad has fully recovered from his injury. He's shaved off his moustache, and his dyed black hair has almost grown out. He has more threads of grey than before, but looks like my dad again. He's rehearsing an Agatha Christie Miss Marple production with the Berwick-upon-Tweed Players. He says it's the only way he can keep sane – losing himself in a role – pretending to be someone else. Ironically, he's playing the murderer.

I guess we all have our methods of survival. Mine was alcohol. But I'm battling with my addiction, getting by without booze and feeling better for it.

Rosamund is awaiting trial. The prosecution are pushing for

diminished responsibility. The distressing, emotional way she lost her baby when she was pushed against the coffee table, followed by the shock of killing Elise, left her in a delusional, psychotic state. Is it wrong that I feel sorry for her? Perhaps I understand more than some how traumatic it is to lose your unborn baby.

*

The doorbell rings. 'That'll be Finn and Julia,' I call to Dad and Thomas, who are in the kitchen preparing dinner. I rise, and fling open the door.

'Hey,' Finn says, brandishing a bottle of wine I know I won't touch.

'Hey,' I say, hugging them both.

We've become good friends – survivors of a terrible tragedy. I've been searching desperately for some good to come out of the terrors we've been through, and believe in Finn and Julia.

But whether they stay in our lives or not, my repair must come from inside of me. 'To thine own self be true,' Mr Shakespeare would have said, and I'm determined I will be.

I'm determined I won't let everything that's happened destroy us.

Gripped by Amelia's story in *I Lie in Wait*? Don't miss *Her Last Lie*, another heart-stopping thriller from Amanda Brittany. Available now!

Acknowledgements

Firstly, I would like to thank my wonderful editor Belinda Toor who has been absolutely amazing. I'm so grateful for all her support in making *I Lie in Wait* the best it possibly can be.

Thank you to everyone at HQ; with huge thanks especially to Anna Sikorska for another fantastic cover design, to my excellent copy editor Helena Newton, to Abigail Fenton and to Christopher Sturtivant.

Thank you to my fabulous agent Kate Nash and her brilliant team, as well as her writers for their support since I joined the agency.

Sending big thanks, as always, to my lovely friends Karen Clarke, Joanne Duncan and Diane Jeffrey for their endless support and feedback. Writing can be a lonely business at times, so to have such supportive writer friends is wonderful.

I've been so lucky to have such support on Facebook, Twitter, and Instagram from so many friends, readers, and writers – huge thanks to every single one of them. I couldn't have got this far without them, and wish I had space to name everyone, but I hope you know who you are.

I'm so grateful to all my lovely readers, and to the blogging community for all their support and brilliant reviews – it means so much. Thank you.

I would like to thank too Sally Maskell and Kate Nussey, who provided the names for Julia Collis and Detective Inspector Kate Beynon in I Lie in Wait, after winning a competition I ran on my Facebook page. Sally's choice was in memory of her sister, Jane Collis. Thank you to everyone who took part in the competition, and donated to my Her Last Lie fundraising page.

Thank you so much to my family and friends for listening to me go on about writing, and for being there for me. Again, you know who you are. I love you all.

Special thanks to my daughter-in-law, Lucy, who once again bravely read an early draft of my novel, and to my sons Liam, Daniel and Luke who tirelessly support me, and to Janni and Amy for cheering me on. Thanks to my mum who still tells everyone she meets that her daughter is a writer, and to Cheryl and my dad who my acknowledgements would never be complete without.

And last but never least a special thank you to Kev who has supported me since I started on my crazy writing journey. I'm dedicating this book to you.

Keep reading for an excerpt from
Her Last Lie …

Prologue

Saturday, 23 July

NSW Newsroom Online
Serial killer Carl Jeffery convicted of triple hostel killings, granted appeal.

Six years ago, the so-called Hostel Killer, Carl Jeffery, now thirty-one, was found guilty of the murders of Sophie Stuart, nineteen, Bronwyn Bray, eighteen, and Clare Simpson, twenty-six. He got three life sentences.

Now his younger sister, Darleen Jeffery, hopes to get him acquitted.

Mr Jeffery was accused of targeting women travelling alone in Australia. He would gain their trust, and when the women ended their relationship with Jeffery, he would tap on their window in the dead of night, wearing a green beanie hat and scarf to disguise his appearance, striking fear. He later killed them.

The main prosecuting evidence came from his intended fourth victim, Isla Johnson from the UK, who survived his attack and identified him as her assailant. She suffered physical and psychological injuries. Following Mr Jeffery's trial, she returned to

England where she now lives with boyfriend Jack Green.

During his trial, Jeffery broke down when questioned about his mother, who left the family home when he was eleven, leaving him and Darleen to live with their abusive father, who died three months before the first murder.

Darleen, who penned the bestseller My Brother is Innocent, has campaigned for her sibling's release for almost six years. She claims her brother's DNA was found on Bronwyn Bray's body because they had been in a relationship, and that this wasn't taken into account fully at the trial. She also insists the court should re-examine Isla's statements of what happened the night of her brother's arrest, suggesting there is no proof that he started the 'bloodbath' that unfolded that night.

Canberra's High Court granted permission today for an appeal, agreeing there are sufficient grounds for further consideration of the case. The hearing will take place on 30 September.

Leaving court today, Darleen, wearing a two-piece royal-blue skirt suit, told reporters, 'I'm over the moon. I believe we have a sound case, and I can't wait for my brother to be released.'

We contacted Isla Johnson in her hometown of Letchworth Garden City, England. She told us she wouldn't be attending the hearing. 'They have my original statements, and I've no more to offer,' she said.

PART 1

PART 1

Chapter 1

Tuesday, 26 July

It was hot.

Not the kind of heat you bask in on a Majorcan beach. No tickle of a warm breeze caressing your cheek. This was clammy, and had crept out of nowhere mid-afternoon, long after Isla had travelled into London in long sleeves and leggings, her camera over her shoulder, her notepad in hand.

Now Isla was crushed against a bosomy woman reading a freebie newspaper, on a packed, motionless train waiting to leave King's Cross. The air was heavy with stale body odour and – what was that? – fish? She looked towards the door. Should she wait for the next train?

She took two long, deep breaths in an attempt to relieve the fuzzy feeling in her chest. She rarely let her angst out of its box anymore – proud of how far she'd come. But there were times when the buried-alive anxiety banged on the lid of that box, desperate to be freed. It had been worse since she'd received the letter about the appeal. Carl Jeffery had crawled back under her skin.

She'd hidden the letter, knowing if she told Jack and her family they would worry about her. She didn't want that. She'd spent too much time as a victim. The one everyone worried about. She was stronger now. The woman she'd once been was in touching distance. She couldn't let the appeal ruin that.

She ran a finger over the rubber band on her wrist, and pinged it three times. Snap. Snap. Snap. It helped her focus – a weapon against unease.

'Hey, sit,' said a lad in his teens, leaping to his feet and smiling. Had he picked up on her breathing technique – those restless, twitching feelings?

I'm twenty-nine, not ninety, she almost said. But the truth was she was relieved. She had been on her feet all day taking pictures around Tower Bridge for an article she was working on, and that horrid heat was basting the backs of her knees, the curves of her elbows, making them sweat.

'Thanks,' she said, and thumped down in the vacated seat, realising instantly why the bloke had moved. A fish-sandwich muncher was sitting right next to her.

Her phone rang in her canvas bag, and she pulled it out to see Jack's face beaming from the screen.

'Hey, you,' she said, pinning the phone to her ear.

'You OK?'

'Yeah, just delayed. Train's rammed.' It jolted forward and headed on its way. 'Ooh, we're moving, thank the Lord. Should be home in about an hour.'

'Great. I'm cooking teriyaki chicken. Mary Berry style.'

She laughed, scooping her hair behind her ears. 'Lovely. I'll pick up wine.'

The line went dead as the train rumbled through a tunnel, and Isla slipped her phone in her bag, and took out her camera. She flicked through her photos. She would add one or two to Facebook later, and mention her long day in London.

Your life is so perfect, Millie had written on Isla's status a few months back, when she'd updated that she and Jack were back from France and she was closer to finishing her book. It had been an odd thing for Millie to say. Her sister knew Isla's history better than anyone. How could she think Isla's life was perfect, when she'd seen her at her most desperate? Felt the cruel slap of Isla's anger?

Eyes closed, Isla drifted into thoughts of Canada. She was going for a month. Alone. Canada. The place she would have gone to after Australia if life hadn't forced a sharp change of direction. Going abroad without Jack wouldn't be easy. But then he couldn't keep carrying her. She had to face it alone. And it would be the perfect escape from the pending appeal.

With a squeal of brakes, the train pulled in to Finsbury Park, and fish-sandwich man grunted, far too close to Isla's ear, that it was his stop. She moved so he could pass, and shuffled into the window seat.

Through the glass, she watched overheated people pour onto the platform, and her eyes drifted from a woman with a crying, red-faced toddler, to a teenage boy slathering sun cream onto his bare shoulders.

'Isla?' Someone had sat down next to her, his aftershave too strong.

She turned, her chest tightening, squeezing as though it might crush her heart. 'Trevor,' she stuttered, suddenly desperate to get up and rush through the door before it hissed shut. But it did just that – sucking closed in front of her eyes, suffocating her, preventing any escape from her past.

'I thought it was you,' he said, as the train pulled away. He was still handsome and athletic. Gone were his blond curls, replaced by cropped hair that suited him. He was wearing an expensive-looking suit, a tie loose in the neck, his tanned face glowing in the heat.

Her heartbeat quickened. It always did when anything out of the ordinary happened, and seeing Trevor for the first time in years made her feel off-kilter. The man she'd hurt at university was sitting right next to her, his face creased into a pleasant smile, as though he'd forgotten how things had ended between them.

'You haven't changed,' he said. 'Still as beautiful as ever.' He threw her a playful wink, before his blue eyes latched on to hers. 'I can't believe it's been eight years. How are you?' She'd forgotten how soft his voice was, the slight hint of Scotland in his accent. He'd always been good to talk to. Always had time for everyone at university. But the chemistry had never been there – for her anyway – and they'd wanted different things from their lives.

'I'm good – you?' she said, as her heart slowed to an even beat.

He nodded, and a difficult silence fell between them. This was more like it. This was how things had been left – awkward and embarrassing. An urge to apologise took over. But it was far too late to say sorry for how she'd treated him. Wasn't it?

'I've often thought about you,' he said, and she tugged her eyes away from his. 'You know, wondering what you're up to. I heard what happened in Australia.'

'I prefer not to talk about it.' It came out sharp and defensive.

'Well, no, I can see why you wouldn't want to. Must have been awful for you. I'm so sorry.'

Quickly, Isla changed the subject, and they found themselves bouncing back and forth memories of university days, avoiding how it had ended.

'You're truly remarkable,' Trevor said eventually. 'You know, coming back from what you went through.'

After another silence, where she stared at her hands, she said, 'It was hard for a time … a really long time, in fact.' She hadn't spoken about it for so long, and could hear her voice cracking.

'But you're OK now?' He sounded so genuine, his eyes searching her face.

She shrugged. 'His sister …'

Would it be OK to talk to Trevor about the appeal? Tell him about Darleen Jeffery? Ask him what kind of woman fights their brother's innocence, when it's so obvious he's a monster? There was a huge part of Isla that desperately needed to talk. Say the words she couldn't say to Jack or her family for fear they would think she was taking a step back. Vocalise the fears that hovered under the surface. The desire to tell someone about the Facebook message she'd received from Darleen Jeffery several months ago was overwhelming. 'I need to discuss the truth, Isla,' it had said.

'His sister fought for an appeal and won,' she went on, wishing immediately that she'd said nothing.

'Jesus.' He looked so concerned, his eyes wide and fully on her. 'When is it?'

'The end of September.' The words caught in her throat.

'Are you going?'

She shook her head. She'd contacted the Director of Public Prosecutions. Told them she wouldn't be attending, that she didn't want to know the outcome. Being in a courtroom with him again would be like resting her head on a block, Carl Jeffery controlling the blade.

'I can't face it,' she said, her voice a whisper.

'I don't blame you.' He shook his head. 'It's sickening that he killed three women. Unbelievable.'

She thought of lovely Jack, knowing how hurt he would be if he knew she was keeping the appeal – and the way it was affecting her – from him. He would be hurt if he knew that within a few minutes of meeting her ex, she was confiding in him – letting it all out. But there was something oddly comforting in the detached feeling of talking to an almost-stranger on a train – because that's what he was now. Someone she probably wouldn't see again for another eight years.

'I'll be in Canada when it takes place. I can forget it's even happening. And I've told them I don't want to know the outcome.' She pinged the band on her wrist, before turning and fixing her eyes hard on the window, a surge of tears waiting to fall. She needed to change the subject. 'So what are you up to now?'

'I'm a chemist,' he said, his tone upbeat.

'Not a forensic scientist, then?' That had been his dream.

'Never happened, sadly,' he said. 'I'm working on a trial drug at the moment.'

'Sounds interesting.' Her eyes were back on him.

He shrugged. 'Not really. Not as interesting as travel writing.'

She stared, narrowing her eyes. 'You know I'm a travel writer?'

He smiled. 'I guessed.' He nodded at her camera. 'You wanted to be the next Martha Gellhorn.'

'You remember that?'

He nodded, entwining his fingers on his lap, eyes darting over her face. 'You haven't changed,' he said again.

She knew she had. Her blonde hair came out of a bottle these days, and there was no doubting she was different on the inside. She looked away again, through the window where fields were blurs of green.

As seconds became minutes he said, 'Maybe we could catch up some time. Now we've found each other again.'

Words bounced around her head, as a prickle of sweat settled on her forehead. She didn't want to be unkind, but she was with Jack, and even if she wasn't, there was nothing there – not even a spark.

She turned to see his cheeks glowing red, and an urge to say sorry for hurting him all those years ago rose once more. 'I'm with someone,' she said instead.

'That's cool. Me too,' he said, with what seemed like a genuine smile. 'I meant as friends, that's all.' He pulled out his phone, the yellow Nokia he'd had at university. 'We could exchange numbers.' His shoulders rose in a shrug, making him look helpless. 'It would be good to meet up some time.'

***

Triple-glazed windows sealed against the noise of heavy traffic rattling along the road outside, and a whirring fan that was having little effect, meant the apartment felt even hotter than outside. Isla hated that she couldn't fling open the windows to

288

let the fresh air in. Sometimes she would grab her camera, jump into her car, and head to the nearby fields to snap photographs of the countryside: birds and butterflies, wild flowers, sheep, horses, whatever she could find – pictures she would often put on Facebook or Instagram.

'Can you open that, please?' She plonked the chilled bottle of wine she'd picked up from the off-licence in front of Jack on the worktop. 'I desperately need a shower.'

He looked up from chopping vegetables. 'Well hello there, Jack, how was your day?'

'Sorry,' she said, tickling their cat, Luna, under the chin before stroking her sleek, grey body. 'I'm so, so hot. Sorry, sorry, sorry.' She disappeared into the bedroom, stripping off her clothes, and dropping them as she went.

Fifteen minutes later she was back, in shorts and a T-shirt, damp hair scooped into a messy bun. She picked up the glass of wine that Jack had poured. 'God, that's better,' she said, taking a swig. She smiled and touched Jack's clean-shaven cheek. 'Well, hello there, Jack. How was your day?'

He laughed and plonked a kiss on her nose. 'Well, Tuesday's done. I'll be glad when I'm over hump Wednesday.'

'Wednesday's the new Thursday, and Thursday's the new Friday.'

'Must be the weekend then.' He raised his glass. 'Cheers.'

She pulled herself onto a stool. 'I saw an old boyfriend on the train home. Trevor Cooper.' The guilt of talking about the appeal made her want to tell Jack.

'The bloke you went out with at uni?'

'Aha.'

'Should I be jealous?' he teased.

'God no.' She took another gulp of wine, before adding, 'He was suggesting I meet with him some time.'

Jack's eyebrows rose and a playful smile dimpled his cheeks. 'Do you fancy him?'

She shook her head. 'Of course not.'

He laughed as he put chicken onto plates. 'Well, go ahead then; you have my blessing.'

'I'd go without it, if I wanted to,' she said, with a laugh. They'd been together two years. He should be able to trust her. 'To be honest,' she continued, 'I'm not sure I want to meet up with him. I'll think of an excuse if he texts. Maybe come down with something contagious.'

Jack smiled and shoved a plate of delicious-looking food in front of her. She picked up a fork and began tucking in, making appreciative noises. 'I probably shouldn't have given him my number.'

'And you did, because?'

She shrugged, remembering. 'I suppose I didn't want to hurt his feelings again.'

There was a clatter, and Luna, green eyes flashing, jumped off the worktop with a huge piece of French bread in her mouth.

'Luna, you little sod,' Jack yelled, diving from his stool. 'Has that "how to train a cat" book arrived yet?'

Isla didn't respond, deep in thought.

'If you don't want to meet him, Isla,' he said, long legs leaping after Luna, 'just ignore him if he texts.' He grabbed the cat, wrestled free the bread, and chucked it in the bin. 'Simple.'

'Maybe,' she said.

Later, Isla sat on her mobile phone watching cute cats on YouTube, as Jack watched a documentary about Jack the Ripper.

Her phone buzzed. Trevor had sent her a friend request on Facebook, and a message saying how great it had been to see her again. She stared at the screen for some moments, and then looked at Jack sprawled full length on the sofa. Trevor was just being friendly, and anyway, her conscience wouldn't allow her to ignore him. She had loads of friends she barely knew any more on Facebook. What harm could another person do?

She added him as a friend.

Dear Reader,

We hope you enjoyed reading this book. If you did, we'd be so appreciative if you left a review. It really helps us and the author to bring more books like this to you.

Here at HQ Digital we are dedicated to publishing fiction that will keep you turning the pages into the early hours. Don't want to miss a thing? To find out more about our books, promotions, discover exclusive content and enter competitions you can keep in touch in the following ways:

JOIN OUR COMMUNITY:

Sign up to our new email newsletter: hyperurl.co/hqnewsletter

Read our new blog www.hqstories.co.uk

: https://twitter.com/HQStories

: www.facebook.com/HQStories

BUDDING WRITER?

We're also looking for authors to join the HQ Digital family!
Find out more here:

https://www.hqstories.co.uk/want-to-write-for-us/

Thanks for reading, from the HQ Digital team

If you enjoyed *I Lie in Wait*, then why not try another
heart-racing thriller from HQ Digital

Some vows are meant
to be broken

DEAR
WIFE

KIMBERLY BELLE

AMANDA BRITTANY

traces
of
her

An unsolved murder.
A missing girl.
Time is running out.

THE
SECRET
SISTER

K A CLARKE
A J BRITTANY

STEVE
FRECH

DARK
HOLLOWS

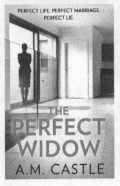

PERFECT LIFE. PERFECT MARRIAGE.
PERFECT LIE.

THE
PERFECT
WIDOW

A.M. CASTLE

HER
LAST
SECRET

Everyone has
something to hide

P L KANE